SHELTERED
Hearts

MARY CRAWFORD

A HIDDEN HEARTS NOVEL

BOOK 2

Copyright

Published on March 28, 2016, by Diversity Ink Press and Mary Crawford.

ISBN-13:978-0692664643 (Diversity Ink Press)

ISBN-10:0692664645

ASIN:B01AAI5KD8

Dedication

To everyone whose hearts
have been stolen by your perfect
match of a different sort—

I write this book in loving memory of my service dogs:
Molly, Boris and Caleigh.

Jessica

1

THE LADDER SHAKES PRECARIOUSLY UNDER my feet as I reach up to fill the hummingbird feeder. For the life of me, I don't understand why Mrs. Bathwell decided that the hummingbirds need to be fed on the highest peak of the rafters. I adore the birds, but this feeding ritual makes absolutely no sense. As a big drop of the bright red syrup splashes on my cheek, the silent cursing that I've been doing under my breath becomes not so silent. Immediately, I apologize even though there isn't anyone outside within blocks. Every other sane person on the planet is asleep at six-thirty on a Sunday morning in this sleepy suburban enclave. I can't seem to outgrow my Midwestern farm work ethic nor my pastor's granddaughter morals no matter how long I've been attending college in sunny Florida.

As I screw on the last feeding spout to the hummingbird feeder, something catches my eye. I've seen that suped-up car before. It was the same one that was racing from the scene where the senior citizen couple was spray-painted with a swastika the other day in front of the local market. Unfortunately, the license plate is partially obscured and they are driving too fast for me to see what it says. It looks like it's not a Florida license plate or if it is, it's not the traditional plate. The only thing distinguishable about the car is that it looks like a sports car of some sort, but it's just grey. Grey and loud — very loud. It is so loud that at first, I don't realize that there is another sound disturbing the early morning quiet.

I can't identify the odd sound, so I take the risk and stand on my tiptoes on the wobbly ladder to try to see over the tall privacy fence. Did I mention that heights aren't really my thing? I really wish that Ivy was here. She was once a cheerleader and she's used to being tossed in the air. I'll keep my five-foot-nothing-self firmly on the ground, thank you very much. From this vantage point, I can just barely see over the fence, but unfortunately I don't really see much. Still, I can hear a rustling sound in the bushes and an odd sound, almost like moaning.

I scramble off the ladder as quickly as I can and start running toward the sound. It suddenly occurs to me that A.) I'm wearing old ratty cutoffs that no self-respecting woman should be wearing in public. B.) My feet are bare. C.) I don't have the lick of sense that God gave me — as my grandfather, Walter would say. I don't know what's in those bushes, and I don't even have my cell phone with me. My grandfather and I don't always see eye to eye. Yet in this case, he would really have a point. I don't even know what I'm doing out here at this ungodly hour in the morning. I always make fun of Ivy for not having very many street smarts. Really, I think her bad habits have rubbed off on me. I know better than to do what I'm just about to do.

I start to turn on my heel and head back home when a flash of brown and black catches my eye. What's even more alarming is that there is some red and silver mixed in with that. "Oh, hell no!" I mutter to myself. As I sprint back to my house, I say a silent prayer of thanks to my grandmother who thought it was important for me to be well-rounded and made me pick a sport to play in high school. If it hadn't been for my introduction to running on the track team, I would've never made it. If left to my own devices, I would happily be a confirmed couch potato.

I open my back door and I'm confronted by the mess that is my kitchen. I don't know why I thought it was a good idea to try to teach myself to cook vegetarian food. I was born and raised on a farm. Maybe I should just accept my roots and move on. I don't think vegetarian cooking is my thing — as is evidenced by the fact that I used every bowl and pan in my entire kitchen. Right now, the most critical question on my mind is how to quickly locate my phone. I'm not really sure where I left it. It could be anywhere in this colossal mess. When I spot my spiral notebook sitting in the middle of the fallout in the middle of my kitchen table, I remember that I stuck my phone in my school backpack for safekeeping. I run to my bedroom to grab it. I snag my tennis shoes from in front of the front door as I go by and slide them on, but in the process, I practically knock myself out on the stairway banister. Let's just say grace isn't exactly my middle name.

Backpack in hand, I run back toward the scene. I punch Rogue's number into the phone. When she answers the phone, it's clear that I've roused her from a deep sleep.

"I'm so sorry, Rogue. I forgot that you guys are on vacation. How is the Grand Canyon? If it's the crack of dawn here in Florida, it must be the middle of the night there."

"Oh, it's all right. I'm not really sleeping all that well anyway. Tristan and Isaac are working on a big case and he's clacking away on the computer and it keeps me awake. What's up?" she asks, barely disguising a yawn.

Her question immediately brings me back to the crisis at hand. "Rogue, I think this could be really bad. There's a hurt dog in my neighborhood. It looks pretty serious. This isn't like back home where we just called the big animal vet or even when I lived in New York City where I knew all the vets at the walk-in clinics because I would take them so many rescued kittens from my neighborhood. I don't know what I can do here. I'm by myself. I don't even know if anything is open on the weekends. Everybody I know in this state is out of town right now. I don't have any medical knowledge. What if I can't help the poor thing? Even if I could call my grandpa, he would probably just tell me to shoot it. He would say that it's all part of the cycle of life and God intended it to be that way. I don't really even know what to think — besides, I can't shoot a gun in the middle of town. I mean, I know how to shoot a gun; I was raised on a farm. That's not really the issue here..." I ramble. "Can you ask Tristan if he knows anybody? Maybe I should call Ivy. Marcus knows everyone—"

I'm only half paying attention to my own blathering as I try to find the dog. He's not in the same spot that I left him. My panic level starts to rise. What if I can't find him and he's walking around injured? The injuries looked really bad when I saw him before. He was actively losing blood. Blood. That's the secret. I'll just look for a blood trail; he must be leaving a pretty substantial one. His injuries looked pretty serious.

I start to feel pretty light headed. Rogue's voice on the other end of the phone is like a splash of cold water. "Jessica, take a deep breath. You survived the streets of New York when you were just a kid. You can deal with this. Just take it step-by-step."

"You're right, I've survived tougher stuff than this. I need to pull it together." I hear a sound off to my left and I whisper, "Gotta go!" before ripping the earbuds out of my ears and stuffing the phone back in the backpack. As I do, my hand brushes across the snack I had thrown in to my backpack for my last late-night study session. Perfect. It's almost as if fate has intervened. I quickly unwrap the pepperoni stick and jam it into my pocket. I don't suppose the puppy is going to care much if it's a little stale and from a discount store.

My heart is pounding. It's been a while since I've been around any animals, let alone one that's been injured. I haven't gotten a really good look at this one — other than to know that I saw blood. I don't even know if this dog is feral or aggressive. The outright insane nature of my mission hits me again — I watch all of those rescue shows on Animal Planet; I know better than to try to do this by myself. I don't have anywhere else to turn. It's a choice between letting this dog suffer or having backup. I forge forward because I really have no choice at all. With grim determination, I crouch down and duck into a hole in the hedge.

This is one situation where being the size of a small third-grader is going to help me. I curse my lack of foresight, as I have to dig out my cell phone from my backpack again to use the flashlight. After I start the flashlight app, I can see that the poor dog has wedged himself up against a cement foundation and a wood fence. He has nowhere else to go and he's shaking violently. As I adjust the flashlight so that I can see where I'm going, I make a horrifying discovery. Duct tape. Lots and lots of duct tape. I'm surprised that he can even breathe. No wonder I had a hard time recognizing the sounds coming from this pathetic creature. It's amazing that he was able to vocalize anything at all.

I edge toward him with a little less trepidation than I had before because obviously he can't bite me — actually, he might be a she. I haven't actually checked, come to think of it. He just looks so scruffy that he reminds me of that character from the movie I saw as a kid, *Benji*. Obviously, my plan to bribe the dog with treats won't work since the poor puppy can't open his mouth. I creep up beside him and quietly sit down. It's really cramped quarters in this little hiding spot. It's a good thing that one of my favorite hobbies as a kid was to cram myself into the smallest possible spaces in my grandparents' old farmhouse and see how long it took people to find me. It drove my grandparents crazy, but I often would spend hours curled up with a good book or an old chunk of charcoal and a pad of paper before anybody managed to locate me.

Slowly, I ease my hand over to him and start to stroke the scuff of his neck. Much to my shock, he rolls over and looks up at me with pleading eyes. Scratch that, *she* looks up at me with pleading eyes as if asking me to scratch her tummy. As I pull my hand back to scratch a different area, I notice that it's covered in blood. I can't believe that she's still so trusting after suffering such egregious maltreatment. I unclip my student I.D. from my backpack, remove the lanyard and hook it to her collar. Of course, her collar doesn't have any I.D. on it. I suppose it's too much to hope that she actually has a microchip. This dog seems to have run out of hopes and prayers an awfully long time ago, I decide as I glance at her concave rib cage and thinning coat. I wonder how long she's been roaming around without any place to call home. It just makes me so sad and angry that I can't even form the thoughts or words to describe my outrage.

Why do people even bother to get dogs if they're not going to take care of them? It boggles the mind.

When I try to stand up, she tries to brace me. The ludicrousness of that situation is not lost on me. This dog is injured enough that she should have difficulty standing up on her own. Yet, she's willing to try to help me. There is something hauntingly beautiful about that simple gesture.

I carefully maneuver us under the hedge so that I don't injure her any more. Intellectually, I thought I was prepared for what I was going to see — but, there. just. aren't. words.

The sight of her juxtaposed against the bright sunny Florida morning is enough to make me retch. If I thought it was horrifying to witness when we were plastered up against the side of the building underneath the hedge, when it's exposed under the bright sunlight, it's the makings of a Stephen King novel. They must have used a half a roll of duct tape on this dog. As I look closer, I can see that at one point, her paws were taped together, but she somehow managed to chew them apart. Even more appalling, it appears that at some point in her young life, probably pretty recently, someone has set fire to this dog's tail. She has raw, open wounds on what should be a thick, bushy German Shepherd tail.

I don't even bother to hide the tears that are streaming down my face. Who in their right mind would do this to any creature — let alone in this quiet, good-natured German Shepherd who is looking up at me with hope filled eyes? I look into her deep, chocolate brown eyes and stroke her ear as I say, "For the time being, I'm going to name you Hope."

Instantly, I regret that I said anything to her because she starts to wag her tail and it thumps painfully on the ground. I coax her into a standing position and start to lead her back to my house. Hopefully, this won't be an ordeal. She's not a very substantial German Shepherd; she's mostly gangly legs and paws at this point. However, if she wanted to make my life difficult, she definitely could. Surprisingly, she doesn't seem to be fearful at all. She falls in right behind me as if she's been heeling for her whole life. As we walk the few blocks to my house, I contemplate what I'm going to do once I get there. I'm not forbidden under the terms of my lease to have a dog, but it's definitely not encouraged and my cat, Midnight, might have a big issue with Hope. He's been the king of my castle since I rescued him. I don't think he'll take too kindly to sharing — especially cross species. Those wounds look deep and somewhat infected. I don't have any way to treat them. I'm a Theater Arts major, minoring in History, I don't have any knowledge about this kind of stuff. I know how to put on Band-Aids when I cut myself with a box cutter when I'm building scenery, but that's about all I know.

The enormity of the challenge ahead of me hits me as I unlock my front gate. My cute little Jeep convertible is parked in the driveway. It's a daunting reminder that I am far over my head. After my Chevy Chevelle died in the middle of the interstate, Tristan and Rogue surprised me for my birthday and got me a vehicle. Neither of them thought that it was extraordinary to buy someone a car for their birthday — which at that time was bizarre, especially since Rogue used to object every time Tristan spent any money on her, but I guess having an engagement ring on your finger changes everything. Still, it's hard to be cynical when I'm the beneficiary of their generosity. I look down at Hope. Her wounds are still seeping and even if they weren't, I'm not sure she has the agility to climb all the way up into my vehicle because I'm not sure how much she hurts right now. Even if I can get her into the Jeep, I'm not sure where I would take her.

I look up animal hospitals on my phone and only one facility is open this early on a Sunday but it's a few miles away. I cross my fingers and hope that I can get her into my vehicle. Hope seems to sense my nerves. She rests her head against my thigh and lets out a big sigh. I reached down to pet her and am once again horrified by the duct tape on her muzzle. I decide that I can't wait any longer and I tie Hope to my roll cage while I run into the house to get my car keys.

Fortunately for me, the concept of a car ride does not seem foreign to Hope. She hops right in to my Jeep and asserts herself as my copilot as she happily sticks her head out the window. I guess it's a good thing that my vehicle is dog friendly. I reach over to pet Hope and I'm dismayed when my hand encounters a fresh trickle of blood. I know that my grandpa preaches that all sin is forgivable, but I sometimes wonder if they should be. Right now I'm not feeling like I should leave the vengeance to the Lord, if you know what I mean.

Mitch

2

"MITCH, I THINK YOU OUGHT to come see what just pulled into the parking lot," Stuart yells across the warehouse where we keep all the extra bedding.

Something in his tone warns me that he's up to something, so I ask, "Are you asking me to evaluate something with two legs or four?"

"Well, Buddy I think that might be the question of the day," Stuart quips. He quickly turns serious as he says, "For the moment though, I think the one with four legs needs the most urgent attention, and if the one with two legs is responsible for the condition of the one with four legs, then you can kiss the one with two legs goodbye."

I've worked with dogs long enough, it only takes me a matter of seconds to size up the situation and when I do, my rage kicks into high gear. Before I can fully engage my brain, I take off into a dead sprint and run toward the bright orange sport utility vehicle.

"Ugh! That's not what I meant!" Stuart calls after me as he jogs around me and runs ahead of me with a pair of blunt nosed scissors and an emesis basin. "What is it about these dogs that makes you lose your ever loving mind?" he wonders, as he stops beside the passenger's door.

When I reach the Jeep, I'm so anxious to reach the dog that I practically rip the hinges off the door. I want to kick my own butt. I know better. I probably just freaked out the dog.

The woman occupant of the car shrieks in surprise at my abrupt intrusion. I hear a strange huffing noise and a growl unlike any I've heard. Like a shape-shifter from the movies, the shepherd mix which had been casually looking out the window moments before, is now fiercely standing over her and challenging me to take one step closer.

"Call your dog off!" I command as I freeze in place, not wanting to agitate the dog any further. Every indication of that dog's body language shows that if I make one false move, I could be spending the night at the hospital being treated for severe dog bites. That certainly is not my idea of fun. I've done it before; I just don't want to do it today. As we have our silent stare down, I take the opportunity to study the dog's predicament a little more closely. What I see makes me angrier by the second.

"Listen, it looks like your dog might have some issues with aggression, but that's not the way you take care of it.

Haven't you ever heard of obedience training? I ought to call the police and have you arrested on the spot," I threaten.

As the volume of my voice increases with each word, the body language of the German Shepherd grows more tense. From the other side of the Jeep, I hear Stuart caution, "Buddy, don't you think you ought to at least hear her side of the story? I know you're mad about the dog's condition, but you don't need to take it out on her."

"The dog can't exactly tell me her side of the story, so the interview would be rather skewed, don't you think?" I retort sarcastically.

The color starts to come back into the woman's face as she turns to address Stuart, "I guess I'll talk to you since you seem to be the only person inclined to listen to me. You're welcome to call the police on me if you want to. I don't really have anything to hide. I came here because I thought you might want to help. Maybe I was wrong. If you aren't going to treat her any better than you're treating me, I guess I'll just keep driving until I find somebody that does."

Stuart starts to apologize, "I'm sorry, Ma'am. He's not usually like this, but something about seeing a dog like this makes him lose his manners and his common sense —"

I'm not ready to give up quite so easily; there's something about this that isn't quite right. "You're going to have a hard time going anywhere else since your dog isn't trained well enough to get off your lap so that you can reach your steering wheel," I observe.

The woman gathers her stunning red hair in a ponytail and twists it before tying her hair in one big knot at the base of her neck. She rubs her shoulder as if it's sore. She mutters to herself, "Oh, for God's sake — it's too early for this kind of garbage."

She blows a puff of air out the side of her mouth and removes her aviator sunglasses.

As far as I'm concerned, she should never wear those shades again. I know that this is Florida, and the shades probably have some good UVA protection, but they are really doing humanity a disservice by hiding her face. As soon as I get a close up look at her, I almost forget why I'm so furious— that is — until she speaks.

"I'd be happy to call this dog off, except I don't really even know her real name or why she's doing this. My only guess is because you scared the bee-jeebies out of me and she doesn't care for your tone. In case you'd bothered to ask, I could've told you that I brought Hope here to be rescued."

"I thought you said you didn't know her name —" I accuse.

"Are you *always* this rude, or am I getting some bizarre two-for-one special today?" she asks with a deep scowl.

"Don't mind my friend here, somebody took the prize out of the bottom of his Lucky Charms box this morning," Stuart says with a smirk. "Why don't you explain to us how you came to find out Hope's name?" he suggests.

"First of all, I don't really think that's her name. I just made it up. I gave her that name because she looked so gosh-darn-hopeful that something good was going to happen in her life for a change."

"How did you end up with her?" I press. "She looks comfortable with you and pretty protective."

"I don't really know why. I was just minding my own business, feeding hummingbirds in my backyard at around six thirty this morning when I recognized a car that has been causing some problems in our neighborhood. After it left, I thought I heard some weird noises. I went to investigate. I didn't have any shoes on so I had to go back to the house. By that time, I lost complete track of her and it took me a bit to find her. I couldn't figure out why she wasn't crying like a normal dog."

"That was a really dangerous situation. You should've called in professionals," I lecture. "She could have been really sick or something. You never know."

"What good would it have done me to call in the professionals? You would've just threatened to call the police on me again," she replies pointedly.

I feel my face grow hot. She's right; I did jump to every wrong conclusion I possibly could have. "How did you get her to trust you so quickly?" I ask, unable to contain my curiosity.

She rolls her eyes at me as she asks Stuart, "Did he forget to eat his Lucky Charms, too? It seems to me that he might be lacking in some brain food or maybe it's because he's eaten too many Lucky Charms over the course of his lifetime and they've caused permanent damage."

Stuart just chuckles and shrugs.

I shoot him an exasperated glance which I hope sends the message, "Gee, thanks for the support, I thought you were my best friend."

The little spitfire looks at me and says, "I'm going to go over this *one* more time with you. Maybe after that, you can actually focus on treating Hope. Are you ready? This is *not* my dog. Before about two hours ago, I had never seen her. I know nothing about her. I found her this way under someone's hedge. I walked her to my car using my student ID as a leash. She is incredibly mellow in the car. She seems to like the name Hope — as much as a dog can like a name. She doesn't particularly care for grey cars or loud stereos. That's the grand total of everything I know about this dog. Oh wait… I know something else. Someone treated this dog like crap and they deserve to have the absolute shit beaten out of them. Someone should tape their mouth shut so they can't scream and set their ass on fire. Of course, that's only my personal opinion."

She gently rubs Hope's ears and murmurs, "I know you were trying to protect me, Baby, but I need you to get out of my personal space because you're squishing me. Out, please."

Hope briefly lays her head on the woman's shoulder as if to apologize and then goes back to the passenger seat as if nothing happened.

The woman looks up at me and says, "I guess I know one more thing —"

"Yeah? What's that?" I ask.

"She responds to the command 'out'," she answers with a cheeky grin.

I can't help but answer with a smile of my own as I concede, "I think you're probably correct. It'll be interesting to see if she knows anything else."

I am once again reminded why Stuart is studying to be a veterinarian. Very quietly without any drama, he opens the door of the Jeep and starts to cut away the layers and layers of duct tape around Hope's legs, feet and tail. He grimaces as he tells the woman, "I can try to start cleaning her up here where she's most comfortable, but we're going to have to move her eventually. This poor girl is just a mess."

A feeling of dread grows in my stomach as I watch the woman try to keep it together and contain her sadness as she attempts to keep the dog calm enough so Stuart can work. It occurs to me that I have completely misjudged the situation and unnecessarily complicated matters. "Can you and I start over?

I'm sorry I jumped to all sorts of incorrect assumptions. I've just become a little jaded, I guess. I'm used to people giving me all sorts of excuses and not enough truth," I try to explain.

A sad faraway look crosses her face as she says, "True. Very true."

I extend my hand for her to shake as I introduce myself properly as I should have done from the start, "Hi, it's nice to meet you. I'm Mitch Campbell. I'm a volunteer here."

I watch in fascination as a blush creeps up from her neck all the way to her hairline. I didn't think I said anything all that controversial. Suddenly she stammers, "Mitch, if I even start to explain to you how small the universe is right now, you would never believe it — not even in a million years."

Stuart and I look at each other and then back at the mystery woman. For the first time today, she looks more than a little nervous. The playful bravado that was there just a few minutes ago seems to have completely vanished. To be honest, her reaction is freaking me out a little. Now, I'm beginning to wonder if my first response to the situation was more accurate than my second. When this all started to unfold, I figured she had something to hide. Now, I wonder if I was spot on. Her body language is suddenly very closed off and, quite frankly, she looks mildly embarrassed.

"What in the world are you talking about?" I demand, feeling defensive again.

"Let me put it this way — of all the ways I anticipated meeting you — this definitely wasn't one of them. I thought that I would get the chance to get all dressed up, looking fierce, like a million dollars — not in my most disgusting Sunday morning   I'm-down-to-my-last-pair-but-that's-okay-because-no-one's-going-to-see-me-today wardrobe."

"Who are you and why do you think that we would meet?" I ask warily.

"I don't know that you would even recognize my name, you interacted mostly with my roommate. However, our mutual friends have been trying to persuade us to get together for more than a couple of years now. I guess maybe fate decided to take a hand." She extends her hand to me and says, "These aren't the circumstances under which I'd hoped to meet, but my name is Jessica Lynn Walker. You probably know me better as Ivy Montclair's former roommate."

Jessica

3

IF THE CIRCUMSTANCES FACING US weren't so dire, the expression on Mitch's face would be worthy of a Vine video. My acting coach at school would've been in seventh heaven if he had seen how clearly Mitch shows his emotion in every muscle twitch in his face. It's a sight to behold.

"Damn that stupid dating site. I don't care if I was raising money for charity by joining that stupid thing. It's going to haunt me for the rest of my life. Tell me, how did you track me down here? Did you put tape on this dog just so you could get my attention?" he asks me, anger accenting every single syllable.

Two can play that game. I am not a natural redhead for nothing. My temper can flare with the best of them. Now that

Hope has moved over to the other seat, I am free to get out. I take advantage of that freedom and I step out of the car. Although, even when I do, it is really not that big of a deal. I had forgotten how tall he said he was in his profile; he dwarfs me. So much for creating a strategic advantage by standing. I might as well be a kid sitting in my timeout chair in the corner for all the impact it has. I feel compelled to poke him in the chest as I set him straight, "Listen before you bury yourself in another hole. You need to know that I didn't have any idea that you still work in Florida, I figured you would graduate from college and take off out of here like every other college student. I didn't even know your full name, let alone your career plans."

"Several of the guys did that. I was planning to graduate with honors, but life got in the way," Mitch admits with a sigh. "I don't think my parents have quite forgiven me for not finishing. I was going to be one of the first people in my family to finish college."

"How can you not have a degree? I read your profile a couple years ago and I thought you were almost finished then," I remember.

Mitch shrugs and answers, "I guess it's like my grandmother used to say, 'I'm a jack of all trades and I'm a master of none.' Originally, I wanted to teach economics at the college level, things didn't go as planned."

"Maybe it's not too late. My grandfather went back to school in his mid-thirties to get his degree from seminary to become a pastor. He injured himself on a combine and wasn't able to do farming full-time," I reply, feeling awkward. It's strange to have this kind of personal conversation with someone that I was just having a hostile interaction with a few moments before.

Feeling awkward about our strange interaction, I retreat to the Jeep and start to gently stroke Hope. I'm not sure whether I am actually soothing her or myself at this point.

I vividly remember the first time I encountered Mitch via the Internet. I was instantly attracted to the person that he projected through his profile on BrainsRsexy.com. It's fascinating to come face-to-face with him. In many ways, he seems radically different from the person he presented himself to be during the brief interactions Ivy and I had with him when we were trying to figure out whether Ivy was being cat-fished through the dating site. Eventually, with the help of Tristan, we determined that she wasn't the victim of fraud at all. She is actually a twin and didn't know it. During those interactions, he seemed open and friendly, almost flirty. Right now, he's not that way at all. Yet his disclosures about his past are giving me a glimpse of the type of person he was when he was talking about his academic career with Ivy. I almost feel like I need to ask him to have the real Mitch step forward. There is one undeniable fact though: he is incredibly cute. He looks like he could be on one of those fundraising calendars for smokin' hot rescue workers. I think he's some sort of heroic volunteer somewhere with search and rescue or something like that.

I can't help but watch as he starts moving dog crates so he can get to a large one at the bottom of the stack. I'm not the only one watching him do his thing. Hope is watching his every move intently. Mitch walks over to the car with a leather lead in his hand. As soon as Hope sees it, she shies away.

Stuart is observing this interaction with obvious amusement. "I don't know what to tell you, Buddy. It looks like you're losing your magic touch with the ladies, both canine and human," he teases with a grin.

Mitch rakes his hand through his short hair making it stand on end. "I don't know what's going on today either. I seem to have gotten up on the wrong side of the bed. I'm generally much nicer to both kinds of creatures. Generally speaking, neither species tends to be afraid of me."

"Then again, you're not known for being rude either, so I guess you have a point," Stuart acknowledges with a grin, but grows serious as he advises, "I've done about all I can do for her here. I need to get her onto a table where I have some better light and can further access her wounds. We need to move her. Do you think she'll co-operate?"

Just then, Hope shifts in the seat and lets out a small whimper, reminding me once again that this is not a social gathering or a TV dating show. I blow my bangs out of my eyes as I impatiently ask, "Do you mind just handing that to me? We need to be doing something for her – sooner rather than later."

Mitch shrugs as he hands the leash to me and says, "Look, I don't mind. In rescue work, there's not much room for ego. Whatever works, works."

After I have the leash in place, Mitch walks up to the side of the Jeep and opens the door to help get Hope out. Unfortunately, she does not agree with that decision and climbs back into my lap. However, this is not a great move on her part because the steering wheel is in the way. There's not a whole lot of room in my small Jeep for a large dog. I'm short and I drive with the seat ridiculously close to the steering wheel so that I can reach the pedals. There is no space for her to be a lapdog, yet it appears she just doesn't care. Mitch sees I'm being squished and makes a grab for Hope. Immediately, the hair on her haunches stands on end.

"Easy, Baby, he's just trying to help you," I soothe. As soon as I speak, she seems to calm down.

"Maybe I should just let you handle her, she seems to react better to you than to me. Maybe her abuser was someone who resembled me," Mitch concedes.

"Hope, out!" I command hopefully. Much to my relief, she complies and returns back to the passenger seat, although she does look really disappointed that she can't sit on my lap. I turn to Mitch as I comment, "That's just a really weird command. It's totally not the word I would use for that. Clearly at one point she was taught that. It doesn't seem to be an accident. I wonder if the rest of her commands are all scrambled?"

"I know, it is strange, but I've learned after so many years in this field never to try to second-guess what people are going to do with their animals," Mitch replies.

"Hey, Mitch, remember that one guy who taught his dog to bring him a Budweiser if his team won and to bring him his Jim Beam if his team lost?" Stuart reminisces.

"Yeah, I remember thinking what a waste of a good dog. That dog would've made an amazing service dog," Mitch responds with a grin.

"You couldn't talk him out of the dog, even for such a good cause?" I inquire.

"No, unfortunately not — not that we didn't try really hard. The guy said his refrigerator was too far away for it to be worth his effort to get off the couch," Mitch answers shaking his head.

For once, I'm glad that my Jeep doesn't have a hardtop on it. I hop out of my side of the Jeep and walk around the vehicle. Fortunately, the leash that Mitch gave me to put on Hope is really long and I'm able to hold onto it while I walk around to the passenger side. Although, I don't think she would really go anywhere. She looks pretty cozy sitting in my passenger's seat. After I open the door, I ask Hope to come. She stays put in the chair as if someone poured rubber cement in the seat. Out of curiosity, I command, "Stay". As I had feared, Hope eagerly jumps out of the Jeep. I glance up at Mitch and ask him, "Care to guess what the command is for h-e-e-l?"

He raises an eyebrow at me and says, "At this point it's anybody's guess; it could be 'run away'. It appears everything in this dog's vocabulary resembles 'Opposite Day'."

Fortunately, my fears are unfounded because much like she did before, Hope follows me with military precision. That is, she does until she sees the exam table in the little room that Mitch leads us into. When she sees the stainless steel exam table, she collapses on the floor and starts to whine. Of course, the sounds coming from her are highly distorted because of the tape on her muzzle.

Alarmed, I look to Mitch for reassurance. I feel tons better when I see a look of heartbreak and devastation on his face as he studies Hope. This is not something he does just to get brownie points in the community. He feels her pain as much as I do.

Mitch pets what's left of her velvet soft ears and murmurs softly to her, "Hope, you have to let me help you. I'll help you feel better, Baby. It's gonna hurt for a little bit, but in the long run, you'll feel way better, I promise." Her body relaxes and her tail gives a feeble wag when she hears his low soothing voice.

Fortunately, Hope collapsed on a pile of blankets, so Stuart and Mitch are able to grab the edges of the blanket and lift her onto the exam table.

Mitch grabs another pair of medical scissors with a blunt point and starts to cut away the duct tape while Stuart takes pictures. I notice that his hands are shaking and it looks like he has tears in the corners of his eyes. "Nervous?" I ask softly.

Mitch looks up at me with a startled expression as he replies through clenched teeth, "Nervous? Oh *hell* no. I'm angry beyond words. There are shelters all over this city. If they didn't want this angel, all they had to do was turn her in some where. That's it. It's not hard. Why do this?"

"I don't know. How could someone look into those brown eyes and do anything like that? She's so sweet even though she's in incredible pain," I empathize, as I lay a soothing hand on Hope's hip and stroke her.

After Mitch manages to remove all of the duct tape on Hope's muzzle, he makes another discovery. There is a laceration on her mouth that needs to be stitched up.

"Can you do that here or do I need to find a vet?" I query with a worried voice.

"I can't, but Stuart here can because he's going to school to become a vet. He's so close to being done he practically is one. I'm just basically a fancy gopher in this organization."

Stuart's eyes widen at Mitch's self-description. "Mitch! You can't go around telling people stuff like that. I can get in trouble for misrepresenting myself," he explains. "What he's not telling you is that our little organization wouldn't exist without his efforts. He can train the untrainable dogs and he's pretty handy at the fundraising efforts, too. Don't let 'Mr. Aw-Shucks' over here fool you. He's pretty indispensable."

Mitch looks over at me and says, "Jessica, can you come over and talk to her? She seems to calm down a lot when you do. Maybe if she's focused on you, she'll pay less attention to what Stuart and I are doing."

I slide off the stool that I've been sitting on. I try to forget the fact that blood makes me a little queasy. I need to be there for Hope. This is bigger than my little phobias. I pull on the strength of my inner nomad. The girl that survived a year in

New York. The one that's not afraid of big rats and cockroaches. If I can handle New York, I can survive anything. I'm a farm girl, I've seen everything, right?

I kneel down on a little stool in front of Hope's head so she can see me. "Am I out of the way here?" I ask.

Mitch nods as he responds, "You should be fine."

"Hope, they're going to make you feel so much better," I soothe quietly. "After you're all better, we'll go get you a giant chew bone. How does that sound?"

I'm trying desperately hard to ignore what's going on in front of me and just concentrate on helping Hope feel better. I'm doing a reasonable job of conquering my phobias — until Stuart makes a whistling noise under his breath and remarks to Mitch, "I've been doing this a while now, but this is the first time I've ever had to remove a piece of Skoal can from a dog's face. I wonder if they were using it as a muzzle?"

"There is no explanation for why there should be a chewing tobacco can embedded in the face of a dog which is deep and ingrown. It's several days, if not weeks old. Even if the dog accidentally got into it, they should've taken her to the vet," Mitch reasons with a scowl.

I can't help but gasp, "Who would do such a thing? She had to be in terrible pain!" Just the thought of it makes me dizzy and I start to sway. It's a good thing that Stuart has finished suturing up her laceration because as soon as Hope sees me become unsteady, she barks to alert Mitch that I'm in trouble — or, at least it looks that way to my untrained eye.

Mitch reaches out to catch me and then turns to Stuart and comments, "Hope has some good instincts. It almost seems like she has some training. Did you check to see if she's got a chip?"

Stuart shakes his head, "Oh man, I completely forgot. I got distracted by the duct tape. I'm not sure if I hope she has a chip or hope she doesn't. It'd be nice if she had a chip so that we can hold somebody accountable for the horrific stuff that's happened to her. At this point, I hope she doesn't have a chip so that we don't have to argue with somebody about her treatment."

Mitch pulls a device out of the cupboard that looks like one of the laser tag toys that the kids used to play with at the arcade I used to work at in New York. His expression turns grim when the machine beeps. He walks over to an ancient looking computer and waits for it to warm up. When he punches the code into the computer, he draws in a sharp breath of surprise. He opens up another program, muttering under his breath the whole time. After a few moments, he exclaims in utter disbelief, "Stu, remember those three puppies that were stolen from the city shelter about a year ago?"

"Yeah, I thought they recovered those—" Stuart replies.

"They did, all except one — meet the one that got left behind," Mitch clarifies.

Mitch and Stuart both look at me and shrewdly ask, "How did you say you came across this dog again?"

"Are we *really* back to this?" I answer with a huff. "Do you guys know what I went through to get her here? I was afraid she might go into shock and die on the way here or something. When I saw Hope, I was out feeding hummingbirds at the crack-o-dawn because that's when my slightly batty landlord begs me to do it and I don't want to upset their routine. I actually crawled through a sewer pipe to rescue my cat, Midnight when he was a kitten. He was smaller than a hot-dog bun. Do I sound like a crazy sociopathic animal abuser to you? Truth be told, I much prefer them to people." I am out of breath when I finish. This man is enough to chap my booty! What a jerk!

Stuart steps forward and extends his hand in a gesture of placation. "Jessica, look… we're sorry. We have to ask these kinds of questions of everyone and confirm our answers. It's more a matter of formality than anything else. We have to make sure we cover our bases to protect the animals."

"I guess I understand that. Still, does it make you feel any better to treat me like a criminal when I was just trying to help Hope? I honestly didn't do anything to her except try to help her. I wouldn't knowingly hurt another creature, ever. I don't even order fish on the menu for that very reason. Even though I know that there are ways to harvest them ethically, I still can't get over holding them and skinning them. I would not make a very good craftsperson who had to deal with animal skins all day long," I answer randomly.

"Just for record-keeping, can we confirm with your roommate, Ivy that you didn't own Hope before today?" Mitch asks.

I shrug as I answer, "Sure, you can ask Ivy if I've ever owned a dog, but she's not my roommate anymore. She just met and fell in love with this guy named Marcus and she and her twin sister Rogue are going to a different school than me now. Ivy and Rogue are identical twins. She never knew she had a twin before they found each other. Oh, wait you already know this. You helped them find each other; I forgot about that for a second. Basically, this story shouldn't come as much of a shock to you."

"Okay, if Hope is not your dog, what can you tell me about the car that you saw drive away?" Stuart asks as he strips off his protective clothing.

"It probably comes as no surprise to either one of you that I am not a real sports car person. Now, put me in front of a Jeep or a John Deere and I could probably tell you the model year, how many seasons it's been run and the last time it had a decent maintenance job, but since my Grandpa firmly believed that his '52 Nash Rambler was a good family car and never needed updating, my knowledge of cars is virtually nonexistent. I do know that the car in question is gray and has an obnoxiously loud stereo system. Whoever does own this car should've probably put less money in the stereo system and more money in a decent muffler and exhaust system. I don't know a lot about cars, but there is something mechanically wrong with that one. It's ridiculously loud and not in a low, sexy 'I-want-more-horsepower' kind of way. This is more of a 'I-may-not-make-it-home' kind of noise."

Mitch just shakes his head and remarks, "As unique as that clue may seem, it's really not all that helpful, kids these days drive those sorts of cars all the time. They use them for street racing. They're pretty much interchangeable, even though the kids don't think so. It's possible the noise being made is from some sort of specialized engine kit. You don't even know if she actually came from that car. That's pretty much a guess on your part; it's unlikely that the police department will actually even do anything about that. So we're pretty much at square one."

As I'm standing there silently stroking Hope's head, she nuzzles my hand and licks it. "Actually, I think that Hope would disagree with you. I think she would tell you that she is in a much better place than where she started this morning. Now, we just have to track down the guys that did this to Hope and decide a reasonable way to make them feel the kind of pain they put her through."

Stuart looks at me and then over at Mitch as he declares, "I don't know about you, but I like the way this one thinks."

Mitch

4

I STOP IN FRONT OF the refrigerator, open the door and stare blankly inside. Finally, I remember what I'm doing. "Stuart, do you want a Coke or a beer?" I ask, tossing the question over my shoulder.

I hear Stuart groan as he lifts his backpack, "It's been a killer day, but I better stick with Coke, I've got to take a test on infectious diseases and the nervous system. Remember the good old days when I only needed to know the human nervous system? Now, I need to know about twenty of them. It's tricky too because even though the test is on the nervous system, the skeletal system of each animal impacts how the nerves run. Basically I just need to know it all."

"You're making my statistics and theoretical mathematics classes sound like a walk in the park," I respond with a shudder.

"Shut up. You are an amazing student. You don't have anything to worry about. You could've done that all in your sleep. Are you ever planning to go back? It's such a waste that you ever left school. I'll never in a million years understand why you left school with only a term and half to go," Stuart halfheartedly scolds, as he walks around me to dig out some half eaten pizza from the refrigerator.

I glare at him as I answer, "You know why I left; that was a stupid thing to say. You almost left your program too," I counter.

"Well, it would have made sense for me to have taken a leave of absence from my program. She was my fiancé, but you guys were just friends from high school," Stuart argues, his voice choking with emotion.

"Yeah, we were friends. The three of us were best friends. We were pretty much the Three Musketeers all the way through elementary school and junior high school before Nora became interested in boys and started dating you. She's the reason I was interested in search and rescue. Her passion for it was infectious. I don't think I'll ever be able to wrap my brain around the fact that of all of us, she was the one that died in the field. She had the most experience and the most passion for it. She did it full time while you and I were only weekend warriors. I'll never be able to sort out the injustice of it all."

"Me either," Stuart answers with a heavy sigh. "I loved her so much. But, Nora had her faults too. She liked the adrenaline of living on the edge. It's what made her fearless in her job. We'll never know if she was too fearless on the day she died. The only way that I can stay sane is to know that she died doing something she loved, you know what I mean?"

"Yeah, I know," I concede. "There wasn't anything she liked better than to be dropped in the middle of a crisis situation like the earthquake she died in. She loved her job like nobody I've ever seen before or since. She gave the word passion new meaning, that's for sure."

"Speaking of passion, what do you think of the little wildfire that we met today?" Stuart probes.

"Honestly, I don't know what to make of her. Part of me really hopes that she's telling the truth. I get the sense that she probably is, but there's something about her that isn't as it seems. She gives the appearance of being flaky and flighty, but I think that there's a whole lot more to Jessica Walker than meets the eye. I'm just really curious to find out what's going on underneath all those different layers of personality. She seems to hide a lot."

"With all due respect, Buddy, I would've held a whole lot back from you too. You scared the living daylights out of her today. I hardly blame her for being a little less than forthcoming with you. I don't know what you thought you were doing with her, but it wasn't a very effective strategy for a nice friendly, get-to-know-you session. You acted like she was an enemy of the state — not a friendly, helpful Good Samaritan bringing in a dog for a little first aid. I thought that you were a little better at reading people than that. I don't know what's going on with you that's making you act all phycho. If you're going to deal with customers, you need to get over this little 'issue' of yours or we're going to lose our community funding. We operate on a shoestring budget as it is, we can't afford to lose a single dime. One of these days, you're going to tick off the wrong person," Stuart cautions.

I roll my shoulders trying to work the tension out as I begrudgingly agree. I knew, the minute the words came flying out of my mouth, I was going to regret them. Unfortunately, that never seems to stop me from spouting off like a steam engine. "I know; I was out of line. I owe her an apology. There was really no excuse for me losing it like that. I should've gotten the facts first."

"Seems to me that you need to be telling *her* this, not me," Stuart counsels.

"Sure, I'll just march right over to her house and hand her an apology, that won't creep her out or anything," I reply sarcastically.

"*Or*, you could just return her student I.D. lanyard and let her know how Hope is doing. I'm not trying to tell you what to do here, but that's just the approach I'd take. Of course, yelling at her some more might prove effective, who knows?" Stuart suggests with a smirk.

I study the grainy surveillance video again. Of course, I've seen some of these clips in the news, but I've never seen the whole tape. I'm hoping to see something that I haven't already seen on television. Sadly, I can't see anything that I couldn't see on my flat-screen at home. In fact, the view is worse here. I turn to the director of the Central Shores Shelter and ask, "Venetia, were the police able to capture any screenshots that showed the thieves' faces?"

Venetia looks at me with complete shock and then amusement as she responds, "Oh Darling, don't ever pick up a side career as a criminal; you'd never make it."

I glance at her with confusion on my face. "What? It was a legitimate question."

"They had oversized sunglasses, bandannas and baseball caps on, there was precious little to identify them with. We could hardly even distinguish a skin tone one way or other."

I scrub my hand down my face in frustration. I can't believe that we actually caught them on camera but it's not going to do any good. What good is Big Brother if all of those stupid cameras don't yield any usable information? "You're telling me there's no way to identify these punks?" I ask, incredulously, unable to process what I'm hearing. "They didn't sign in or anything? I thought that all visitors had to sign in."

Venetia sighs deeply as she replies, "That's how it's supposed to work, but they managed to sneak in during a really busy adoption fair. It was crazy that day. We had so many people here that you could barely find room for your own shadow. A bunch of our staff was out sick with the flu so people weren't supervised as closely as they usually are. It was just a catastrophe waiting to happen and it did. As nearly as we can tell, it must've been a ring of them — because they got away with three puppies. It breaks my heart to find out what happened to this little one. She was the runt of the litter to start with; she was always more legs and paws than anything else. Here at the shelter, we named her Lucy because she was never very coordinated and she reminded us of Lucille Ball. You be sure to thank that young lady for finding her, you hear?" Venetia insists.

"It's funny you should say that, because that's exactly where I'm headed. Thank you for your time today. I was hoping we would be able to find out more information about who did this, but it looks like maybe I've hit a dead end here, too. Maybe that information that Jessica has about the car will help the police narrow the list of suspects a little. I don't know, it's not much to go on — but it's something," I hope as I grab my coat and head out the door. I reach down and untangle Lexicon's leash from his legs. He's a new dog we've just started working with for search and rescue. His owner surrendered him to us after he was diagnosed with pancreatic cancer because he figured he wouldn't be able to deal with an active German Shepherd puppy. Right now, the jury is still out about whether he is going to have what it takes to be a search and rescue dog. On the upside, he's really curious about what's going on in the world, but it's hard to hold his focus for very long. Apparently, he hasn't been walked on a lead very much either. Some dogs instinctively know how to untangle themselves if they get stuck on a leash. Lexicon is *not* one of those dogs. He's baffled every time it happens.

By the time I finally find Jessica's address, I can tell that Lexicon is eager to get out of the car and take a walk.

I spot a patch of grass in the side yard that doesn't look like it would be too damaged by an exuberant puppy in training. I walk around the side of the house and let Lexicon do his business. As I do, I see something through the open gate. The flash of color is mesmerizing. I lean up against the edge of the old picnic table and just watch in amazement.

I should probably feel voyeuristic, yet somehow I don't. I can't look away from the artistry of her movements. Jessica is in a word — stunning. One word is not enough to describe her.

She is not only stunning, but exotic, earthy, sensual and ethereal all at once. There isn't a trace of tomboy here. I don't even know how she can dare to describe herself that way.

My eyes drink in her beauty as if I've never seen a woman before today. She is wearing a jade colored bra and some sort of deep purple and blue tutu thing ballet dancers wear. She has hot pink headphones on with black zebra stripes. It's obvious that she has no idea that I'm even here because she's lost in her own world of music. She is standing inside of a little gazebo that's surrounded by hummingbird feeders. She's performing some exotic belly dance. I've never seen anything like this. It's like watching poetry: intricate, yet sexy. It's clear that she knows what she's doing; unlike that stripper that Stuart took me to see when we turned twenty-one. She was just a poser compared to Jessica's skill.

I wonder where she learned to belly dance. I think she told me that her grandpa is a pastor. I can't imagine that belly dancing is standard curriculum in the church. Lexicon comes up and nudges my leg. It's then I realize how long I've been sitting here, staring at her. Now I'm in an awkward situation; do I acknowledge how long I've been sitting here, or do I just pretend I haven't seen anything?

The decision is quickly taken out of my hands as Lexicon gives a quick bark of excitement. "Mitch? What are you doing here? As you can see, I wasn't expecting company," Jessica exclaims as she blushes scarlet red.

Oddly enough, it's my turn to blush. I thought I had outgrown that in junior high, but I guess not. Perhaps it's what I deserve for spying on her for so long. I fish her lanyard out of my pocket and hand it to her as I stammer, "I stopped by to give you this."

For a moment, Jessica looks at it with confusion before saying, "Umm... thanks. I appreciate it, but you could've mailed this."

I blush even more because she's seen through my transparent ruse to visit her. Awkward! "You're right, I could've, but I also needed to come and apologize to you in person for my behavior yesterday. There was no call for the way that I treated you. You were doing absolutely the right thing and I jumped to all the wrong conclusions. I was way out of line. I came to say that I'm sorry; I want to thank you for taking the time to bring Hope to us. She is doing much better this morning. It looks like maybe we were able to get antibiotics on board in time. We'll probably be able to save her tail from the burns."

Jessica sags so abruptly that she almost lands in my lap. "Oh my gosh, I'm so glad you said that. I worried about her all last night. I had a paper due in my History of Ancient Greece class, but there was no way I could concentrate on it because I was thinking so much about Hope. I think God probably got tired of hearing my prayers about that poor dog."

"Let me tell you, he heard his fair share from me, too," I admit. "Stuart tells me she's doing much better this morning. She was even doing well enough to eat soft food this morning, so she must not be in excruciating pain."

A second ago, I was looking into Jessica's eyes, but now I'm just staring into space because she just suddenly disappeared. Though, it's not difficult to figure out where she went. She's currently on her knees, hugging the stuffing out of Lexicon and having a conversation with him like they're long-lost buddies. Of course, he's eating it up like nobody's business. He has a pitiful expression on his face that would put Eeyore to shame.

I gently tap her on the shoulder and instruct, "This is beautiful and worthy of a Hallmark moment, but technically you're not supposed to be touching Lexicon because he's wearing a service dog vest."

Jessica shoots up to her feet so quickly, my father who is a field instructor at the Firefighter Academy would be proud. Her hand flies over her mouth and she whispers in a horrified voice, "Oh my gosh! I even *know* better than to do that. I went to high school with someone who was blind. I don't know why I didn't think about that when I saw the vest. I'm so sorry."

I chuckle under my breath as I respond, "Don't worry about it, Jessica. Lexicon is a pretty compelling little dog. Stuart calls him the 'Con Dog' because he can persuade you to do pretty much anything even when you know better. He's just that cute and cuddly."

"I think it would be really hard to say no to him on a regular basis. Then again, I pretty much have a hard time saying 'no' to any animal. I'm probably not your best test audience. My grandma drew the line at me keeping pet spiders like in Charlotte's Web," she reminisces with a grin.

I smile as I relate, "My mom's hard line was snakes. She wouldn't even let me have a garter snake. I never understood that. She didn't believe me when I told her they wouldn't poison her. She told me that I must've misunderstood all of my library books."

"With as much as you love animals, I'm surprised you didn't become a veterinarian like Stuart," Jessica observes.

"I thought about it, but I don't have money for all the years of schooling that it would take. My grandpa was helping me pay for college until he passed away and he taught at the college level for years and years. That's what he wanted me to do and it seemed reasonable at the time. I really like business and economics. I even thought about going to law school."

"Why don't you? You seem pretty smart to me. You could probably do either career. Maybe you could get a scholarship or something," Jessica suggests.

Her innocent words feel like burning embers to my soul. I have felt completely lost in the two and a half years since Nora died. It's like I can't find my bearings. People don't really understand my grief and I can't really explain it to them. The conversation would get really awkward if I actually told anyone the truth. How do you say to someone, "You know that person you thought was my childhood buddy — my best friend's soon-to-be fiancé? I've actually been in love with her since she took me to a Sadie Hawkins dance in the ninth grade." Unfortunately, my best friend had already laid a claim on her. So no one understands why Nora's death completely derailed me because everyone assumes we were just casual friends. I can't even share the truth with my best friend because it would completely destroy him. Consequently, I'm left to figure it out on my own. I'm not doing a very good job with that either. They say that time heals all wounds; I guess that just isn't true for me. I keep waiting to get over the pain, but it's still there like an unwanted shadow.

I must have grimaced because Jessica lays her hand on my forearm and asks with concern, "Hey, are you all right? Are you hurt?"

I swallow hard as I answer with a wry shake of my head, "Not in the way you think, but I'll survive." I shift positions and call Lexicon over to my side as I try to change the subject. "Hey, is there any way that you can show me where Hope got out of the car? Maybe Lexicon can use some of his new training to help us track down some clues."

Jessica looks down at her attire and attempts to cover herself with her arms as she asks, "Okay, but do you mind if I throw on some clothes first? I don't usually let anyone see me like this. You can grab yourself something to drink from the refrigerator and if you're feeling really brave, you can try the hummus and garlic pita bread that I made the other day when I was trying my hand at vegetarian cooking. I can almost guarantee that it won't kill you. I've eaten it for two days and fed it to my coworkers and no one has died yet, so I think it's relatively safe."

I grin at her as I respond, "What's a farm girl like you doing eating hummus?"

She shrugs as she answers, "Beats me; it was one of those things that seemed like a good idea at the time. I was watching this really great cooking show. It convinced me that for the health of the planet and everyone I know, I needed to learn to cook like a vegetarian. After completely destroying my kitchen, I'm thinking that maybe for the health of the planet and everyone I know, I should probably just stick to cooking what I know how to cook. It was kind of a disaster. I think I doubled or tripled my carbon footprint just from all of the dishes I had to wash."

I laugh out loud at her description. "That sounds like the first time that Nora, Stuart and I tried to make our moms a chocolate cake for Mother's Day. If the instructions told us to mix it on low, we were pretty sure that it would've been much better and fluffier if it were mixed on high. Stuart's poor mom was cleaning cocoa powder out of her drapes and ceiling vents for months," I explain, chuckling at the memory.

"I bet that was a colossal mess. Is Nora your sister or Stuart's?" she asks as she flips on lights as we walk through her kitchen. A black cat takes off like a bolt of lightning as soon as it sees Lexicon. Much to Lexicon's credit, he does not go chasing after the cat. I guess at least some of his training is sinking in. I'm very encouraged. When he first came into our program, he had absolutely no manners at all.

I'm trying to come up with a socially acceptable answer to that question and eventually I decide to tell Jessica the unvarnished truth. I figure it's not much of a risk because she doesn't really know me from Adam. She's probably not going to judge me too harshly, given the circumstances.

I scrub my hand over my face and notice that I probably should've shaved this morning, I'm not really sure why I didn't. What a bizarre thing to notice at this very second. Oddly, that's the way my brain works sometimes.

"Nora was Stuart's high school girlfriend, she was also the reason that we got into search and rescue work. Unfortunately, she lost her life on a rescue mission."

Jessica interrupts me and exclaims, "Oh, I'm so sorry. That is so sad, but how sweet was it that they were high school sweethearts—"

I take a deep breath before I confess, "Sweet for them, but not so sweet for me. Sadly, I was in love with Nora almost as long as Stuart was."

Jessica

5

"YOU ARE AN ASSHAT," I assert through clenched teeth.

Mitch reacts as if I've slapped him.

"Let me get this straight. You think I'm an asshat because I fell in love when I was fourteen years old?" he asks incredulously.

"Yes! Only a jerk steals his best friend's girlfriend," I explain angrily.

"I don't recall telling you that I actually stole Nora from him. To this day, Stuart has no idea that I had any sort of romantic feelings toward her — in the ninth grade or on the day she died; I've stayed loyal to him throughout our whole friendship," Mitch retorts.

"How could he not know if he's your best friend? Your grief is like a neon sign," I counter.

"I don't know, I always figured it was because he had his own crap to deal with and he didn't have the emotional energy to deal with my stuff too — or maybe he just didn't want to see it. Who knows? The bottom line is that we both loved her very much… and now she's gone. I'm having a little trouble sorting out my life without her in it. I can't exactly turn to Stuart and explain to him why everything was so messed up. If I did, he would know how much I loved Nora. That's why I just keep my emotional stuff to myself."

"You don't have anybody you can talk to about this? What about your family?" I ask, feeling remorseful about my snarkiness.

Mitch shakes his head. "No, that won't work either. His family and mine practically live out of each other's pockets. They play Bunco, golf and go RVing. They even sponsor a local Little League team. I don't want to put them in a position where they would have to choose sides between us if we ever started fighting, particularly if it was over a woman. It's just a no-win situation all the way around."

"You can talk to me about it, I'm usually a really good listener. I have to warn you though, I may have some pre-existing bias, because this is a really hot button issue for me."

"That listening thing goes both ways, you know," Mitch offers.

I blow my bangs out of my face as I pull a pitcher of sweet tea out of the refrigerator. Thank goodness my grandma always taught me to be prepared for guests. This is pretty much the first time I've actually ever had to use her southern lady training, but it's handy nonetheless.

"That's okay; you don't need to hear about all the drama in my life. It's not even really my drama. My mom just never could figure out who she was in love with between two best friends. She just bounced back-and-forth between both of them like a pinball. I was the one that got left behind in the equation. It just stings a little," I acknowledge.

Mitch nods as he replies, "I can imagine so. That's one of the reasons I never said anything about my unrequited love. I didn't have to put Nora in the position of having to choose between the two of us. We were also close growing up; it would've been really unfair to ask that of her."

"But what about what you ask of yourself? You made some pretty big sacrifices for your friends," I point out.

"I didn't really have any choice. Stuart was the closest thing I had to a brother and Nora held my heart in her hands. I did my best to keep them both happy."

"You're a remarkable guy, Mitch, I hope someday I have somebody in my life who is as good a friend as you," I remark, as I take a tray of vegetables out of the refrigerator.

Mitch's eyes widen as he watches the pile of food grow in front of him, "I thought you said you weren't expecting anybody," he teases.

"I wasn't. If I'd been expecting you, this wouldn't be served on paper plates. You'd get the good china and crystal glasses with flowers and the whole shebang — this is just a snack, Southern style... well, Southern style meets vegan, I guess. Okay... I'm just going to shut up right now. It doesn't even sound appetizing to me. You can eat it if you want or not. I'm going to go upstairs and put some decent clothes on," I say in a rush. I'm embarrassed to be half naked, rambling and sounding ditzy.

45

A slow grin crosses Mitch's face as he examines me slowly from head to toe. "I don't know, I think I'd have to argue that you look more than decent to me. That dance was the most exquisite thing I've ever seen."

I run upstairs and hide in my shower. I turn the water on and barely notice it's freezing cold. My skin is so hot from embarrassment that I could be standing under a glacier and I don't think I'd even notice. I can't believe he caught me belly dancing. Yes, I belly dance — but I can count on one hand the number of people who actually know that I do.

It started during my freshman year of college. I went to school in New York. I had a roommate, Natasha. She was like, the coolest person I'd ever met. She started getting really sick about the second week of school. She went to tons of different kinds of doctors it turned out she had some bizarre form of hereditary autoimmune disorder. A bunch of the girls in the dorms decided to take a belly dancing class and put on a little show for her when she was in the hospital. I'm so clumsy; I thought that I was going to hate the class. Initially I just did it because I felt pressured by my friends to do it. It turned out that I really liked the control that it gave me over my body. For once in my life, I felt strong and sexy. After my parents decided that their drama was more important than raising me, they turned me over to my grandparents, so I was raised as a pastor's kid or grandkid as the case may be. Conservative values were the name of the game.

The thought of a belly dancing class was ludicrous to me, but I love the dichotomy of the freedom from rules but the discipline and tradition of belly dancing. It is exhilarating for me. Having said all that, I very rarely dance in front of other people. And when I do, I'm usually heavily made up and in costume. When I have made public appearances for charity, I performed under the stage name Jinger Jessane. So far, I think

SHELTERED
Hearts

that Mitch is the only person I know personally who knows that I belly dance besides Natasha.

Speaking of Mitch, I guess I better hurry up and get back down there, so instead of lingering in the shower like I love to do, I give myself a speed shower and throw on some sweats. I figure he's basically seen all of me and there aren't really any secrets left so I throw my hair in a ponytail and head back downstairs. I guess it's time to go face the music. I figure the upside is that I have already been just about as embarrassed as I'm ever going to get in front of Mitch — it only can go uphill from here.

Before I reach the bottom of the stairs, I pause to listen to Mitch. It takes me a moment to figure out what he's doing and I have to peek my head around the corner to confirm what my ears are hearing. Sure enough, Mitch is down in the floor using Midnight as a training tool for Lexicon. I cannot believe my eyes. Midnight is the pickiest cat ever. He particularly doesn't like men. He has only granted his gift of friendship to very few people. To the best of my knowledge, he doesn't like any men at all. In fact, it is not an understatement to say that he absolutely hates them. For him to tolerate a guy, let alone a guy with a dog, is absolutely astounding. Not only does he appear to be letting Mitch pet him, he appears to be enjoying it.

I almost blow my cover when Midnight allows Lexicon to lay his muzzle across his back and doesn't flinch. It's almost enough to make me suspect that Mitch swapped out my cat for a stunt cat. It is truly remarkable. A few moments later, Mitch praises them both and gives them both a thorough tummy scratching. By the way they both react, you would think that they were lifelong friends instead of new acquaintances. After Midnight saunters off, I quietly walk around the corner and then give a thumbs up to Mitch as I comment, "That was almost too

47

impressive for words. What did you say you do for your day job again?"

An odd look crosses Mitch's face as he replies, "I am a bookkeeper for the school district."

"That's a perfectly honorable job. Why do you sound like somebody asked you to eat day old liver and onions?" I probe.

"Let's just say it's not the stimulating use of my education that I was hoping for," Mitch answers with a grimace.

"Why don't you find something else that's a better fit?" I gesture to the couch where Lexicon is quietly sitting at his feet. "You obviously are a man of many talents."

"I wish my decision was that easy, but I've got a lot of people counting on me to make the right choice."

"I can totally understand where you're coming from. I've made some doozies in my own life. How about we set aside personal reflection for a while and go try to catch some bad guys for Hope?"

"Sounds like a plan to me," Mitch agrees as he leverages his long frame off my dainty couch. It's a rather comical sight. I didn't choose the couch, it came with the cottage, but its quaint style doesn't fit Mitch's lanky body very well.

It's going to be funny to see how we kiss. *Woah! Back up, Jess, where in the world did that come from? You might want to rein it in a little—you barely know the man.*

Suddenly, I look up and notice that Mitch is looking at me with an amused grin. He points to my feet and says, "I'd recommend shoes unless you're planning to completely reenact the scenario, complete with running back to your house."

I want to smack my forehead. "I swear I'm not this dense. Most of the time, I'm a fully functioning adult — capable of dressing myself without assistance. I can even comb my hair and brush my teeth," I finish with a smirk.

Mitch shrugs as he responds, "Okay, I won't tell you the number of days Stuart has to remind me to tuck in my shirt or make sure it's not on inside out. He has designated himself to be my fashion police because I'm pretty helpless. Lord, help the woman who marries him. Most of the clothing budget in their house is going to go to him." "Really?" I ask, in surprise. "I guess I really wouldn't know that since I only saw him in scrubs, but he didn't really strike me as a fashion bug."

"We have a room in our apartment dedicated only to his clothes and shoes," Mitch explains with a raised eyebrow.

"Oh… wow!" I breathe. "That's impressive dedication. I'm sure that there is a match for him somewhere. As my Grandma Wilma says, there is a lid for every teapot."

I run over to my front door and slip on some Keds. I grab my keys and automatically start to clip them to my lanyard but realize that it's not there. Mitch walks over to my kitchen table where I dumped my phone and headphones and grabs it. He gently slips it over my head and pulls my ponytail through it. Such a simple gesture shouldn't be intimate, but somehow it is.

I give myself a mental shake as I try to remember — despite our Internet chats — Mitch is pretty much a stranger to me. We may have bonded over the dogs, but we might not have much else in common. Besides that, he is scorching hot. The kind of hot guy that probably has a girlfriend or two waiting in the wings. I have no business letting my thoughts wander. Just as I'm thinking that, Mitch puts his hand on the small of my back as he escorts me out the front door and all of my good intentions go flying out of the window.

We stop at the trunk of the car and he presents a piece of gauze from one of Hope's wounds. Mitch gives a low command to Lexicon. The dog instantly assumes a different posture. He is more alert and focused than I've seen him. Immediately he takes us on a sharp turn to the left.

"How did he do that? I didn't tell you guys which way to go," I whisper as I try to keep up.

Mitch shrugs as he responds, "It's what I teach these guys to do. It's a critical skill in search and rescue. I'm trying not to put any pressure on Lex. To him, this is all just a game. He thinks this is fun stuff. He doesn't realize that he's learning a job. This is his first real world test. Up until now, he's only done it at our training facility; it'll be interesting to see if he can stay on task and not get distracted."

"He seems to be doing spectacularly well so far. In fact, this must be where Hope went when I went back for my shoes. Poor baby, she probably came back here to eat something from Mr. Martinelli's dumpsters, but her mouth was all taped," I lament.

There is a jagged chain-link fence with a hole in it. I'm getting prepared to crawl through the hole when all of a sudden Lexicon sits down and refuses to move. "Hold up!" Mitch commands abruptly.

"Okay," I agree as I freeze in place. "What happened?"

"Lexicon alerted to something. I need to check it out, it's possible it's a false alert, but it very well could be real," Mitch explains as he puts on some neoprene gloves.

I hold my breath. My heart is pounding so hard. I'm not even quite sure why I feel like I'm the one on the spot. I've always suffered from really severe test anxiety. It's one of the reasons that I prefer the arts to more traditional learning settings. Don't get me wrong; I'm a really big nerd. I love learning about the science-y things especially if they involve animals. In a perfect world, I would love to be a marine biologist and save the whales and other endangered sea life. But I know myself well enough to know that I would never be able to handle that academic rigor of all those science and math classes. I just don't have the ability to buckle down and hold still. I would melt down under the pressure of tests. Not to mention getting high-level PhDs and all the stuff you would need to be a professional in the field. I also think that I would miss performing on stage. I like pretending to be somebody that I'm not. It gives me a great sense of freedom.

I watch as Mitch carefully scours the area for any clues. Lexicon's body is tense with concentration and focus as he watches Mitch for cues. Finally, I see Mitch pull out a plastic bag from his backpack and deposit something in it. The relief that courses through my body is palpable. It seems that Lexicon must've been successful. I don't want to interfere with what Mitch is doing, but I am so curious about what he found that it's difficult to resist my urge to run over there and ask a million and a half questions. After a few minutes, it appears that they've finished whatever it is they're doing and Mitch boxes up everything. He tosses Lexicon a toy that looks a bit like a deranged sock-puppet and starts to praise him effusively. In that moment, all of Lexicon's professional behavior vanishes and he becomes a quintessential puppy with absolutely no boundaries; he suddenly starts randomly bouncing about four and a half feet up in the air.

Mitch laughs out loud at Lexicon's antics. I don't know what I expected his uninhibited laughter to sound like, but I guess I didn't expect it to sound so free and unrestrained. It's contagious and I start to laugh too. "You should do that more often," I comment absently. I'm a little shocked when the words actually emerge from my mouth. I was thinking them, but I didn't actually mean to repeat them out loud.

Mitch looks up at me with a puzzled expression on his face as he asks, "I should do what more often?"

Blushing, I explain, "You should laugh more often. You have a great laugh. It makes me happy. I guess it reminds me of my grandpa's laugh. He can bring a whole church full of people to smiles just with his laugh. Your laugh is a lot like his."

"Gee, I don't know how I feel about that," Mitch responds with a grin. "Isn't your grandpa kind of old?"

"Well, technically yes," I concede, "but to hear my grandma tell the story, he was quite the dashing young man when they met. She fell in love with him even though he had a farmer's tan and had a black eye because a bull had kicked him."

"It does seem like it would take a whole lot of charm to overcome those deficits for sure," Mitch teases as he pulls a bottle of water out of his backpack and offers some to Lexicon in some sort of foldable bowl.

Finally, I can't contain my curiosity any longer "What did your dog find?"

"Well, I don't know for sure. That'll be up to the police to decide. But I have a guess. I think that Hope was wearing some sort of training harness when they dumped her off. She must have caught it on a fence or maybe part of the car when they pushed her out. I've seen this logo before. I trained a service dog once for a lady in a wheelchair and she had a couple of harnesses specially made from a leather company and they had the same logo. If my hunch is correct, we might have these guys. This company is pretty small. They hand make everything," he explains, the excitement building in his voice with every single word.

"Oh, you have no idea. If they bought it over the Internet, my friend Tristan and Ivy's dad, Isaac can bust them so hard that they'll have a cyber concussion," I declare, practically bouncing up and down like a kid who has just seen my first parade.

"Remind me who they are again?" Mitch asks, his brows drawn together in concentration.

"I don't know how much of this story Ivy ended up telling you. She talked to you online via BrainsRSexy because she was trying to figure out why guys were telling her that she'd gone on dates that she never went on. Eventually, she figured out that she had a twin sister. When she met Rogue, she actually fell in love with Rogue's best friend, Marcus. Rogue fell in love with Tristan, the guy who helped track Rogue down. It was all very romantic. It was even more romantic when together they all went on a grand adventure to find their long-lost dad, Isaac. When they found Isaac, they discovered that he had been told that everyone passed away and that he was still desperately in love with Rogue and Ivy's mother. Now, everyone is one big, happy family."

Mitch is looking at me with his jaw slightly agape. When he can finally find the words to speak, he says, "That's a really romantic story, but it doesn't really answer my question about why you think Tristan and Ivy's dad can help us?"

I wave off his concerns as I continue, "Well, if you had had an ounce of patience, I was getting there. You have to let the story ripen and percolate before you get to the climactic ending; don't you ever go to plays?"

"I can respect your art, but this is real life and we're trying to get justice for Hope here," he answers impatiently.

I feel rightfully chastised, as I respond, "Point taken. I don't fully understand what Isaac does, but he's in the upper echelons of law enforcement and he has whomever he needs in the alphabet of agencies pretty much at his beck and call if things get serious here. He's not one of those people who throws his name around just for the thrill of it, but if he needs to get something done, he'll do it for a good cause. Tristan owns an identity theft prevention and investigation company called Identity Bank. When those two joined forces, they became a pretty unstoppable business in the fight against evil. If the bad guys are hiding online, they won't be doing that for long. I suspect that once you sic Tristan and Isaac on their case, they'll be found within a matter of hours," I state confidently.

Mitch looks a little skeptical as he replies, "The trick may be getting local law enforcement to work with them. They have a difficult time letting civilians in on their cases."

I shrug casually as I respond, "That's just the thing, Tristan and Isaac aren't even considered civilians even though Isaac is pretty much retired. They have some sort of connection with law enforcement and they aren't treated like outsiders."

"That's good to know, I'll pass on the information when I drop off this evidence," Mitch promises.

"Okay, just tell them that Isaac Roguen and Tristan Macklin are available to consult on the case if they're interested."

Mitch's face suddenly distorts into an approximation of a cartoon character as he responds, "Remember when you were telling me that it's a really, really small world? I now know what you mean. In my business law class, we were learning about copyright law and rare books. I'm familiar with Isaac Roguen's name because he was involved in the recovery of some really expensive art theft and rare books. How weird is that? The guy is the stuff of legends — do you have any idea how famous he is?"

"I can tell by your reaction that he's a little more famous than I even knew," I respond with a smile. "I guess that's good. Maybe it will open a few doors with law enforcement."

"I think we could probably consider them blown clear off the hinges — this probably became the brightest day in Hope's whole life."

Mitch

6

THE SOUND OF STUART'S LAUGHTER echoes in my head as I turn off my car in the precinct parking lot. He thought it was hysterically funny that I couldn't wait to bound out of bed this morning, even though we were out ridiculously late last night on a local rescue. A local toddler with severe autism had escaped his bedroom without his monitor. His mother was frantic, but fortunately we were able to find him without any injuries and return him home safely. Those rescues always make my heart skip a beat or two. Still, I couldn't wait to get up this morning and bring the evidence in to the station.

I walk over to Darya's desk and place a cup of coffee in front of her as I inquire, "Are you busy?"

"It depends on why you're asking," as she takes a long gulp of coffee. "Mmm, on second thought, I don't really care. How is it that I dated the same guy for almost four years and he could never figure out how I take my coffee, but I just transferred here five months ago, and you can get my order perfect? Are you sure you don't want to marry me?"

I grin as I respond, "Darya, I think your standard needs to be a little higher than who can bring you the most accurate coffee order. Don't get me wrong — I like coffee as much as the next guy, but I'm not willing to base my whole relationship on it. Sadly I think I'll have to decline your offer of marriage."

Darya pokes her bottom lip out like a petulant child as she responds, "Will you at least go dancing with me? We would make a striking couple you, with all your blonde hotness and me, with my mysterious dark vixen thing going on."

"We would look spectacular up until the point where the music started. All of your illusions would then be shattered because I am a terrible dancer. You would be profoundly disappointed in my dancing skills."

Darya shrugs as she replies, "Well, I guess if you're not going to let me flirt with you, I suppose I have to actually do my job. Whatcha got for me?"

"Are you still working the case involving Central Shores?" I ask.

Her mouth turns down in the deep frown as she takes another sip of coffee. "Working it? Yes. Making any progress? Not so much. It's like that poor little puppy disappeared off the planet. How could three or four teenagers pull this off and nobody say a word? This case defies logic!" she complains as she adjusts the tie in her uniform. She's not required to wear one as a female detective, but she said she doesn't want to be treated any differently than the guys, so she wears a whimsical tie every day. Today her tie is covered with Tweety Bird.

I carefully hand her the baggies that I collected and marked from the scene, as well as a USB drive from the lipstick-camera that was attached to Lexicon's service vest. I use those to document all of his searches from start to finish. It helps me as a trainer to know if I am subconsciously queuing him and skewing his results one way or another, but in these cases is absolutely critical for me to be able to show in court my actions and process my dog went through to find the evidence.

"What's this?" she asks pulling a stack of evidence envelopes out of her desk.

"Oh, just a little something that might help you crack Hope's case wide-open," I deadpan as I wait for her to respond.

"Hope? Who's Hope? I'm a little lost here. I only took a couple of weeks off while my dad had surgery, so I can't be that far out of the loop. How about a little help?" Darya suggests with exasperation.

I have been waiting for nearly a month to be able to see her expression when I tell her this news. She's been worried about Hope for months and months so it's going to be a great pleasure to show her this file.

I slide the manila folder onto her desk. Not knowing what to expect, she cautiously opens it. I purposefully put an adorable picture of Hope with an almost lopsided grin on the front of the stack of pictures. I saved the more difficult ones and put them toward the bottom. Hope has a ways to go in her recovery, but even the three and a half weeks she's been in our custody have made a world of difference. Her burns have scabbed over well and her ears are healing up nicely. Initially, Stuart was afraid that he might have to do more surgery to repair a particularly vicious laceration on her right ear. However, Hope has done a remarkable job of just leaving it alone, so it appears she may be in the clear.

Darya looks up at me with befuddlement on her face as she inquires, "Is this the puppy? Oh listen to me... I'm supposed to be a detective... Of course this is the puppy... otherwise you wouldn't be showing it to me, right? I guess I had forgotten how quickly puppies grow up and I was still looking for a puppy that more closely resembles the pictures in our files. Oh, poor baby... look how beat up she is!" she exclaims as she thumbs through the pictures. When she reaches the pictures of Hope's tail she pales a little as she exclaims, "Oh my Gosh! Please tell me there is something in those little bags that's going to tell me who these creeps are."

I nod as I reply, "Actually, I think I have some good news on that front too. But it's going to take some legwork to track it down. There is a piece of leather that I believe belongs on a training harness. I trained another dog that had a harness from the same company. It's a custom harness maker out of Ohio. The family is Amish. The parents don't use a computer, but the son does. It's kind of hit or miss whether you can reach them."

A pained look crosses Darya's face. "It's just my luck that you give me something to run down when all the cadets are studying for the big state qualifying exam," she complains.

I smile again as I respond, "Just wait, I didn't even tell you the rest of my news—"

Darya raises a skeptical eyebrow in my direction as she asks, "There's more?"

"So much more," I declare. I pull out a chair from her desk and turn it backwards. "Do you mind?" I ask.

She gestures toward the chair and says, "No, by all means, help yourself."

I set my briefcase on her desk and throw my leg over the chair, straddling it backwards.

Darya covers her mouth as she snorts with laughter. "You do realize that you sat on that chair just like my fourteen-year-old brother, right?"

I shrug as I answer, "I don't know, I've never really thought about it, I guess it must be a guy thing."

I grab my legal pad from a briefcase and look at Darya as I ask, "Are you good and anchored in your chair? This is going to totally blow you away—"

"Okay, okay, enough buildup. I just want to get to the punchline. What's the big announcement? Does it have to do with this case — or your personal life—what's the big deal?" Darya challenges.

"It most definitely has to do with this case. Although, if you don't believe in fate now, you're really going to believe in it after this story. There's no other way to explain all of the things that occur in this case. You absolutely, positively have to believe that a higher power of some sort is involved in this dog's life or our lives to make sure that everyone involved in this case intersect in some way or another. To believe otherwise would totally boggle the mind."

"Mitch, do I need to ask if you're under the influence of something?" Darya asks pointedly.

"Geez Louise! Darya, you know I work for the school district and I'm randomly drug tested. Besides, I work for you guys when I go on a search. I could be called out at any minute of any day. I'm not using anything. Even when I drink a beer, it's largely ceremonial just so I can say I have some in the fridge. I don't want my senses to be dull in case I get called out on a disaster. How could you even almost think that I would use any substance?" I protest.

"Can you blame me?" Darya argues. "You're not making any sense at all."

"That's because this whole situation is so full of coincidences, it's like some weird classic soap opera history. They would've written a radio drama about this or something like one of those mysteries, I don't know."

"What are you talking about?" Darya pushes with a confused expression.

"Bear with me here, it gets a little complicated. A while back, a radio station morning show challenged a bunch of rescue workers to join a wacky new dating website called BrainsRSexy.com to raise money for charity. Since I was trying to raise money for the shelter, I gladly did it. I thought, 'What harm could it do?' I was single at the time, so I didn't think there would be any fallout from it so I filled out their stupid questionnaire and put a profile online. I thought that would be the end of it. Well, I was going to school at that time and my roommates got wind of what I was doing and may have started answering posts on my behalf so, I figured I should start checking my email before they did because I didn't want them to get me into trouble with any of these ladies. Soon I found myself sucked into conversations with some of the women on the site. A lot of them were really nice and I started corresponding with this girl named Rogue. One day she seemed to undergo a personality change, but she looked the same. It was really bizarre. To make a long story short, it turned out that Rogue and Ivy were twins and they didn't know it."

Darya looks spellbound by the story as she slowly sips her coffee and mouths the word, "Wow!"

I acknowledge her and continue with the conversation, "One of the people who helped them figure it out is this guy named Tristan Macklin. He runs a company called Identity

Bank. I guess that he is really well plugged in with all sorts of contacts within the law enforcement community."

"I'm aware; his class on anti-skimming devices and spotting credit card fraud is worth its weight in gold. I got to go to one about two years ago over in Charleston at a national LEO conference; for someone so young, he is certainly impressive."

I lean back in my chair and let out a deep breath. Okay, I get it. The guy is the greatest thing since Sherlock Holmes and amazing. Everybody seems to have a massive case of hero-worship when they talk about him. I remember some of the messages that I used to get from Ivy. She would talk about the dude in the same reverent tones. He must be pretty incredible — her sister fell in love with him. "That's what I've heard, I've never actually met him, I've just heard about him. Anyway, I guess Tristan and the girls joined forces and worked together to track down the twins' biological dad who had been absent from their life basically from the time they were born. If I gave you a hundred guesses who he was, I don't think you would be able to."

"Is this somehow germane to the case? Or did you just come to tell me stories over my lunch hour?" Darya asks me.

I smile as a random thought occurs to me. Apparently, hanging out with Jessica has already managed to affect me. Telling this story is starting to take far too long — I guess I've taken a cue from Jessica and added a flair for the dramatic.

"Mitch Chambers! What are you smiling about now? Does this story have a point?"

"I'm smiling because someone I know recently accused me of not having any appreciation for the drama of the story or the story arc, and I'm thinking that I've added plenty of drama to this story. What I'm trying to tell you is that I've brought you an offer of outside help — probably some of the best outside help you could find and it's not going to cost you a single dime. They've donated their services for free because it's for Hope," I explain.

"Who has donated their help?" Darya clarifies.

"Tristan Macklin and Isaac Roguen," I answer with a rather smug grin.

"*The* Isaac Roguen? The one we study in the Police Academy?" Darya asks with astonishment in her voice.

"One and the same," I announce, unable to keep a straight face. "We're going to catch ourselves some dog-nappers."

Darya sighs and tries again, "Are you sure you won't marry me?"

"Yes, my friend, I'm sure. I've met a little sprite with hair the color of a wild summer sunset who's stolen a piece of my heart."

Jessica

7

"IVY, I THOUGHT YOU HAD TO get ready for your big art show?" I ask as we enter Ink'd Deep, her fiancé, Marcus's tattoo shop.

"Normally, I would, but Marcus ordered me to back slowly away from all of my pieces because I was having a really bad case of 'fiddle-itis'. He assures me that they're perfect the way they are and I just need to accept that I'm a genius. Since I'm completely exhausted and I need a manicure — like, yesterday — I'm going to take his word for it. He said that he wants to add a little something to my tat because I got second place in the senior art show, even though I'm only a junior. Do you mind waiting a few minutes before we have our little spa date?"

I shake my head, as I respond, "No, that's all right. I've got some lines I need to memorize for my senior production. I can't believe I'm about to get my act together and graduate. I think I should send that guy from the Registrar's Office some chocolates or something. He helped me track down all my transcripts from three different community colleges and that funky arts school in New York who changed their name four times. It was crazy trying to cobble together a graduation path. I didn't think it was all going to come together because every school wanted me to take something different to get to the same degree — but I finally have enough credits to graduate. I really thought I was going to be in school forever."

Ivy sighs as she commiserates, "I know what you mean, changing my major from Accounting to Art set me back a year and a half, but I'm so much happier now. I love going to school here with Rogue, even though the move from Tampa was hard."

I stick my tongue out at her as I tease, "I know you do, but you don't have to rub it in so much. I miss having you as my roommate. Nobody whips up chocolate cake for me in the middle of the night any more. If I want to cook, I have to do it myself. It's a real bummer."

Ivy looks a little sad as she replies, "I know. Losing you was the only downside of my new, happy life. I wish I could have both things. It looks like Marc is ready for me now. Do you want to wait in the front of the shop or the back?" she asks me.

"I need to study, so I'll wait in the back. There'll probably be less distractions back there," I reason. I grab my backpack and go through the privacy curtain to the back.

When Jade sees me, she says, "Hey, Red, what's up?"

I examine her as I respond, "Hey — well, I'm not exactly sure what color to call that — so I'll stick with Jade."

Jade grimaces slightly as she puts her hand on her hair and says, "It's something, isn't it? I call it 'Don't take a gamble on a person who's struggling at beauty school hair'. I think I'll go back to my usual black after this."

"Oh… that explains so much," I declare sympathetically. "What are you going to do?"

She shrugs philosophically and replies, "I'll wait for it to grow out, chop it off and start over again."

"You are way more laid-back about this than I would ever be. If that ever happened to me, I think I'd be comatose for a month. It has taken me so long to grow this out. I don't have the lovely hair genes that Ivy and Rogue have. I've fought for every inch of this," I answer as I take my hair down from the beret I have it tucked under.

"Wow! It's been a while since I've seen you, but it's grown a lot," Jade compliments.

"Thanks. Mama Rosa turned me onto some natural remedies and essential oils and stuff to make my scalp healthier. I don't know if any of that stuff really works or just makes me feel better about myself, but my hair feels healthier and it seems to be growing faster — either way, I'll take it."

"So, why aren't you hanging out with the twins?" Jade asks, as she blows on the Hot Pocket she's just pulled out of the microwave.

"I'm not even sure where Rogue is and Ivy is doing something unbearably romantic with Marcus right now. It makes me feel intrusive, so I'm hiding from all the mushy stuff in the back room."

Jade rolls her eyes. "I so feel you. It's like some weird episode of a dating reality show around here. I feel like the weird contestant who can't get a date. Do you want to kill some time and get a tattoo? I could draw something up for you real quick," she offers.

For a second, my heart feels like it just stopped in my chest. I actually have to consciously remind myself to take a breath. Jade has absolutely no idea she's just granted one of my most private secret wishes. As the granddaughter of a preacher, the idea of getting a tattoo was so forbidden that I didn't even dare bring it up as a topic of conversation. Still, I used to go to the library and hide in the reserve room and look at photography books about body art and just admire the beauty. I almost got a tattoo when I lived in New York, but I didn't want to face the idea of letting my grandparents down after they had done so much for me. Until this very moment, the idea of getting a tattoo was just something like a theoretical and ethereal idea that just flitted around in my head that was never obtainable or within my grasp. I have studied her portfolio in person and online many, many times. Her work is phenomenal. It's been featured in magazines and even on a television show — you know one of those 'cover my bad tattoo' shows. This guy had fallen asleep at a party and his friends had tattooed obscene words all over his hands and forearms. Jade was able to tattoo an amazing natural forest scene. It looked so much like a photograph and you couldn't even tell that anything had ever been on his arms before, let alone filthy, disgusting words that should never be uttered out loud.

I chew on my bottom lip for a couple of seconds before I summon up the courage to answer, "I'd really love to but—"

Jade crosses her arms and looks at me as she responds, "You know, some people actually consider me to be pretty decent at this—"

My jaw drops open in shock. This is my worst nightmare. "Oh geez, it's not that at all, Jade. It's the whole way I was raised and whether I'm willing to disappoint my grandparents by turning my back on a whole lifetime of what I was taught just so that I can have something on my skin that looks pretty. I just don't know how I feel about that. My traditions and the way I was taught mean the world to me. My grandpa is a preacher; I was taught my whole life that tattoos are wrong. Yet, I've been drawn to them since I was about nine. I feel really conflicted about all of this. I personally would love for you to give me a tattoo. There isn't anything I'd love more — really if I'm honest. But, here's the deal: it goes against everything I was taught. So, I have to sort out the puzzle in my head and I don't know that I can do that today."

"Someday, when I'm not at work, you and I can have a really long conversation about who people think we are and who we think we should be versus who we need to be to make our souls happy. That's really too heavy a conversation to have here at work. Suffice it to say, something happened in my life that made me realize that life is too flippin' short to live it to make other people happy. If you're not happy with who you are as a person, none of the rest makes any sense at all," Jade answers philosophically.

Much to my shock, Jade looks a little shaken and emotional. The guys in the shop call her 'The Rock' because absolutely nothing shakes her, so for her to show this side of herself is a little bit unusual.

Suddenly, I hear a shriek from the other room. I've lived with Ivy long enough to know that it's atypical and I run in her direction. Much to my surprise, she's actually grinning from ear to ear. She's frantically waving a piece of paper in front of me. Finally, I grab her wrist and hold it steady so I can see what the paper says.

This motion seems to snap her out of her happy-haze and she takes a deep breath as she shows me the piece of paper. I haven't had a whole lot of time to get to know Marcus during our short visits. They've mostly been best-friends-night-out-on-the-town type of deal. From the expression on Ivy's face, he seems to have the romance thing down flat. The piece of paper that she hands me appears to be the stencil of her tattoo that Marcus is adding.

"Look!" she exclaims excitedly, practically hopping up and down on one foot as she hangs onto my arm.

"I'm trying to — but you're making it awfully hard for me to read this," I tease.

I examine the paper a little more closely and I notice that there is a date on it for this coming Thanksgiving with two interlocking rings and a question mark.

She turns around and shows me the design as he stenciled it on her shoulder. "I couldn't figure out why he wanted me to look at the stencil. He never works from a stencil. He always free-hands all my designs. It didn't make any sense for him to change all of a sudden, but he was really insistent that I look at his design."

My complete bafflement must be spelled out on my face because Ivy quickly clarifies, "Don't you see? Marcus finally set a date. I'm really going to get married!"

Ivy envelops me in an exuberant hug. I return the hug and reply, "Congratulations! He's a really great guy. I'm excited for you."

Ivy spins around in an excited circle as she says, "You know what this means, right?"

"I hesitate to ask," I comment with trepidation. "I'm not sure I really want to know."

"You're so silly!" Ivy chastises lightly, "It just means my mom gets to take us dress shopping."

I roll my eyes as I respond, "Yeah, that's kinda what I'm afraid of, I'm going to look really silly up there in the land of giants."

"Come on, Jessie, you have to be in my wedding party. You're the only person who knows how to dance. Otherwise, my wedding reception will be an epic failure."

Marcus calls her from over his side of the shop, "I hate to break up your celebration, Ivy Love, but if you guys are going to make your appointment, I need to get going on this tat."

Ivy gives me one last hug before she skips off to join Marcus. I slowly walk over to my spot on the couch in the back room.

"That was exciting," comments Jade as she wipes down the lunch table.

"Yeah, one more wedding to go to where everyone asks me why I'm still single and tries to fix me up with their cousin's brother's best friend who is the hottest catch around. I can't tell you how many awkward, ugly bridesmaid dresses I have in my closet — no matter what they tell you, you can never, ever wear them again," I lament.

Jade grins at me as she responds, "Sure you can. I slash mine up with a razor blade, put fake blood on them and wear them as zombie bride outfits. They work spectacularly well as costumes. The added perk is that it's an amazingly cathartic activity. The next time I have a dress slashing party, I'll invite you over."

"Sounds like a plan to me," I respond as I rub my temples. I feel guilty that I'm not more excited about Ivy's wedding. But I feel like we've started traveling in different worlds. She's got this psychic bond thing with her twin sister. It is something that I'll never have with her — I mean, they can communicate without talking. It's like she has to struggle to fit me into her life now. We don't even go to the same school or have the same interests anymore. When I hang out with her, it's just awkward; I feel like I'm the quintessential third wheel. It's not anybody's fault, really. It's just the reality of it all. So, I don't know how to fix it without hurting somebody.

"Why the big sigh, Red?" Jade probes. "I thought you and the Spooky Doubles were going to go get beautified. That should be fun."

I laugh out loud at her description of Ivy and Rogue, although I can't say it's wrong. "That's just it, it should be fun. It's just not so much fun anymore because their lives are so perfect now and mine is pretty boring and predictable. Unless you count the people I sell cheaply made cell phone cases to out of the kiosk in the mall, I don't have much interaction with real people these days. It's me, my books, my cat and my fellow Theater Arts geeks. If you examine my life closely, you'll see that I've pretty much turned into my grandparents before my twenty-fifth birthday. That's pretty darned depressing."

"Didn't Ivy tell me that you were going out with that Mitch guy from BrainsRSexy? Seems to me that just looking at his picture would count as mega-social interaction. He's pretty cute. Anybody that rescues dogs gets bonus points in my book," Jade remarks with a knowing snicker.

"Oh, I don't disagree that he's cute. Still, I can't help but wonder if maybe he's too cute, you know what I mean? We've gone out a few times for a coffee and to a couple of movies. We even took the dogs out to play at the dog park. It was a real blast. He's pretty shy, but he has a great sense of humor if he can get over his nerves. I can't really tell if he likes me because he seems awfully busy. So, maybe he's trying to avoid me and I'm just not getting the clue and he doesn't know how to let me down easy. I'm terrible at reading situations like this," I explain it as I throw my hands up in the air. "Maybe I should just hole up in my house with my cat and stalk people on the Internet."

Jade chokes back a snort of laughter as she says, "Well, we'll always have social media to hide behind; we can post whatever pretend life we want to have."

"That's the sad thing, my grandpa outclasses me there, too. He has more Facebook friends and Twitter followers than I do. He posts an online Bible study group every week and he posts a new Scripture every day and gets hundreds of likes and comments. Last time I got brave enough to post a selfie, someone told me that my eyeliner was crooked."

Jade's phone beeps and she briefly looks down to check the message. She mutters to herself, "Okay, that settles it. I'm not part owner of this business for nothing. I'm going to give myself the afternoon off. We single girls — or in your case quasi-single — need to stick together against the onslaught of couple-dom. Besides, I need to see if I can get a professional to do something with this mop that's sitting on the top of my head. It drives me crazy to look at it every time I go past a mirror."

If I thought shopping trips with just Ivy and her mom were crazy, I was in for a rude awakening. Rogue together with Jade and Ivy are a whole other category.

Ivy and Rogue have taken to being Floridians with money quite nicely. It's hard to believe that these were that same girls that had a hard time coming up with rent money. Ivy has never been as poor as Rogue because her adoptive parents were pretty solidly middle-class but she never was comfortable spending money. It's funny how quickly she's acclimated to her change in circumstances. When I asked about it, she just shrugged and told me that Marcus finally showed her the books to the shop and told her that as long as she didn't try to buy the whole store and all its inventory, and every stock option, he'd probably be fine.

I finally acquiesced and agreed to the full treatment. That announcement alone made Jade's day, I was pretty much her own personal, living dress-up doll. I've never had an experience like that in my whole life. I have to admit that she has an eye for what looks good on me. Usually, I'm so petite that everything looks like I'm a kid trying to play dress-up in grown-up clothes. Somehow Jade worked around that and for once, I look really sophisticated — not Theater Arts sophisticated, like throw on a bunch of black and bright lipstick and call it good — but, stop and take notice good.

Rogue insists that we meet everyone for dinner since we look so fabulous after our day at the spa. I am trying not to let my sadness show. I know that this day is supposed to be a happy treat, but all it has done is underscore how lonely I really am. I miss my family more than I care to admit. Today is especially hard. I try to hide my tears as Jade holds the door for me. "I don't think you need those today, Red," she comments vaguely.

Her comment is so odd, it makes me stop in the middle of the doorway, but I don't know her well enough to question her further. Puzzled, I just follow Rogue and Ivy into the restaurant. When I look around the dim interior, I'm not surprised to discover that it's a karaoke joint. If there's one thing that unites this group of friends, it's their love of karaoke. It's pretty legendary for sure. For the first time all day, I breathe a sigh of relief. I actually like karaoke. As a Theater Arts major, I'm pretty much in my element here. It's not like we're going to get into any deep relationship talk here and no one's going to grill me about my lack of significant other. Jade taps me on the shoulder and asks, "How're you feeling about this now?"

"Only about a hundred and fifty percent better!" I shout over a guy who is trying to sing a really bad version of Robin Thicke's *Blurred Lines*. "This might turn out to be pretty bodacious after all."

"Good, glad you feel that way, because it's going to get even more outrageous," Jade warns.

Just then, the guy on stage did a really strange pubic thrust. "More outrageous than that guy?" I ask with a snort.

Jade just shakes her head in disbelief as she corrects herself, "Maybe that was a poor choice of words, but I think you're going to have fun tonight in the best sense of the word."

The hostess leads us to a back room, through a couple of really heavy doors. I thought this was really strange because the restaurant isn't really all that full and I want to see the people performing on stage. Before I can ask Ivy about it, I figure out what's going on. There are a couple rows of tables and a bunch of balloons. Disconcertingly, Ivy's mom — well, I guess you call her the adoptive mom — Lenore is standing next to what I can only guess is my birthday cake. I only know it's my birthday cake because it's done up in my favorite colors of teal and royal blue. A few months ago, after Ivy got engaged to Marcus, I was at her house for a preplanning wedding party and Lenore was there. She was shocked to hear that I had never had a Barbie cake. I was equally surprised to learn that this was a pretty standard rite of passage for most girls. My mom never bothered to do anything like that for me. My grandma is talented at many things but she is simply not all that gifted in the kitchen — especially when it comes to baking. I suppose it never occurred to her to bake me a cake like that or, if it did, it may have just been above her skill level. My grandparents put every last dime they had into saving the farm so there wasn't much left for any extra luxuries. Extravagant birthday parties were definitely considered a luxury. This is huge — especially considering the fact that Ivy doesn't even live with me anymore. I haven't left any clues for anybody about it for over two years, so I'm surprised that anybody actually remembers that it's my birthday.

Just when I finish absorbing the shock from the fact that Ivy's parents are here to help me celebrate my birthday, I hear a bark of familiar laughter from the other side of the room. Startled, I look up and I notice that Mitch is standing around talking to Marcus and Isaac.

"Wait! Stop the bus. What the heck? What in the world are you doing here, Mitch?" I demand. "In case you haven't noticed, I'm on vacation in a completely different city. How in the world did you even know that?" The hair on the back of my arm starts to stand up. This is starting to have stalker vibes all over it. I've seen stories like this on the news.

"I wish I could take some credit for spectacular planning and claim to have phenomenal romantic instincts, but in reality, it was a happy little accident of fate. It turns out that I was invited to this little shindig," Mitch answers with an embarrassed look on his face

Mitch

8

ARE YOU SURE IT WAS really that random?" Jessica asks me pointedly. "I thought you had search and rescue training this week."

I nod solemnly as I answer, "Scout's honor. I was in the area to deliver a search and rescue dog to the Alachua County Sheriff's Office and I called Tristan to see if I could meet with him to hand over a copy of the surveillance tape that I have on the punks that we suspect took Hope. I didn't want to risk having it corrupted on the server when we uploaded it. At some point, our county is going to do a system wide upgrade, and I'm not exactly sure when. I don't want the upload to get caught in the middle of that system change. So, I thought I would drive up to Gainesville to make that switch possible without any threat of corruption."

"That explains why you're in town, but that doesn't explain why you're at my birthday party," she challenges.

"When these guys mentioned that today's your birthday, I didn't want to miss it, so I rather rudely invited myself along. If I had known that it was your birthday this weekend, we would've done something really special. Although, it would have been nice if you would have told me at some point during the last two months we've been going out. It would've been really fun to be able to surprise you," I tease.

I watch as a wave of emotion passes over Jessica's face. It takes her a couple moments to collect herself enough to speak. "I don't have very many people left in my life to do anything special on my birthday. I like to pretend that days like today don't matter, because to most people, I don't matter."

"Please never say you don't matter. You do matter. You most definitely are important to Hope because you saved her life and you are pretty special to me. I've been wearing a smile on my face ever since you and I crossed paths. I can't remember the last time I've been this happy. You matter a lot to me. Let's go celebrate your birthday, Jess."

A woman with dark hair elbows Jessica in the side and practically yells, "Red, I thought you said you didn't have a boyfriend. He sure looks like a boyfriend to me — he sounds like one, too. I sure wish I had some random guy drive all the way across the state to see me. Can you make him look like that, too?"

Jessica flushes bright red before she answers, "Gee, could you work a little harder to embarrass me?"

"I was a bit embarrassing, I'm sorry, That was uncool. I propose that we declare a truce over chocolate ganache cake," Jade announces graciously.

A crease mars Jessica's delicate brow as she vacillates, "I don't think I could do that. I haven't had dinner yet."

Rogue walks up beside us and says, "Hi, Mitch. It's nice to finally meet you in person. Jessica, come on join us on the dark side and eat dessert before dinner. It's not going to kill you, I promise."

Jessica looks down at the ground in embarrassment before she says, "I know it's bad. I've been away from home so long you think I'd be over all my hang ups. I fell for the stereotypical bad boy and lost everything that was important to me in the process. The ironic thing is that my grandfather hated Dex on sight and it didn't get any better the whole time we dated. As much as I wish it wasn't so and as much as it cramps my style, my grandparents are usually right about this kind of stuff."

"I know that I'm not always the brightest guy in the room, but I'm completely confused," Marcus admits. "I mean, my mom could start a mug book with all the people my brother dated that she couldn't stand. I'm not really sure what any of this has to do with whether we can dig into this chocolate cake before the pizza comes. The homemade pizza dough in this restaurant is to die for, but it takes forever for them to make food. Jessica, blow out those candles."

Tristan makes a big show of holding Marcus back from the cake as he says, "Geez, man, let the lady decide for herself how she wants to handle her own birthday party. It's her day."

I watch as Jessica seems to give herself a mental shake and visibly straightens her spine. "Oh, all right. It's not as if a little chocolate cake is full-on debauchery or anything. Besides, these ladies ran me ragged today; my blood sugar must be a little low," she justifies, as she walks over to the cake.

Isaac pulls out a vintage Zippo and lights the candles. "Wish carefully, *Mi Pequeña*; wishes made in the presence of friends and family are especially powerful," he cautions, as he puts his arm around Jessica. "I heard your *padre* is not interested in the job. Just so you know, there is room for you at my table just as there is for my daughters."

Jessica blinks away tears as she kisses Isaac's cheek. When she bends down to blow out the candles, her hair gets in the way. Impulsively, I step behind her and gather her hair in a loose ponytail to prevent her from singeing it. I've spent far more time than I care to admit in recent days thinking about running my fingers through her hair, but my fantasies pale in comparison to the actual experience. In order to behave like the gentleman I was raised to be, I try to concentrate on what's going on in front of me instead of the sensation of her hair resting like silk in my hand.

Jessica looks around at her friends and declares, "You guys are simply the best. This is the best birthday I've had since... I can't remember when."

"I'm so glad you are happy. Between your job at the mall and your Theater Arts commitments, you are one hard chick to surprise. I almost had a heart attack this afternoon when Jade said that you were thinking about not coming with us. That would've thrown everything out of whack," Ivy admits.

Jessica looks at Jade with narrowed eyes as she accuses, "You were in on this, too?"

Jade looks at Jessica and shrugs, "Sure, I couldn't let the Spooky Duo down, although unlike some people, I actually have to use my cell phone to communicate."

Her friend looks a me and remarks, "It was a stroke of genius for them to include you though. I'm pretty good at surprise parties, I couldn't have pulled that one off."

I hold my hands up in a gesture of supplication as I proclaim my innocence, "Actually, I am here entirely by coincidence. I had no idea that it was Red's birthday until today. If I had known, I would have done some elaborate planning all on my own. Although, I don't know that I could've topped all this — but, I can tell you one thing: never in a million years would I have chosen karaoke."

I can tell by the look that crosses Jessica's face that I have said the wrong thing. Her eyes light up with pure mischief as a sly grin splits her face.

"Really? Did you just say that out loud *in a karaoke bar?* Are you for real? You know what that means, right?" Jessica asks with almost a maniacal laugh. "Everybody knows it's pretty much a universal, unwritten rule that the person who admits that they don't want to be in a karaoke bar and insists would never get on stage absolutely, positively, without a doubt has to be the very next person on stage. That rule is pretty much written in stone," she states matter-of-factly and then she turns to her friends to confirm, "Right, everybody?"

Almost as if they're puppets, the whole entourage nods in unison, as if on cue. My throat immediately dries up and my palms start to sweat. I don't know why I am at all shocked. Everything that's happened in my life since I've encountered Jessica and her friends has been akin to an episode of the Twilight Zone. Nothing has followed any sense of logic or pattern.

I take a bite of cake as I try to formulate an argument that might get through to Jessica. As I take a drink of soda, I tug her down into my knee and start to state my case, "Jess, I know we haven't really done the whole-bare-your-soul, get to know you thing, but, this would probably be a really good time for me to tell you that I don't sing. I don't sing or dance. By that, I mean I *really* don't sing in public. Like never—not in the car, or in the shower. I work with animals and they would flee if they heard me sing — that's how truly terrible I am. If I'm bad at singing, I'm even worse at dancing."

Jessica looks at me with mirth in her eyes as she says, "Nope, I'm not buying it. A cute guy like you? I bet you went to all the high school dances. In fact, I bet you dated a cheerleader. In fact, I suspect you were named Homecoming King a time or two."

I flush a little as I realize how uncannily correct all of her guesses are. "You're sort of correct. I was never personally Homecoming King. That honor always went to Stuart, because he was always more popular than me. I tended to be more shy. He is Mr. Personality-and-a-Half. Besides, he and Nora always made the storybook couple. Everybody always named them the golden couple. That was okay with me because I didn't like the limelight much. Remember, I don't dance and the Homecoming couple always had to dance. I did date a cheerleader, but only because she had a crush on another guy and didn't want anybody to know. So, we held each other's secret all the way through school. Her story turned out a little less tragic than mine, because she finally told the object of her affection, and last I heard they've got three kids. When she and I went to the dances, we basically hung out with the faculty members. We never actually danced."

Jessica looks at me with a shadow of pity in her eyes as she remarks, "I guess I'll have to make up some ground."

I groan as I reply, "I don't think I'll be able to make my body do what yours does."

Jessica immediately slaps her finger over my lips as she harshly whispers, "Shh! These guys don't know. You're the only person who knows both sides of me."

At first, I'm surprised when she tells me this, because I thought she mentioned that she began belly dancing in college, but then I remember she told me she began dancing when she was in New York. Ivy only knows her from Florida. I make a zipping motion with my fingers and whisper, "Don't worry, you're safe with me."

Jessica gives me a long assessing look before she responds, "You know, I think you're probably right. For the first time in a long time, someone in my life is probably telling me the truth. It's a little bit weird, honestly."

"I'm sorry your life experiences have taught you those lessons. Maybe we can build some new memories together," I suggest.

Jessica smiles as she squeezes my hand, "I'd like that. Now, it's my turn to keep you safe—"

"What do you mean?" I ask with trepidation.

Jessica grins as she answers, "I'm not the only person who needs to break out of a rut, am I? You've been rather beat up by life, too. Here's to putting the past behind us and stepping into brand-new horizons. Would you like to perform under your own name or do you have a snazzy stage name picked out?"

"Stage name?" I stammer, "Why in the world would I need a stage name?"

"You and I are going to go up there and sing a duet," she explains. "I've chosen a Joe Cocker song, so the expectations won't be super high. Based on your speaking voice, I suspect that you might have a gravelly singing voice, so Joe Cocker is a perfect fit for you. If it's not, just mumble — that's what he did. I'll play nice. I'll even do the Jennifer Warnes role tonight."

My mouth opens and shuts like a trout that's been hooked. "You want us to sing a romantic movie classic for our first time up there?"

Jessica shrugs as she responds, "Sure, why not, what's the worst that could happen?"

"Never ever ask a search and rescue worker 'What's the worst that could happen?' Someday, I might get tired and loopy enough to actually tell you and that would be enough to give you nightmares for the rest of your life."

Jessica shudders as she says, "Thanks for the warning— but for now, we're going to go face down one of your nightmares. Are you ready?"

"No, not really — something tells me I might be more prepared to face down my kind of nightmare —" I admit honestly.

"Don't worry, I'll keep you safe—" Jessica offers.

"Oh, I'm counting on you being my battle buddy, there's no doubt about it. If you weren't here, I would've been out of those doors in a nanosecond."

Jessica

9

AS I'M UNLOCKING MY KIOSK and setting out merchandise, I see Sam Taylor approaching out of the corner of my eye. I take some extra time to rearrange my display because I know it's going to take a while for Sam to cover the distance from his shop to mine. I once asked him if walking with crutches was painful and he explained that it doesn't usually hurt unless he has blisters on his hands. Still, I feel awkward just watching him walk, so I make myself busy cleaning my display. When he arrives, I pull out the stool for him because he's breathing a bit hard. I hand him a bottle of cold water from my mini fridge.

"Hey Sam, what brings you into my neck of the woods?" I ask after he's taken a big swig of his water.

Sam looks at me with great concern as he states somberly, his speech strained and slightly slurred, "Jessie, you didn't tell me you were robbed."

I'm not sure which one of us looks most surprised at his announcement. I quickly go back around the counter and through the little Dutch door to the inside of the kiosk and scan the interior space. Everything appears to be intact, including all of the inventory and the little wall safe that's built into the under-counter area. I scurry back to the front of my display area and survey all of the displays. Even though I have moved some things, everything seems to be there. I look back up at Sam with abject confusion on my face as I ask, "I don't understand — I don't think I was robbed; nothing is gone. Maybe they have the wrong store," I reply as I study his face for answers.

Sam shakes his head so violently he almost throws himself off balance — although with his cerebral palsy, that's not all that unusual. He's not known for his subtle gestures. Encyclopedic knowledge of diamonds and other gemstones — yes; subtle gestures with his body — not so much.

"No, I don't think so. They asked for Jessica Lynn Walker specifically. When I told them that your kiosk doesn't open until 10:30, they informed me very briskly that they would be back. They wouldn't give me any more information than that. The cops wouldn't even tell me if you were safe. I thought you'd been injured in a car accident or something. They were very infuriating. I thought about trying to pretend to be your fiancé like they do in the movies to try to get your information, but the one police officer looked at me as if someone like me couldn't possibly have a fiancé and I lost my nerve."

"I'm sorry they worried you like that. They could've at least told you that I wasn't hurt or anything," I commiserate. An alarming thought suddenly occurs to me, and I ask, "Did they say anything about my family? I hope it doesn't have anything to do with my grandparents, they are pretty elderly and they don't live anywhere near here."

Sam looks crestfallen as he answers, "G-Gee, Jess, I forgot about that, b-but I don't think they would have told me butkuss anyway." I can tell the stress is starting to affect him. It shows in his speech first. He looks at his watch and frowns. "I've got to go. My break is about over and management is being especially paranoid because the higher-ups are coming from corporate in a couple of days and no one is sure why. Everyone needs to mind their P's and Q's for while."

I hold Sam's crutches while he uses the counter to stand up. I straighten out the back of his jacket and refold his handkerchief in his pocket. "Thanks, Sam, I appreciate the head's up. Go sell a bunch of people in love a bunch of pretty little rocks, okay?"

Sam winks at me as he says, "One day, I know you're going to be in my store with your perfect Prince Charming. Who knows, he could be right under your nose."

It's an old joke between us. We've spent many lunch hours lamenting our very dry dating spells. We even went out with each other once, but we quickly decided that there just was no spark between us other than friendship. He needs to find someone who doesn't get the elements on the periodic table mixed up and who actually knows who the characters are on Star Trek. I don't meet either of those criteria. Sadly, we were not a good match.

As I watch Sam walk away, I can't help but remember my last run in with Mitch. I thought I had pretty good chemistry with him, but I guess I misread the whole situation. I don't know what to make of the last week of absolute silence.

I'm beginning to wonder if Mitch and I are such a great match. It seemed like things were heating up between us nicely and I thought we were getting along great. We never seem to run out of things to talk about and it never feels awkward or strange to hang out with him. For once, I feel like I don't have to pretend to be someone else. It's a refreshing change. We're different, of course, but that makes things intriguing and challenging. I never know what to expect. My birthday party was downright poetic. It was like something out of an 80s epic romance movie; I couldn't have scripted it any better. Despite his protests to the contrary, Mitch was actually a really good sport about karaoke. He also underestimated his singing talent. Granted he wasn't the best singer I've ever heard, but he definitely wasn't the worst — a little quiet maybe, but still a solid crooner.

Surprisingly, it wasn't Marcus that brought him out of his shell as much as Tristan. It turned out that the two of them both speak fluent 'computer geek,' so they had plenty to talk about. When you added Isaac to the mix with his law enforcement background and his interest in Mitch's search and rescue work, Mitch was feeling right at home. I even convinced Mitch to dance with me. I'm a huge fan of The Fray and it made me feel romantic and daring to dance in and out of his arms like candlelight.

I thought that the night ended well. He was much more bashful than I expected him to be. Instead of kissing me goodnight, he just brushed his lips against my cheeks and squeezed my hand. He thanked me for reminding him how much fun it was to laugh again. Then... nothing.

As I watch the minutes on my cell phone tick down to ten thirty, I can't help but notice the little calendar widget staring me in the face reminding me that it's been eight days since I've heard from Mitch. Not a single cell phone call, email or text message. Like Sam and I have said many times, I am the queen of failed relationships. I am not new to the brush off game. Usually, if I think things have gone reasonably well, the guy will at least give the appearance of a good college try, at least for a few days. Even after all the time we spent together, Mitch hasn't even given me the courtesy of that. I just got the full on brushoff mode. I'm completely confused. Granted, I'm not the best in relationships, and I tend to screw things up but I'm usually not that clueless. I'm mentally kicking myself in the butt, because I had begun to hope that maybe Mitch was a little different from the scumbags I typically involve myself with. I guess I should've known better than to be delusional. I knew better than to think that my friends' luck would rub off on me.

Just as I'm beginning to boot up my computers for the day, a couple of people wearing suits walk up to my kiosk. Actually, I can't say that they're regulation suits, really. The woman's suit is classically tailored and she looks phenomenal with her long black hair artfully styled in a chignon. What wins her all sorts of points with me is her pop art Bugs Bunny tie, complete with a carrot as the tie clip. She hands me a card, but before I can look at it, she sticks her hand out for me to shake. Reflexively, I shake her hand. I'm not the granddaughter of a pastor for nothing. I can shake hands with the best of them.

She smiles widely as she says, "Hello, you must be Ms. Walker. I'm Darya — Detective Darya Virk. I'm from the Hillsborough County Sherriff's Office. I understand you're involved in a crime I'm investigating."

Something about the way she laid that out, makes me bristle and I automatically straighten my spine and glare at her as I reply, trying not to clenched my teeth, "If you are here about Hope — which incidentally is the only 'crime' that I've been remotely involved with recently — I was not at all 'involved' in committing the crime. I merely rescued that poor dog. Did anybody take a really good look at that dog? Had I not been there that day, Hope would be dead! Doesn't anybody get that? I don't understand why nobody understands that I stopped to help that dog. Does everybody treat people who help animals this way? If so, I can understand why more people don't get involved. This is crazy!" I finish with a huff.

Detective Virk looks down at her notes and pinches the bridge of her nose as she looks at me with chagrin. "May I call you Jessica?"

I roll a shoulder as I nod mutely.

"Look, it was an unfortunate choice of words on my part. This is already my third stop this morning. I've been crazy busy and I don't have enough caffeine onboard to make my brain cells fire appropriately. What I meant to say was: 'I understand you're helping us out on a case. If it's possible, I'd like to compare notes with you about some new information that we have on her suspects to see if we can narrow the pool down a little further? I need you to come down to the station and see if you can identify some suspects that we have in custody. Can you do that, please?' If my brain would engage a little faster, I would've said that the first time. I'm sorry if I upset you."

"Oh, that happens to me all the time, but I'm not really sure what I'm supposed to do. I needed to be open about five minutes ago. I'm not supposed to leave the kiosk unattended. Then again, these are kind of extenuating circumstances."

Darya holds up her hand and replies, "Don't worry about it. My partner Booker has taken care of it."

I can't help myself; I raise by eyebrow in curiosity and ask, "Booker?"

The detective, who quite frankly looks afraid of his own shadow, just nods grimly and answers, "Yes, Booker, as in Booker C. Jones."

As wildly inappropriate as it is, I cannot contain the giggle that erupts like champagne bubbles as I confirm, "Seriously? Your parents must have a really odd sense of humor."

The detective nods tightly in my direction as he responds, "You have no idea, Ma'am." He looks toward the mall entrance and sees Rachel in her uniform. "Oh good, it appears your replacement has arrived. Now you are free to go meet with the third-party consultants."

For the first time in a week, I feel like dancing. I resist the urge to hug Darya and Booker as I probe excitedly, "Tristan and Isaac are going to be there?"

Booker stares right through me as he replies in a monotone, "I'm not at liberty to discuss the details of this particular case."

Darya rolls her eyes as she says, "Booker, they sure taught you by the book at that fancy academy you went to, but sometimes you have to use your common sense. Get off your high horse and use your brain. Obviously, Ms. Walker knows the parties involved in this case. She's also going to recognize who's in the room when we walk in. I don't think it would hurt to confirm what she already knows."

"Ma'am, we're supposed to keep witnesses separate at all times—" Booker argues.

Darya sighs. "Yes, of course we are, no one is suggesting any differently, I'm not sending them on a Disney cruise for lunch. We're going to offer Ms. Walker a ride to the station because traffic is awful — which she's free to turn down since she's not in custody — and then she's going to discover that Mr. Macklin and Mr. Roguen are already waiting at the station and have already given statements which may or may not have been helpful in our investigation. None of that is top secret, classified information. We are investigating a dognapping, not the Pentagon papers."

Booker looks a little demoralized as he responds, "Yes, Ma'am, I understand. I was just trying to follow proper protocol."

Darya looks at him with sympathy as she responds, "I'm not saying that following protocol isn't important, you just have to do it in a common-sense way which will allow you to do the rest of your job. So, Jessica, would you like to ride with us?" she asks me.

I nod in relief as I reply, "Yes, it doesn't matter how many other places I've lived. I still drive like a farm girl. Any time that I can get out of driving in the big city, it's a win for me — even if I have to do it in the back of a cop car."

My heart starts beating faster as Isaac hands over the enhanced surveillance tape to Booker. Isaac perches on the edge of the table as he addresses me, "Jessica, we have been able to collect and digitally enhance images from surveillance cameras from throughout the area surrounding the shelter from the day in question from vehicles that may match the one that was described. The one we're looking for may be in this video, or it might not be. So I don't want you to get worried if it's not there. The suspects may have driven an entirely different vehicle that day, or they may have come to the shelter on foot. We just don't know. At best, this is a shot in the dark, but it's worth taking so, take a deep breath and see if you might recognize something. If you do, just tap the mouse and it will mark the screen," Isaac instructs.

"What if I get it wrong? What if I've gotten everything in this case wrong? I took a class on criminal justice and I learned that eyewitness testimony is the least reliable testimony out there. What if I made one huge mistake about everything and I'm just compounding it right now?" I fret, starting to panic over the responsibility of it all.

Darya lays her hand on my shoulder as she reassures me, "I think you can relax, Ms. Walker. Only very rarely do we ever have to rely exclusively on eyewitness testimony these days. Usually, there is an extensive forensic record tying a defendant to a case. Whether it's DNA or an electronic footprint, there is nearly always something else concretely tying a suspect to a crime. In this case, you, most assuredly, will not be the only thing tying the perpetrators to the crime. Once we can definitively tie these particular suspects to the dog you named Hope, we will be able to go back and match her hair to hairs found at the place of residence and we'll be able to do some DNA testing that will definitively identify the dog. If the conditions are as deplorable as you say they are, there will be grounds for a cruelty investigation and everything will be documented quite thoroughly."

I swallow hard as I capitulate, "Let's do this for Hope."

Ten or fifteen minutes go by and I see a bunch of gray cars and SUVs. It's so tense in the room I can hear the sound of my own breathing. Frustratingly, nothing in the videos matches the description of the gray car. I'm just about to give up when the corner of a brightly colored license plate catches my eye "Wait! Stop!" I practically yell.

At this point, every pair of eyes in the room focuses on me as seemingly they all ask in unison, "What?"

I force myself to take a deep breath as I explain, "I'm pretty sure that I recognize that license plate. When Ivy was here, we used to take watercolor classes together and I have a thing for color. I tend to notice random patterns of color everywhere. I can't tune it out, sometimes it's obnoxious. I remember noticing it when they talked about the car on the news because it struck me as funny that everything about it was totally monochromatic except for the license plate. They tried to obscure it with mud, but it didn't work. It was the same way when they were in front of my house. The plate was obscured enough that I couldn't see the numbers or anything, but I could still see the colors."

Darya nods in Booker's direction as she remarks, "I wish all of my witnesses were as observant as you. That's really helpful information." She takes some notes down in a file and then closes it. "That's all I need from you today, Ms. Walker. If I need anything else, I'll let you know. In the meantime, if you remember anything else, here's my card. Don't hesitate to call me."

To be honest, I feel a little bit deflated. I thought that there was going to be some dramatic development. It doesn't feel like we're any closer to finding the monsters who tortured Hope than we were the moment that I found her. I try not to let my disappointment show as I shake Darya and Booker's hands and exit the interrogation room. Booker offers to drive me back to the mall, but I feel guilty when I see the stack of files on his desk so I politely decline.

I know that smartphones are supposed to make it easier to navigate in the world, but I'm about to throw mine across the room as I'm trying to pull up the bus schedule. I guess that's why I practically run over Mitch in the hallway. Today, he's working with a completely different dog. I'm not sure if I'm more surprised by his mere presence or his abrupt command, "Dizzy, halt."

I scowl at Mitch as I snap, "Look, I don't know what I did to upset you, but a simple hello would've been nice."

Mitch looks baffled as he asks, "What?"

Out the corner of my eye, I see the city bus pull into the parking lot of the business complex. I gasp as I grab my bag and place it on my shoulder and sprint to the door.

Mitch clicks his tongue and says, "Diz, come," as he quickly follows me and soon overtakes me and holds the door open for me. He looks me in the eye as he directs, "When you get somewhere private, call me."

Mitch

10

"I KNOW WE JUST FINISHED our latest round of first-aid training, but I'd really rather not use it on you," I remark as I chuck a roll of paper towels across the room at Stuart. He's currently laughing hard enough that he's aspirating his strawberry milk. "Seriously, dude, how old are you? Why are you drinking that crap?"

"Didn't you ever watch Saturday morning cartoons? It's good for you," he responds with a shrug. "Did your fiery, red-headed Tinkerbell really flip you off in the middle of the police department? I would've paid money to see that. What in the world did you do to her?" Stuart asks between chuckles.

I hold up my hands in a gesture of innocence, "Nothing, I swear."

"I just think it's too funny. Usually I'm the one who's all sorts of awkward with women. I've never seen you have trouble. Normally, they fall all over themselves just to be in your presence. This is fascinating to watch," Stuart retorts with a chortle

"I think all the studying has damaged your brain. That's not how it's been at all. You're the one who's Mr. Popular. You and Nora were the 'it' couple all the way through high school. I'm the one that was always the third wheel, did you forget that?"

Stuart shakes his head at me and counters, "I don't think we'll ever agree on how things went down back then. I think the girls steered clear because no one was a hundred percent certain whether Nora's heart belonged to you or to me. I don't blame them; some days, I'm not sure Nora knew either."

Before I can even absorb what he said, Stuart follows that world-tilting statement with an insightful question, "You guys were hitting it off big time, especially at her birthday party, right? Didn't you go out on several dates with her and take her out with the dogs to see what they think of her? I thought she passed the dog park test with flying colors."

I nod as a reply, "Yeah, I told you all about that. She's amazing. All the dogs love her. For once, I'm glad I signed up for that stupid dating site because in a roundabout way it's responsible for our connection."

"So, why are you disconnected now?" he prompts with a knowing smirk and his arms crossed.

"I went on a rescue," I answer defensively.

"Yeah, so? Did you fall into a vortex where every form of modern technology failed? Did you lose her cell phone number, her email address, or my cell phone number? You know, she gave me her cell phone number the day we stitched Hope up. I could have called her for you — if you were that hard up. I think she's pretty hot so if you're going to give her the brushoff, I'd like to know."

"I'm not giving her the brushoff!" I bellow.

Stuart arches his eyebrow at me as he probes, "Does *she* know that?"

I sink back into the old dilapidated couch. I feel like banging my head against the wall. I can't believe how stupid I am. I wish I had some grand excuse, but I really don't, other than I was stressed out, exhausted and distracted. "You know, I hate it when you're right. There's no living with you for weeks afterwards."

"Someone has to save you from yourself. Do you need some help plotting your recovery?" he offers with a grin.

"No, but I might need a loan. It could be costly to get myself out of the doghouse, so to speak," I admit.

An agitated sigh escapes me as I refresh the screen on my cell phone again. Stuart dips his fry in catsup as he rolls his eyes at me and complains, "Do you mind? Some of us are trying to study. What is your problem? I know it's not your job because you're on vacation."

"Didn't I tell you? I've commenced 'Operation Earn Red's Forgiveness'. Stage one should launch any second now. I'm waiting for the package to be delivered."

Stuart's eyebrows shoot straight up as he asks, "Do I even want to know what hare-brained plan you've come up with?"

"Well, it's like you always say: 'go big or go home'," I reply with a shrug.

"Mitch, you know that you're the closest thing I've got to a brother, but since when do you take my advice on anything? This might actually be a really bad time for you to start. Your parents always thought I was a bad influence, remember?"

"Stu—" I turn toward him and pin him with a lethal gaze. "Seriously, now is not the time. I may have blown the whole thing and I don't want it to be over before I have a chance to figure out if I even stood a chance to make it work."

Stuart looks a little shocked by the anger in my voice. "All right, I was just messing with you. I think Jessica is cool. She's definitely not one of those interchangeable girls that are like the female equivalent of Legos that you seem to date just so that you can say you check off some mandatory dating box. I never quite figured out why you do that. Obviously, you don't even have a connection with these women and you don't even seem to be enjoying yourself much, so why put yourself through the torture? That never made much sense to me. The fact that Jessica seems to hit all the right buttons for you makes me want to root for her that much more. It's good that she makes you think on your feet and strive to be better."

My anger rolls to the surface as his words hit a little too close to home. "Geez Stuart, why don't you tell me how you really feel? I don't see you going out and finding your perfect match either. I see you playing a whole lot of dating games and working the field, but I don't see you getting serious about anybody. Do you really have a whole lot of room to talk about the way I date?"

Stuart recoils as if I've just decked him. His jaw clinches; he sticks his earbuds in his ears and starts to gather up his books and notecards. He looks back over his shoulder and remarks, "As your best friend, I really shouldn't need to explain this, but put this on your balance sheet, 'Mr. Accountant'. The one person I thought I was going to spend my life with died in the middle of an earthquake. You'll pardon me if I'm not real excited about jumping into another relationship. I feel like part of me died that day, too. I don't know that it's ever going to change. So, if I want to play around the edges of dating for the rest of my freakin' life, I don't see how that's your business or anyone else's. I really figured you, of all people, would get that."

I watch in stunned silence as my best friend since second grade strides away, leaving a cloud of dark rage hanging in the air.

Fortunately, the restaurant is pretty quiet and there aren't many people around to witness my quiet struggle. I fight with my urge to follow Stuart to make sure that he's okay. I deeply despise the knowledge that my presence might actually make things exponentially worse. Even though I want to argue with everything Stuart said, I know, deep down, I simply can't.

Although Stuart doesn't make a habit of being blunt, everything he said was absolutely spot on. His remarks over the last few days make me question again how much he knew about my feelings for Nora. If he knew the depths of my feelings for his girlfriend, why didn't we ever talk about them? If Stuart knew about them, was Nora aware of the full extent of my crush too? Did they ever discuss them together? If they did, how did they feel about it? There are so many unanswered questions, I can barely wrap my brain around it. It almost seems like the whole paradigm of our friendship has completely shifted long after Nora passed away. It's almost too much to contemplate, especially since Stuart is obviously furious with me right now.

This isn't a good time to consider even having a rational discussion about the past. And even if I were to consider having a conversation about our relationship between the three of us, what purpose would it serve? I don't know that solving any of my past would help sort out my current relationship with Jessica. It's also confusing. In some weird way it all seems intertwined like a crazy ball of yarn that's knotted and twisted in so many ways that it might never come unwound. I haven't quite figured out why my past and my present have become so enmeshed when the two women would have never, ever crossed paths. Yet, one feels dependent on the other.

My phone beeps with the special ring tone that I assigned to Jessica. My mouth turns dry and the palms of my hands are sweaty. I almost laugh out loud at my own body's responses to a simple text message. I haven't been this nervous since I went on my first search and rescue assignment. This is ridiculous. I stop to take a drink of my soda and wipe my hands on my jeans. I open the message and breathe a sigh of relief as I read, "You're lucky I'm a sucker for a good mystery."

Latching Hope's working harness, I tuck a single red rose into the backpack. I present Hope with a scarf that Jessica left behind in my rig and I softly give the command for her to seek Jessica. This will be a real test of Hope's recent training. It's one thing for her to be able to find things in a confined training ground. It's another thing for her to be able to do it in a busy shopping plaza with all sorts of foreign scents, outside in the elements with the public distracting her. I purposely haven't looked for Jessica. I'm not entirely certain she showed up. I don't want to know exactly where she is because I don't want to give Hope any nonverbal cues; I want Hope to be able to do this all on her own. It's vital for me to know what her actual skill level is before I use her in the field.

It doesn't take more than a couple of seconds before Hope is apparently on Jessica's trail. Her focus is laser sharp. When a child squeals with delight and starts to approach her, Hope doesn't even look up. In fact, she just speeds up. Very quickly, I need to jog to keep up with her. She is weaving in and out of traffic so quickly that I'm not even sure where she's going. Abruptly, Hope sits down, which is her signal that she's found what she's looking for. Initially, I'm concerned that it might be a false positive because I don't see Jessica anywhere.

Just as I'm ready to dismiss Hope's find, I hear a peal of laughter I would recognize anywhere. I peer around a really large older gentleman walking with a cane only to find Jessica kneeling at his feet tying his shoes. "I gotta say, these are the hottest kicks I've seen in a while; but you need to get yourself some lace keepers, I'd hate to see you trip on your laces again. That could have been a nasty fall," I hear her say.

"Much obliged, Missy. My granddaughter moved away. She used to take care of me — now I gots nobody. I just wanted to take me a walk today. It's a nice day and all," the gentleman explains uncomfortably.

Jessica's eyes tear up as she answers, "It's all right. Tying your shoes was the least I could do. If I didn't already have a date for this evening, I would take you out to dinner."

"Oh… go on now, don't you be wasting your time on an old man like me; love is for the young," he says with a shake of his head.

Jessica throws back her head and laughs as she replies, "You never know... maybe I like my gentlemen older and refined."

"Quit whisperin' sweet nothins' in my ear and go find yer beau," the old man replies with a chuckle. He looks up and catches me watching the interaction with bemusement. "Never mind that, I think he found you." He helps Jessica to her feet and advises, "Now, that's a right handsome young man. You make sure to treat him right. Look-see that dog thinks the world of him. That right there tells you everything you need to know 'bout him. You two have a good date. If you ever need someone to watch the dog, let me know. I lost my Charlton to cancer couple years ago. He was the best bulldog ever."

As soon as Jessica hears my voice, she spins around. Comically, she almost loses her balance and the gentleman has to catch her. As soon as she sees Hope, she drops back down to her knee and encourages Hope to come for a snuggle.

"Missy, I don't think you should do that, looks to me like that dog is on the job or somethun'," he cautions with a shake of his head. "Maybe you should save your kisses for your man."

Jessica reluctantly stands up and replies, "You're right, but what if it's more fun to kiss the dog?"

The man gives a full-bodied belly laugh and advises, "If that's true, I need to have a good long talk with your beau. He needs to have some lessons from somebody who's been around the block a time or two."

I put Hope in a down and fervently pray she stays there because her body language is screaming anything but compliance as she's practically vibrating with anticipation. I smile to myself as I sympathize with her because I've been feeling the same way all day. I carefully step over Hope as I reach down to get the rose out of her side pack.

I carefully study Jessica as I try to read her expression for clues. Her eyes are wide with surprise as I stride toward her with purpose. The color in her eyes reminds me of a swirling sea with waves of color, sometimes blue and sometimes green. Her expression is teeming with emotion. She appears both hopeful and wary, anxious and excited, defiant and accepting.

The old man chortles as he remarks, "Missy, I may have underestimated your man, he's on a mission — you best brace yourself."

Jessica nods in agreement as she murmurs, "I think you might be right, but something tells me that may not be a bad thing."

When I stop directly in front of Jessica, she looks down toward the ground. I reach out with my index finger and tilt her chin up. Without a word, I boldly kiss her lips, taking time to leisurely savor the soft texture. For a moment I am completely lost in the pure sensory nature of it all as I bury my hand in her rich fiery hair and respond to her lips dancing with mine.

When I reluctantly pull away, Jessica sighs and rests her forehead against mine. "Umm… hi," she stammers, after she catches her breath. "I take it you missed me?" she asks.

"More than you can imagine," I admit as I hand her the rose I've been hiding behind my back.

She arches her eyebrow at me and asks, "Really? You could've fooled me. I thought for sure I gave you my phone number."

I stroke her cheek with my thumb as I answer, "You did. If I had any brains, I would've used it every single day. I was an idiot and let the stresses of my job get to me. I'm here to show you that I'm willing to do things differently and step out of my comfort zone."

Jessica closes her eyes and leans her cheek into my palm for a moment before she opens her eyes and nails me with a piercing glance. "Why?" she asks with trepidation.

"Despite appearances to the contrary, Jess, I like you. Whether it was an accident of fate, a bizarre coincidence or divine intervention, something brought us together and I'd like to see where that leads," I confess with raw emotion.

I glance over the top of Jessica's head and catch the eye of the older gentleman and note his silent salute of support.

Jessica

11

MY HEAD IS SPINNING — OKAY, I'll admit that kiss would have been enough to make me weak in the knees all by itself. I can't believe that this is the same guy who was almost too nervous to give me a peck on the cheek. The change is startling, baffling and intriguing. I'm once again struck by the thought that I'm not really sure who the real Mitch Campbell is. I wonder if he has a real sense of himself either. Sometimes, I think he might be as confused as I am.

At the moment, we are making quite a spectacle as we proceed down the street. Mitch doesn't want me to pay attention to where we're going so he's asked me to look down at the sidewalk and not out at our surroundings. To the casual observer, it probably looks like Hope is my guide dog. It appears as if Mitch and I are taking our grandfather out for a night on the town.

I have to give Mitch credit — although this kind of thing isn't anything new for me, given my grandpa's calling — it was Mitch who graciously came up with the idea of inviting the man, whose name we learned was Mr. Houser, on our date to serve as our unofficial chaperone and tour guide.

It isn't long before we pause and Mitch opens the door for Mr. Houser and me. I am immediately assaulted by the fragrant smell of spices. I recognize the smell of Indian food immediately, Ivy and I once had a roommate who was a waitress at an Indian restaurant and she used to bring home food all the time. We were so spoiled. I turn to Mitch, "How did you know that Indian food is one of my favorites?"

"I didn't. Tonight is about showing you that I'm flexible and can operate outside of my comfort zone. I figure that this is just about as far outside of my lane as I can get. You probably don't know me well enough to know how difficult this is for me. This is pretty much the culinary equivalent of jumping out of a helicopter for me. You know that stereotypical kid who only eats peanut butter and jelly sandwiches with two carrots on the side, that can't be touching? Well, that was me as a kid. Who am I kidding? That's pretty much me to this day. I like my steak exactly medium rare with a baked potato with only butter and green onions on the top with salt-and-pepper. Please serve my steak sauce on the side."

I chuckle softly as I ask, "So, I'm guessing no Hungarian goulash for you?"

I watch as a shiver travels up Mitch's spine and he answers, "No, I don't think that would be happening on my plate."

I pat him on the forearm and suggest, "Mitch, you don't have to prove anything to me. The whole idea of us going out on a date is for both of us to have a good time. If you're torturing yourself to prove a point, that kind of defeats the purpose of going out to have fun."

"I can appreciate that; thank you for offering, but I really want to follow through with my mission on the date tonight — especially now that I know that you love Indian food. I really think I can work through weirdness for just one night, don't you?"

I reach out and interlace my fingers with his and give his hand a squeeze as I murmur, "I really appreciate the gesture. It's been a while since anyone has gone out of their way to make me happy."

When the hostess starts to seat us, Mr. Houser refuses to sit with us, deciding instead to sit at a nearby table. Mitch excuses himself to go speak to him while I study the menu. Well, that's what I'm pretending to do. What I'm really doing is watching Mitch interact with the kind gentleman I met this afternoon. Mr. Houser seems so lost and alone. I wonder if that's how my grandpa feels. I used to be really close to him until I ran away to New York with Dex Cantillate. The difference between Dex and Mitch is pretty stunning as well. I don't remember Dex ever doing anything to help anyone except himself.

I watch with a smile as Mitch reaches into Hope's saddlebags and pulls out a dog-eared paperback and hands it to Mr. Houser. I fan my self a little. Let's face it — men who read are just hot.

Mitch brings Hope back over to the table and commands her to lay under it. "Sorry about that, I just wish he would've decided to eat with us. Although, I can understand why he would feel like he was intruding. It would be a bit unorthodox for him to include himself on our date."

I nod my head as I respond, "Let's play it his way: we'll do part of our date at our table, then we'll take it to his table. Mr. Houser reminds me so much of my own grandpa that it makes me homesick. Walter is stubborn like that, too. You just have to be a little creative sometimes."

Mitch looks at me and shakes his head, "Is that the secret of women everywhere? You decide what you want and then just set out to get it done by being creative?"

I wink at him and respond, "Do you think I'll ever tell?"

The waitress arrives and lays out the sampler plates with a virtual cornucopia of Indian food.

"Wait a second, I didn't even have a chance to look at the menu," Mitch protests as she continues to unload her tray.

"I know," I concede. "I figured with your hang-ups, it would probably be easier for you just to dive right in. This way, if you don't like something, you're not all in. You can just move right on to the next dish. There will be no commitment issues one way or the other. Since I like it all, if you get attached to one dish, I'll just eat what you don't."

Mitch regards me with wide-eyed astonishment as he admits, "You know, there is a certain convoluted logic to that. I'm glad you thought of it."

For a self-professed picky eater, Mitch is doing an admirable job working his way through our little buffet. I think it helps that we're talking about his last rescue and some dogs that he recently encountered at the shelter. He doesn't seem to be paying much attention to what he's eating. Finally, I get the nerve up to ask about something that's been bothering me for over two weeks. "Mitch, I'm a little confused. What happens to us now? I thought I knew where we were headed and then you didn't even try to talk to me."

Mitch picks at some grains of rice left on the edge of his plate as he confesses, "I may be book smart, but no one ever accused me of having a whole lot of common sense. I just blew it and I hope you'll give me a chance to start over. For now, let's get some dessert and head over to Mr. Houser's table."

If I didn't already have a colossal crush on Mitch, I would definitely have one now after witnessing how he treated Mr. Houser with such respect.

When Mitch learned that Mr. Houser was retired and alone, he to offered drive him to the shelter to help work with the dogs. He explained that many of the dogs just lack opportunities to interact with people and could use some lessons in basic socialization. I really thought that Mr. Houser might actually break into tears at the thought of being able to have the dogs in life again — even only temporarily.

Even though we invite Mr. Houser to hang out with us for the rest of the evening, he begs off citing fatigue. So, I give him a big hug and program my phone number into his cell phone and make him promise to call if he needs anything. After Mitch collects the newspapers from his stoop, sees him safely inside and double checks his locks, he meets me at the bottom of the stairs and places his arm around my waist. "I really wish I would've gotten to know my grandfather better. To me, he just represented a bunch of expectations. I never got to know him as a real person. I don't even know how he met my grandma. I wish I could tell stories to my own kids like the one Lee told us tonight about Clara," Mitch comments wistfully as we walk down the sidewalk.

I pull him a little closer as I respond, "I'm sorry. I know what that feels like, I've taken my grandparents for granted too. I wish I could go back to the way things were before I ruined things between us with my bad choices."

Mitch reaches up and brushes some hair out of my eyes and gently kisses my temple, "Is there any reason you can't patch things up now?" he asks as he pulls me into an embrace.

I shrug as I bury my face in his shoulder. "I don't know. It almost feels as if any dream of a normal family life has been so far shattered that nothing can rebuild it. I'm so different from the little girl he remembers, I'm not even sure he would recognize me."

"People change and grow, Red — even your Grandpa," Mitch reasons.

I smile against his chest as I answer, "You've never met Walter Walker. If you think I'm stubborn, he's the original 'It's my way or the highway' guy. Of course, he was totally right about my pig-of-an-ex, but that's beside the point."

Mitch pulls away and lifts my chin until I'm looking him in the eye. "I know this sounds simple, but have you told him that?"

"Not in so many words," I admit, emotion breaking my voice. "The last time I saw him was during the middle of Isaac and Rosa's wedding. It would have been a terrible time for me to talk about our private business."

"I understand — family stuff is hard — but if you ever need me, I'll be in your corner," Mitch assures me as he stops abruptly in front of a heavy wooden door. He checks his phone for a moment and then looks back up at the door. "It looks like we've arrived at the 'put up or shut' up portion of the evening," he comments with a grimace.

Before I can ask him what he's talking about, he opens the heavy door. The smell of the waxed floor together with talc and the familiar stench of sweat hit me about the same time as I notice the full-length mirrors and the barre surrounding the whole room. It's surreal to watch myself spin on my heel and run into his chest as I ask, "Did you sign us up for belly dancing lessons?" Sheer astonishment drips from every syllable as I regard him with wide eyes.

The side of his mouth quirks up in a half grin as he responds, "I'm feeling a little crazy, but not that crazy. No, tonight you and I are going to learn the tango. Or, at least that's what's supposed to happen — like you've already discovered, I don't have very much coordination so who knows what could really happen."

I lean up and kiss the bottom of his chin. "Relax. The only one I'm worried about is Hope. Won't this to be hard on her ears? The music can get awfully loud."

"Believe it or not, it's actually part of her training as a service dog. I try to expose her to as many different environments as I can. Rescue scenes can often be loud and chaotic, so I need to know that she won't panic around noise. If she's sensitive to noise, then I know that I'll need to place her in a different environment. If it gets too intense for her, I'll take her back to the training center for the night, but I really want to see how well she does."

"So, what should I do with you if you panic?" I ask, trying desperately hard to keep a straight face.

Mitch grabs both of my hands and replies, "Hold me tight and kiss me all over until I stop shaking." There is enough intensity in his gaze that I'm not exactly sure that he's kidding.

Mitch

12

IT'S FUNNY HOW IDEAS THAT YOU hatch on your couch seem inspired by some genius force, yet when you actually have to carry them out in real life, they lack the true spark you were sure was going to dazzle the world. I cringe as I feel a bead of sweat roll down the middle of my back. What in the world was I thinking? Dancing? Not only dancing but Argentine tango? Up close and personal dancing — complicated dancing! It's official, I've gone completely, certifiably insane. There is no other explanation for what's happening here.

Jessica looks down at her tight dress in dismay as she remarks, "I admit, I figured you had something much more sedate in mind."

The dance instructor notices her dilemma and offers, "I've got some clean clothes from the lost and found that I was going to donate to charity, would you like to see if there's something that would fit you?"

Jessica starts to balk, "I hate to take something away from charity."

The instructor waves off her concerns as she admits, "Oh, that's quite all right, It's just a bunch of old T-shirts that we're no longer using because we changed our studio logo."

I step forward with some money and hand it to the instructor as I offer, "Why don't you let me pay for a couple of T-shirts since I didn't give Jessica any warning about what we were going to do today."

The instructor takes it with a smile. "Great! Now everybody wins; you get new clothes and the charity gets extra money. Why don't you go change, and I'm going to go grab myself something to drink. I have a feeling you and your boyfriend are going to keep me on my toes tonight."

While Jessica is changing, I set out to make sure that Hope is comfortable in her surroundings. I give her water and lay out a small survival blanket for her to rest on. So far, she doesn't seem at all fazed by the environment, even though there is music playing through the speakers and it's vibrating through the floor.

I wish I could claim to be that calm, cool and collected when I next see Jessica. The truth is I have to remind myself to breathe. She is wearing her wild red hair up in a high, sleek ponytail and her long, elegant neck is exposed as she stands near the barre doing stretches. The cropped T-shirt she's wearing droops down over her shoulder exposing the lacy strap of her tank top. She's wearing a skirt that looks like it's made up of several panels of brightly colored T-shirt material, but when she moves her legs just right, it splits all the way up to her hip. I know she complains all the time about how short she is, but I think her body is beautifully proportioned. She's just the right height to cuddle under my arm; her head rests perfectly against my shoulder.

I walk over to the barre and manage to croak out, "Are you excited?"

Jessica nods as she answers, "Yes, very. It's been a really long time since I've done any Latin dancing. I've always wanted to take formal lessons. I don't think my classes at the Y count."

"Sure they do. That's way more than I've ever had. You'll have to be patient with me. I think the last dance lessons I had involved world culture day in PE in the third grade," I confess.

I fumble with my hands as I hold her in a traditional waltz hold. Right now, I'm cursing my tendency to show every nervous tic. I wish I could be one of those guys with nerves of steel who knows exactly what to say and how to say it. Realistically, I feel like one big ball of sweat. I'm pretty sure that Jessica can feel me shaking like a nervous Chihuahua.

Jessica looks around the room, her eyes resting on each woman. Finally she looks at me and asks with a teasing grin, "Is there someone else you would like to dance with?"

Her question takes me off guard and I drop her hands for a moment as I stammer a response, "No, of course not! Why would you think that?"

Jessica giggles as she steps closer and grabs my hand and places it at her waist and positions my other hand on her shoulder. "I don't know, you tell me. You're treating me like I ate garlic and anchovy pizza for dinner. In case it's a newsflash to you, I kinda like you, Mitch. Dancing is a really good excuse to get right up close and personal and Argentine tango is a really good dance for that. I don't mind if you touch me," Jessica instructs as she scoots her body even closer to mine.

I'm sure that this is the spot where I'm supposed to have some witty, sexy retort. However, since the mere sight of Jessica tends to short-circuit every logical thought in my brain, the best I can come up with is, "Umm, okay… sounds good to me." I mentally kick myself. Really? *You do daring search and rescue work, you went to a good college, and you run a volunteer program with rescue animals and you can't think of one intelligent thing to say?* Fortunately, Jessica doesn't seem to notice my lapse in conversational skills, as she rests her head on my shoulder.

Suddenly the instructor introduces herself as Suzanne. An incongruent thought hits my brain when I hear her name. My mom used to be a huge fan of the television show, *Three's Company*. Suzanne's perky attitude reminds me of Suzanne Sommers.

Suzanne tells us to introduce ourselves to each other and tell each other our greatest fear. I freeze a little at this instruction. It seems a little silly to be introducing myself since my hands are a fraction of an inch from some very intimate parts of Jessica's body. I'm just about to say something lighthearted and glib when Jessica looks at me with somber eyes and admits in halting speech, "My name is Jessica Lynn Walker and I'm afraid that once you discover who I really am, you're going to be disappointed and leave just like everyone else does."

I cup her face in my hands and gently kiss her before I reply. "Jessica, I don't think you understand the difference you made in my life in just the short time that I've known you. I wake up with a smile on my face just because I thought of something that you said or did. I look forward to checking my phone to see if there's a text message from you. I know I didn't make it clear, but when I was away on the rescue, one of the things that made it easier to have a positive outlook when things were very bleak was the fact that I had someone waiting for me when I came home."

"What if I'm not really the belly dancing, life of the party, concert-going fiery redhead that you think I am? What if I spend most of my time doing homework, reading books and trying not to burn down my kitchen with disastrous cooking experiments," Jessica counters stubbornly.

I try a different tactic. I reach out to shake her hand as I say, "Hi, I'm Mitch Carver Campbell. The world sees me as some sort of hero, but I've been so busy making everybody else happy, I haven't bothered to figure out what makes me happy and who I really am. I'm afraid that once I figure that out, I'm going to let a whole bunch of people down."

Compassion swirls in Jessica's expressive eyes as she just shakes her head. "Mitch, I don't see how that could possibly be true. Everything you do is extraordinary on some level. Whether you choose to volunteer at the shelter or continue your work with the search and rescue team or even if you keep your job with the school district, it's all honorable. I don't see how anyone could be disappointed in what you do."

I sigh as I try to explain, "I know it's hard to understand, but so many people need such different things from me that it's hard to balance them all. Sometimes I feel like I can't keep everybody happy. Eventually, I'm going to devastate someone because I can't continue to juggle everything."

Jessica runs her fingers through the hair at the nape of my neck, "It sounds like both of us could use a little more friendship and a little less judgment in our lives. Regardless of how tonight turns out, I promise to be your friend through all of this, okay? You have the right to be who or what you decide to be. I'll be proud of you — no matter what."

I briefly rest my chin against the top of her head as I pull her into an embrace. "The same is true for you, Jess. Just for the record, I'd much rather spend an evening reading books than being the life of the party."

Whatever Jessica might've said in response is drowned out by the tapping of Suzanne's timing stick on the floor. I'm really lucky that Jessica knows what she's doing. She immediately pulls me back into proper dance form. All I can say is that I'm glad that I really like Jessica because, it would be really awkward to do this dance with a stranger and it would be downright terrifying to deal with someone I didn't like. Jessica wraps my arm around her so tight that my hand is nearly brushing the underside of her breast and my other hand is cupping the back of her neck. "Am I supposed to be this close or are you taking advantage of my virtue?" I joke.

"*Shh*," Jessica cautions, "Just watch in the mirror. See what she's doing with her partner? We're supposed to do that. You're the leader and I'm the follower."

"Wouldn't it be easier if you led and I followed since you know what you're doing?" I suggest, as I watch the instructor go through ever more complicated steps.

Jessica giggles as she responds, "I suppose in theory, yes, but that's not the way Latin dances work. You're the man and you're supposed to lead."

"What about equality and treating everyone fairly?" I challenge, arching my eyebrow.

"Mitch Chambers, stop procrastinating. This is not a gender studies class and you're not going to talk your way out of this. You're not expected to be an expert at it the first time you try. That's why this is called a *class*. You are learning to do the Argentine tango. For that matter, so am I. We're on this adventure together, and we'll look silly together along with every other person in this class, understand?"

Wow! It didn't take her long to nail my perfectionistic phobia. I guess it comes from being an only kid. A lot of times my fear of not being perfect the first time prevents me from trying new things. I didn't think it was that transparent, but maybe it really is. The fact that it's obvious makes me more determined than ever to break out of my shell and try something new and outrageous. I'm tired of being defined by the person that I've always been. I've been stuck in place by grief and indecision for too long.

I take a moment to really study Suzanne's movements with her dance partner. Fortunately for me, his movements don't seem to be the most difficult. Actually, they seem really similar to the waltz I learned as a teenager. Perhaps this won't be quite as difficult as I had envisioned. I can still count and do a basic box step.

Placing my hand in the small of Jessica's back, I escort her to an empty spot in the front of the lineup so I have a good vantage point and plenty of room to maneuver Jessica. I start to count off steps in my head. Soon enough, it becomes apparent that I'm not exactly quiet when it comes to counting off the steps because Jessica comments, "Thanks Mitch, I think I have the count. I've been dancing for quite a while; I can count the beat in my sleep."

I flash her a quick grin as I respond, "You might be able to, but some of us can't walk and chew gum at the same time. We have to do things the old-fashioned way. I hope it doesn't bother you."

Jessica shrugs as she responds, "No worries. Do whatever you need to do to make it work for you. I think it's endearing.

Just make sure you count correctly, otherwise you'll throw me completely off."

I place her back in traditional hold and put my foot in the starting position as I whisper, "Is this the foot I start with?"

Jessica nods and whispers back "If that's your dominant foot, yes."

Thinking back to the way I climb rocks when I repel, it is my dominant foot. I shift my weight to it and begin the box step. I am about to congratulate myself on how coordinated I am, when all of a sudden Jessica does a complicated cross step and I become lost. Jessica reads the panic in my face and instructs me to breathe. She murmurs in my ear, "Relax, you don't have to do that — only the women do. We have a couple of extra fancy moves in there to show off our sexy selves."

I breathe a sigh of relief. "It'd be nice if I had some advance warning of that, so I wouldn't have a heart attack," I mutter to myself.

Jessica smirks and raises an eyebrow as she responds, "I suppose I could whisper, 'Ta-da!' before I'm scheduled to make a big move, if that would make you feel better."

I grin as I retort, "Could you? That would be helpful. Then I could be prepared for when you dazzle me."

Jessica groans, "You're such a cheese ball. Do women actually buy this stuff?"

I shrug as I respond, "I don't know, I don't get much chance to be nice to women — usually only on Mother's Day and Secretary's Day."

By the fourth run-through of the dance, I am feeling pretty competent. Jessica and I are starting to have some real fun. We're even starting to add our own creative flourishes to the dance. Suzanne is so impressed that she even brings us up to the front of the class so that we can do a demonstration. It's then that I realize how much I've really changed the last few weeks. Since meeting Jessica, I've sung karaoke and danced in a club and in front of a group of strangers. I would've never done those things without her encouragement — it's strange how things work out.

Just as we're about to start another set of dance moves, an unusual ringtone breaks through the tango music. Much to my surprise, it's country music. It's quite jarring in the middle of the Latin dance class. I guess I really am caught up in the environment. At first I don't realize that it's from Jessica's phone because everyone had placed all of their duffel bags in a central location on a big mat-table. I look behind me to see if Jessica has noticed the odd music. When I do, I watch in brief shock as she almost collapses to the floor. I run to catch her before she falls and hits her head on the mirror or bar. "Jessica, what's wrong?" I am alarmed as she sinks to the floor like a falling kite.

"That's my phone, that song — it's *Flyover States* — it's for Kansas. It's my grandpa. You don't understand; my grandpa never, *ever* calls. He hasn't called since we had the riff over Dex. This must be the worst kind of news. It's either my grandparents or my parents. You have to answer it, Mitch; I'm too scared. I guess deep down, I knew that all those thoughts of my grandparents must have been some sort of premonition — don't you think?"

I scoop her up off the floor and carry her over to some folded mats on the side of the room. "Jess, it's too early. You don't know that yet. There are a lot of people in this room. It might even be someone else's phone. You just don't know. You need to breathe, Red. If you panic, you won't be able to help."

Suzanne rushes over with Jessica's jacket and purse. Out of respect, I start to hand Jessica her purse, but she waves me off and says in voice clogged with tears, "Can you check, please? I don't know how I am going to handle it if it's 'the call'. "

I nod tightly as I respond, "I understand. What am I looking for, Jess?"

She becomes almost impossibly pale as she stammers, "Six... six-two-oh... I don't know... I'm sorry I don't even know if it's still listed under the Parsonage or if it's back under the farm or under Walter Wal—" Jessica's speech breaks as she starts to sob. An older lady from the class brings her a bottle of water and a wad of paper towels for her to wipe her face.

I cringe as I realize that her phone doesn't have any security features installed, but that can be a topic for another day. I swipe her phone open and have to fight to school my expression when I read the list of missed phone calls and see 'Almost the Voice of God' listed in her contacts list. The sarcasm is oozing right through her screen; it must've been really interesting in that household when she was a teenager. No wonder she's regretful about things that happened in their relationship. When I glance over at her, she's speaking up at me through fingers, clearly anxious to see my response. "Is there anything there?" she asks with trepidation. I nod carefully. "It looks like you missed a call from your grandpa," I reveal softly.

"Well? Did Grandp... Walter... leave a message?" Jessica inquires anxiously.

"I didn't find one yet, but I didn't know exactly what I was looking for." As I start to thumb through her messages, the phone rings in my hand. It's the same ring tone I heard before. As soon as Jessica hears the familiar notes, tears start to stream down her face again.

Knowing her family must be concerned, I answer the phone, "Good evening, this is Jessica's phone."

"Why on earth are you answering my granddaughter's phone?" A voice on the other end of the phone demands.

"I'm Jessica's friend, Mr. Walker. I'm helping her out because she got a little scared when she got a call from home. Jessica's just taking a minute to collect herself so that she can talk to you. We're in a rather public place right now. Do I need to get her somewhere private for the news you need to share?"

"Well, if she would call home more often, the sound of my voice wouldn't reduce her to tears," Jessica's grandfather asserts, with pain in his voice.

"Sir, I don't know the whole story, but I get the impression from Jess that she feels that you might not welcome her call," I explain cautiously, reluctant to step on anyone's toes.

"Oh, for the love of Pete," Mr. Walker mutters, "where in the world would Jessie get some silly notion like that? My Missus waits for her call every week after church."

I can't disguise my relief as I reply, "I'll be sure to convey your message, Mr. Walker. Is there anything else I should tell her?"

"I'd like to talk to my little Buttercup if I could, but if I can't, just tell her that Wilma is having more of her spells and she's just not bouncing back like normal. I think it might do her spirit some good if Jessica could come for a visit."

Jessica taps me on the knee and whispers, "Is everything okay? Did anybody die?"

"Sir, how are Jessica's parents? No one else is gravely ill, correct? She is quite concerned."

Through the phone, I can hear Jessica's grandfather say some very un-pastor-like things under his breath, before he sighs and says, "My little Buttercup always had a heart bigger than the surface of the sun. Between you and me, as far as I know, they're on some beach somewhere in California. We got a call from some collection agency trying to get some money for one of those newfangled Jacuzzi things. I told the guy if they were stupid enough to sell an oversized bathtub to two beach bums with no job, that was more his problem than mine. Her parents always did care more about chasing the good life than they cared about her. It was the saddest thing I ever did see. If you're as good a friend as you say you are, I don't need to tell you that she's one of the kindest souls the good Lord ever put on this planet. She didn't deserve to be given to those parents of hers."

"I agree with you, Mr. Walker. Just thinking about her makes me smile," I concede. "Give me a second to assure her that you don't have catastrophic news for her."

Jessica

13

THE ROAR OF MY RACING HEARTBEAT is so loud in my ears that I can hardly hear what Mitch is discussing with my grandfather. Of course, it doesn't help much that Suzanne has resumed teaching the class. It wouldn't be fair for me to expect her to do anything else. The whole world can't stop just because I'm having a family emergency. I laugh at my own hubris that I would even expect anyone to remotely care about my mini meltdown. Even so, people are amazingly kindhearted.

I'm still trying to determine how alarmed I should be when Mitch rests my phone up against his shoulder and moves his face closer to mine and starts to explain, "Jessica, come on. It's safe for you to start breathing again. It sounds like there's no immediate emergency. Your grandma is just feeling a little under the weather and your grandpa thought it might make her feel a little bit better if you were able to come home for a visit. They both miss you."

"Are you sure that's all it is? Nothing is wrong with my parents?"

"Nope, apparently not. It appears they are in California."

I nod as I inelegantly let out one last little sob and hiccup at the same time. "Unfortunately, that sounds just like my parents," I acknowledge. "They've always had more wanderlust than a sense of parental responsibility."

"I'm sorry they've missed out on somebody so great. Speaking of that, your grandpa would like to take a minute to say hi," Mitch fills me in, as he hands me the phone.

I'm so surprised that I almost drop the phone before I work up the nerve to break the ice with a tentative, "Hello?"

"Buttercup? Is that you?" my grandpa asks from what seems like a million miles away.

"Yes, Gramps," I respond falling back on a childhood name I haven't used in forever, "it's me. What's wrong? Why are you calling? Is someone hurt? Are you all right? Is Grandma all right?"

"Aside from missing you, Jessica, I'm right as rain. Unfortunately, I can't say the same about your grandma. She's been having her spells. I thought maybe since your exams are over, you might come for a visit. Maybe you could cheer her up a bit and snap her out of it. What do you think, Buttercup? You can even bring your friend."

"I'll have to ask for time off at the mall. Wait... How did you know that my exams are over?" I ask as my brain finally catches up with what he just said.

My grandpa just laughs as he responds, "Buttercup, don't you ever check the Dean's list? They post it on your school's fancy website every term and you're almost always on it."

I blush a little when he says that, even though I know he can't even see me. "Um I- I g-guess I knew it was there. I just didn't realize anybody I knew actually paid attention to that stuff," I stammer.

"Well, I don't know about anybody else, but your grandma and I do. We download it every term. We have viewing parties of your little recital thingies too. I have to say, young lady, that costume you wore last year was a little risqué for my taste. It was a little difficult to explain to the church ladies."

I blush even more as I recall the can-can girl costume I wore in last year's play. "I'm sorry, Grandpa, I wasn't in charge of costuming."

"Should I tell Wilma to set two extra plates for dinner after church?"

I look up at Mitch with total panic in my eyes; I didn't expect my grandpa to back me into a corner with no way out, yet here I am.

Much to my relief, Mitch just shrugs and nods his head yes.

Home. That word ricochets around my brain like some runaway pinball in a crazy arcade game. What will it be like after all of these years? I've been lurching from place to place, trying to make families from my collection of friends. Sometimes, I've gotten really lucky — like with Ivy and Rogue — and I have been able to create a reasonable facsimile of the family experience. I certainly wouldn't trade my experiences in New York for anything. They helped me discover who I am as a person and I developed a great deal of inner strength by living through them. Despite all of my inner growth, there has never been any outside experience which has fulfilled the need for my own family, as dysfunctional and unconventional as it is.

As I glance over at Mitch quietly reading a thick crime novel, I wonder what he will think of my odd little family. My grandfather can be overbearing, authoritarian and downright cantankerous even when he is not undergoing massive stress. I can't imagine what he's going to be like right now. I know he told Mitch that he's not upset with me. Still, I wonder how much of his statement was just for show. After all, during all of those years, I never changed my phone number and he was able to reach out to me when it really counted. It's hard to know where the real truth lies in our situation, since we both have our own perceptions of what happened.

I guess I'll know soon enough, because we're very close to landing. The flight attendant comes by to pick up our garbage from the snack we were just served. She looks down at Mitch's feet and says, "Sir, you'll have to put away your briefcase."

Puzzled, Mitch looks down to see if he inadvertently left his computer case on the floor.

"I don't have any bags on the floor," he argues.

The flight attendant points to Hope and declares, "Yes you do, it's right there; I see the strap."

"Hope, sit!" Mitch commands.

Hope snaps to attention, her jowls quivering with excitement.

The flight attendant cannot cover her astonishment as she exclaims, "How in the world did you hide a dog as big as that on this plane?"

My gaze jerks from Hope to the perky, picture-perfect flight attendant. I stifle the urge to ask her how many times she's flown in oxygen-deprived environments as I attempt to explain, "Hope is a service dog. She's been lying in that same spot for the last two hours. You've walked by her at least a dozen times."

The flight attendant chews on her bottom lip as she says, "I'll have to talk to the captain, I'm not sure that's allowed."

The man who is sitting next to Mitch in our row just chuckles as he responds, "I'm not sure what the captain could possibly do. It's not like he can stop by the nearest kennel and let the dog off. He wouldn't need to anyway, that dog hasn't let out a peep the whole time we've been on the plane. I've never seen a dog be so good."

"But, the dog might upset the other passengers," the flight attendant argues stubbornly.

We're on a small puddle jumper plane because Great Bend, Kansas is practically in the middle of nowhere. About twelve other passengers start shaking their heads and one older lady wags her finger at the flight attendant as she asserts, "Young Lady, the only person here who's upset is you. We all think it's wonderful to get to fly with a dog who is providing such a noble service to the country."

The flight attendant looks startled for a moment and then she looks around at all of the passengers who are nodding. She carefully examines everyone's expressions before she asks, "Really? No one has an issue with this? Not even the dog?"

I shake my head as I respond, "No, remarkably, she seems to be a much more even keeled flyer than I am. I'm usually a nervous wreck. It's easier with Hope here."

The flight attendant has the good grace to look chagrined as she amends her statement, "It appears that I stand corrected. You do not have to put your service dog in the overhead compartment. She is free to roam throughout the plane as long as she is under your control."

Mitch lights up with an unintentionally sexy smile as he responds, "Thank you for your understanding. Service dog teams everywhere are grateful for people like you."

I have to admit, it's rather amusing to see the formerly stern professional young woman practically melt on the spot. I can almost see her mentally fight the urge to fan herself as she blushes and stammers, "You're welcome, it was no problem."

I mentally salute her response because he can render me almost speechless with just his smile, too.

I lean over to Mitch and whisper, "Careful where you aim that smile, you might cause some poor innocent female to trip over something and hurt herself."

Befuddled, Mitch stares at me for a second, he shakes his head and states empathically, "I'm sure that's not true."

I smile at him with bemusement. I still can't believe he has no concept about his power over women. "I am sure it is," I insist as all the women within eavesdropping range nod in agreement.

When we finally get a chance to exit the plane and enter the small airport, I'm surprised to see my grandpa holding a sign that reads, "Welcome Back Buttercup!" The enormity of half a dozen years catches up to me as I run those last few steps to land in my grandfather's arms. It's such a weird dichotomy. In some ways, I can feel the pain of the last few years be washed away, yet in other ways, it feels as if it's being placed under a magnifying glass. Why did I waste all those precious years over a matter of simple pride? I'll never get those years back. How utterly stupid am I?

Tears slide down my face as I kiss my grandpa's cheek and whisper, "I'm sorry, Grandpa, you were right — I should've listened."

"You were right too, Buttercup, they were your mistakes to make. I couldn't live your life for you. I shouldn't have been so critical. Believe it or not, I was a teenager once, too," he responds, as he gathers me in a warm embrace.

"I've missed you so much," I confess as I pull away and try to collect myself. Mitch pulls a Kleenex out of my backpack and he hands it to me as Hope tries to nuzzle my hand.

Grandpa gives him the once over with an openly skeptical gaze. "I see you still have boys following you around. Although, I can't say I blame 'em. You've grown up prettier than a speckled fawn under a rainbow. I just hope your choice in boys has gotten better over the years."

I'm not even sure how to respond to that. Part of it's a compliment and part of it is meant to be a dig, but the part of it that is intended to be a dig isn't even untrue, so it's not even an insult — so I decide to go for straightforward.

"Thank you, Gramps. I work hard every day to try to make you proud of me. My taste in men has improved dramatically — Mitch is among the best I've ever met. You two should get along famously. He reminds me a lot of you. He is compassionate and good through and through."

My grandpa looks at me with the sadness in his eyes as he responds, "Jessica, I know we battled something fierce back in those days, but I was always fighting for you, never against you. I was trying to help you fight against the notion that you weren't worth anything and that no one loved you. Nothing could be further from the truth. Still, it wasn't a message you were willing to hear back then. You were so desperate for approval, you were willing to look for it in the first fly-by-night boy who said pretty words to you whether he meant them or not. It was like watching my biggest nightmare come true. This Mitch-boy here is mighty handsome, I hope it's not history repeating itself."

"I agree with you. Although Mitch is fun to look at, the situations are not similar at all. In fact, if I had to guess, I'd say that Mitch puts himself last in his life instead of first. He's very good at taking care of everyone else around him. Let me formally introduce you, Mitch, this is my grandfather, Pastor Walter Walker. Grandpa — this is my... umm... f-friend, Mitch Campbell." I stumble over the word. I'm not sure how to categorize our relationship myself, let alone explain it to my grandparents.

"Mitch is a bookkeeper for the school district and he does search and rescue work. He also trains search and rescue dogs in conjunction with a local shelter in our area. That's how we met. I helped rescue Hope here. She was in pretty bad shape a few months ago."

"That fine specimen of a dog was a rescue?" my grandpa asks incredulously.

I nod somberly as I answer, "Yes, she had to have a couple of surgeries to correct what was done to her. Somebody actually set her tail on fire. Can you believe that?"

My grandpa just shakes his head as he responds, "I can't believe the things that people do to God's creatures. It's just pathetic."

I grab my grandpa's hand and squeeze it as I press him, "Okay, Grandpa, I'm here. What's really going on with Grandma? What's important enough that you essentially called a big family meeting?"

My grandpa squeezes my hand gently as he takes a deep breath and continues, "You know, I was never really able to sugarcoat things with you. You always did get to the heart of the matter. I'm just going to tell you straight-out."

Even though I'm only wearing jeans and tennis shoes, I sway a little when I hear those words. As a pastor, my grandpa has a flair for the dramatic. Therefore, it could be something relatively mild that he's built up. Conversely, it could be something very, very serious — there's just no real way of knowing. Mitch reaches out to catch me and places his arms around my waist to steady me.

Mitch looks up at Grandpa and asks, "Sir, do you mind if I ask what you mean?"

"Wilma used to be really active in all the church committees and goings-on, but lately, she feels so tired that she can barely pop a roast in the oven. She seems to forget her own shadow. It's not like her at all. You know her. She won't set foot in a doctor's office. She just says it's a symptom of growing older. I know that's not true. I'm older than she is and I don't have the same symptoms as she does and neither do any of my friends. I was hoping that maybe you could help persuade her to get herself to the doctor just to make sure that everything is okay. I don't know what I would do if I lost her. She is my exhale to my inhale — one doesn't happen without the other. I really believe that God created her just for me."

"I'll take her to see Dr. Everett myself. Try not to worry about it, okay? If we're all working on the same team, it should be easier. Maybe Grandma just has a lot on her mind or something. Hopefully, it won't be anything serious," I offer hopefully.

As we drive up the bumpy drive in my grandpa's old Suburban, careful to avoid the age-old ruts in the roadway, I notice a bunch of new fencing. "What happened to the Totter place?"

My grandpa sits taller behind the steering wheel and grins slyly. "I bought it. Got it for a steal, too. Tom and Sheila were too busy thinking about vacations in Hawaii to worry about making sure they got top dollar for their property. They were just done being farmers. 'O course I was more than happy to expand my land, so it worked out well for everybody."

"That's great, Grandpa, but where did you come up with the money for this?"

"Well, you know how your grandma used to think it was so funny that I had all those magazines on farming?"

"That's not quite the way I remember it; I remember her being frustrated that you would use your bath time as your own private reading sanctuary when we only had one bathroom," I answer with a teasing grin.

"That's true enough, but all my leisurely reading eventually paid off. I became fascinated with all that organic stuff a few years back and started transitioning my fields, one at a time before it was trendy to do so. When the market became hot, I had a bunch of land ready to produce crops. I had already done a ton of research so, I knew all the right stuff to try and how to rotate the crops the correct way to make the land the most fruitful. Even though a lot of people tried it and failed, I was really successful my first go around. Then, this hotshot health food blog did a web article on me and my work with the men's mission — you know the one I do with the prison ministry. Well, that got picked up by one of those viral websites and then it was all over the place and my daily scripture reading group picked it up and they started sharing it. It was like trying to control crabgrass after that. I've never seen so many messages on my Facebook. There were some mean ones for sure, but most of them were nice. A lot of people wanted to know where to get my produce. I even had one person from Guadalajara, Mexico ask me. Can you imagine? Of course, I couldn't ship from our neck of the woods in Kansas all the way to Mexico. The produce wouldn't stay fresh — I was flattered just the same."

"That's very impressive," Mitch compliments.

"I got so much national attention, our local news station did a couple stories on my little farm. That led to the local health food store offering me a produce contract. It's funny how God works it all out in the end. That's how I ended up buying our neighbor's farm. The only downside to that plan was I ended up with his not-so-smart donkey. That creature is as backwards as they come. He stands out in the rain and then when it's sunny outside he goes in the barn and hides in the shade."

"What does Grandma think of all your newfound fame?"

"She keeps quoting scriptures to me and reminding me that technically I'm retired from farming and I'm actually a pastor now. I can't argue with her. She's right, of course. But, there will always be a part of me that wants to go out there and work my fields. I hate that my body can no longer do what I love to do. At heart, even though I love being a minister, I am still the farmer that gets up with the roosters and loves to feel the dirt fall through my fingers before I plant the seeds. I love to see the new growth of seeds and the anticipation before birthing season — it's all very cyclical and predictable. I miss the rhythm of life and death, of renewal and hibernation."

"I know, Grandpa, but look at how you are using your knowledge to teach a new generation how to farm. Think about how many people you've helped through your prison ministries. Your love of farming is helping countless generations of people, even if you're not directly driving a tractor. I've seen how you help people as a minister, that's equally powerful, if not more so. I wouldn't downplay that either."

My grandpa looks in the rearview mirror at Mitch as he comments, "See what I mean? Buttercup here always sees the best in everyone, even if they don't always deserve it. It's a rare gift to always see the most optimistic picture in every situation. If Jessica here believes you can conquer the world, hold onto that — because it's a priceless gift."

I turn in my seat so that I can see Mitch's response. He catches my eye as he smiles in the mirror at my grandfather and replies, "I hear what you're saying, Mr. Walker. I feel pretty invincible knowing that Jessica's cheering me on."

Something about his tone alarms me, "Mitch! You work in search and rescue. I don't *want* you to feel invincible. I want you to feel calm, alert and very, very cautious."

Mitch's eyes cut to me as he somberly replies, "Jessica, I won't ever lie to you and tell you what we do is one hundred percent safe, because it's simply not. I know that probably better than anyone since I lost one of my best friends in an accident at a rescue site. We use safety gear and we practice a lot. I don't take shortcuts and I refuse to work with a team who does. That's just not how I operate — but that's the only kind of promise I can give you, Jessica, I'm sorry."

"I watch the news. I don't think there's a safe job out there now. Honestly, I worry about Grandpa too. Between the farming equipment and upset parishioners and protesters who may be trying to make political statements in the name of faith, I don't know that any of us can truly be safe anywhere. Tristan and I were talking about this the other day. Believe it or not, he was teaching me about strategic ways to get out of a dark movie theater. I think it's just an occupational hazard with him, you know. He and Isaac both live and breathe the security business.

They've both seen and heard about more bad things than anyone deserves to know about in a hundred lifetimes. I don't know how they absorb all that and still lead halfway normal lives. It must be really hard on Rogue and Rosa to help them slough off the pain of their jobs."

Mitch sighs deeply and says in a quiet, somber voice. "Jess, this really isn't the place to have this conversation — but remember when I was telling you that I have some hard choices to make and regardless of how I make them someone is going to get hurt? Part of those hard choices is having to deal with what happens when a rescue doesn't go well and what's left behind. It's not pretty for anyone, especially not the rescuers and first responders and their support system. Unfortunately, it's often the people who love and care for the rescuers that end up paying the highest price and I'm not sure I'm willing to put you in that situation."

Mitch

14

I DISCOVER SOMETHING VERY INTERESTING in this instant. Apparently, my words can actually impact atmospheric conditions — because as soon as I say those words, I swear the temperature in the SUV drops about thirty degrees even as all hell broke loose around me.

"I'm of a mind to dump you off in the middle of my cornfield, Young Man. Just who do you think you are? Treating my granddaughter like that — if you were going to up and dump her like yesterday's trash, why didn't you do that in Flo-ri-da? I never did trust that place anyway! Why did you have to follow her home to do it?" Mr. Walker bellows, hitting the steering wheel for emphasis.

At the same time, in a timbre so eerily quiet I almost miss them, Jessica's words float by, "Just one time, I want to be important enough that someone stays." The utter hopelessness and dejection in her voice makes the hair on the back of my neck and my arms stand on end.

By now, Mr. Walker has caught his second wind and is about to unload with a second volley of verbal ammunition. I hold up my hand and sharply retort, "We can talk later, Sir."

He angrily throws his truck in park in front of an elegant farmhouse and turns to glare at me. He starts to speak but seems to think better of it when he catches a glimpse of tears rolling down Jessica's cheeks. I tilt my head toward Jessica and nod tightly at him as I plead quietly, "Please, may I have a moment to explain myself privately? It's a simple misunderstanding. I wouldn't hurt her this way."

Mr. Walker runs his hand over Jessica's hunched shoulder and advises, "The BB gun is behind the seat if you need it. It's the one with the tricky trigger plate, so be careful."

Jessica's head snaps up and her mouth drops open in astonishment. "Grandpa! You did *not* just tell me to shoot my boyfriend."

"To be fair, I didn't say you had to. I just said the option is there if you need to."

I meet Mr. Walker's gaze over the top of Jessica's head and hold it as I reply, "I understand where you're coming from. Your warning is received and understood. Trust me, it's not needed. I didn't come all the way here to break your granddaughter's heart. It's been a really long time since someone's gotten as close to me as Jess has — I like and respect her a great deal. I'm trying to make decisions about my life, which make sense for both of us. My statement earlier today was about leaving my job, not leaving Jessica."

Jessica gasps and I watch with new dread as her eyes fill with tears again. Luckily, I stashed a couple of napkins from the plane in my pocket and I wipe the tears from her cheek as I murmur, "Red, you might want to stop crying before your grandpa decides to put some buckshot in my backend just on principle."

She takes the napkins from me and blows her nose before she gives me a teary smile. "If you don't want a girl to break down into tears, you have to stop doing mushy things."

I look at Mr. Walker and shrug slightly as I raise an eyebrow in question. Finally, I look back at her and ask, "Mushy?"

"Maybe not entirely mushy, maybe a little crazy and mushy at the same time but I'm going to give you the benefit of doubt and say you didn't intended to come across quite so mushy —"

Mr. Walker opens the SUV door and remarks, "I'm gonna let her explain woman logic to you, I've got chores to do and I've gotta check on the missus. Don't stay out here too long, Buttercup, Wilma's been waiting years to see you."

After he closes the door, I turn to Jessica and say, "Jess, I didn't mean to upset you. I never intended to leave you. I need to make sure you know that I have the right priorities. Being a first responder is really hard on relationships."

"I understand that, but if you make your choice based on me, I'm no better than all of the other people who want something from you. It's incredibly sweet that you want to, but that's not right either. You have to make the decision based on what you want out of your life — not what I need from you. Does that make any sense? If you go to work every day, but it doesn't make you happy — then I've sentenced you to a prison.

I don't want to ever be that person," she reasons, as she strokes my cheek.

I lean my cheek into her hand as I struggle with the questions swirling in my mind. "How can I not factor in the impact of my choices on you? That concept is absolutely ludicrous to me," I argue.

Jessica runs her fingers through my hair as she concedes, "I don't know. There has to be some way to balance it all so that you don't have to sacrifice who you are to keep me safe and I don't have to pretend not to be scared to give you permission to be who you need to be."

Abruptly, Hope sits up in the backseat of the SUV and gives a sharp bark. This is such an unusual behavior for her that Jessica and I both turn toward the house to see what's happening. Mr. Walker is jogging toward the car with an uneven gait. His face is red and his eyes are wide with fear. He's holding his cell phone to his ear. In a flash, Jessica and I are both out of the car — yet even more surprising, Hope beats us both there and is sitting at Mr. Walker's feet looking expectantly up at him.

"Mr. Walker —" I start to ask

"Walter. For Pete's sake, call me Walter — Mr. Walker was my dad," he snaps.

"Walter," I correct myself, sliding into my professional voice. "Can you tell me what's going on?"

He looks at me with watery eyes, which closely mirror Jessica's in color. They look haunted with fear and worry. He seems a little stunned as he declares, "I can't find Wilma."

Jessica catches his cell phone as he starts to stumble a little and I reach out to give him an arm to lean on. "Come on, Walter, let's go inside and you can give me a few more details."

The first thing I notice when we walk into the house is the smell of cooking food. Actually, more accurately it's the smell of overcooking food. Jessica runs ahead of me and takes a pot of potatoes off of the stove that are boiling over. She starts to put them in the sink but then changes her mind and takes them right out the back door. When she returns, she says to Walter, "Sorry, Gramps, I know mashed potatoes are your favorite, but those were beyond saving. They were pretty scorched."

"Were they burned black or just scorched?" I ask.

"Well, the pigs won't mind them, but they're not edible for us," Jessica clarifies. "I wouldn't say they were black, though."

I look around the kitchen a little more and I notice a testing kit on the table.

"Is this your wife's?" I ask Walter.

He nods as he confirms, "The doc says she has bad sugars. That's part of the reason I started reading all those health-food magazines. The organic stuff is good for her sugars. I don't do any of that artificial sweetener stuff."

"Does she test like she's supposed to, Grandpa?" Jessica asks, trepidation clear in her voice.

"Sometimes, if she remembers or if she hasn't been eatin' right."

I pick up the gauge and read the date and time. "The good news is that she apparently took a test about an hour ago, the bad news is her blood sugar was only forty."

"What does that mean, Mitch?" Jessica asks as she starts to wipe up some milk off the counter.

"It means Wilma is likely not feeling real well right about now. Walter, does Wilma sleep in a nightgown?"

He understandably bristles at the question. "Do I need to remind you that you are in a God-fearing home, young man? That's none of your cotton-pickin' business."

"I'm sorry, I haven't explained myself well. I'm not trying to be intrusive; I just need an article of clothing that your wife has worn for an extended period of time for Hope to use."

"Well, why didn't you say somethin'?" he asks as he turns to Jessica and instructs, "Buttercup, it's under her pillow just like always. Run up and get it for him."

"Thank you." I cringe as I look down at my clothes. "Walter, I didn't really come dressed for a search. The TSA even took my sunscreen. What has the weather been like?"

"Well, we've had a good stretch of rain as of late, fields are going to be pretty muddy. Need some boots? Wear about a ten, do you?"

I shrug as I respond, "I'm a little more comfortable in a ten and a half, but I can make tens work in a pinch, anything is better than trying to do it in these lightweight sneakers."

"Wilma picked me up a pair of Danner's at the church rummage sale with the price tag still on them. They're big on me, they'll probably be perfect for you. I'll get you a hat too."

Jessica runs into the living room where I'm sitting on the Ottoman changing my shoes. She hands me the phone as she breathlessly explains, "It's Sheriff Foster. He wants to talk to you."

After listening to him speak for a few minutes, I hear the same theme that I hear in every jurisdiction that my team goes into — big or small. I try to intercept him and address his concerns upfront to see if I can save some time. I look at Jessica and mouth the name Foster. When she confirms that I'm correct, I start to address the officer's concerns.

"Sheriff Foster, if I were in your shoes, I'd be concerned too because I understand you don't know me from Adam. I have had over seven years of international search and rescue experience, not only as a team member, but a team leader. I'm well aware of protocol and I know how not to disrupt a crime scene if it comes to that. I'm not here to usurp your authority or take any glory from your department. Actually, I'm just here on vacation. I brought Jessica home to see her grandparents. As far as the paperwork is concerned, I'm not even here. I'll play it however you want me to. If you need me to be on the record, I will be. If you want me to disappear, I'm fine with that too. I just want to help Jessica find her grandmother. It's critically important. If my hunch is correct, Wilma could be really, really ill. I can have my search dog in the field in approximately five and half to seven minutes. It's up to you. All I need is your permission to go ahead."

I can practically hear the gears in his head spinning as he thinks about what I just told him. Those beats of silence are about the longest I've ever heard. Finally, he asks me in a long southern drawl, "You're not really spinnin' some tall tale; you do know what the heck you're talking about?"

"Yes, Sir. I do. I even have credentials from Quantico to back me up."

The sheriff clears his throat as he instructs, "Then go do your stuff and do it well. Miss Wilma is my kids' Bible school teacher and they would be devastated if something terrible happened to her."

"I'll do my best, Sir. I'm going to leave Jessica with her grandpa. While I'm out in the field, she can be the point of contact. We will have to use cell phones for now, because I didn't bring all of my equipment with me since I wasn't planning on launching a full-blown rescue while I was here.

This trip was only supposed to be an evaluation of how well Hope does during air travel."

"Do you have all of the equipment you need?"

"Yes, I think I can manage. Walter decked me out with all sorts of appropriate gear to face the elements in Kansas. I've got to go now, Sheriff. We'll touch bases later," I pledge, as I hang the phone up and hand it back to Mr. Walker.

"Jessica, I need to run back out to the SUV and grab that orange backpack from my suitcase. It's got my rescue pack in it. The airlines wouldn't let me put all my stuff in the carry-on bags, so I decided to check it."

"Oh, I know exactly where I stashed that. I can go get it," she offers, as she sprints out the door.

Right before we're ready to go, Walter says a quick heartfelt and tearful prayer over me that I can find his wife. Hope holds statue still for the blessing.

Jessica pulls me into a tight hug and tugs my face down so that she can whisper, "Are you sure that you don't want me to go with you? Wouldn't it be safer to have two of us out there? I could help you look," she offers quietly, trying to keep our conversation private.

"Jessica, right now I need you to keep your grandpa calm and man the telephone. In a town as small as this, word is going to soon get out that she's missing and people are going to start calling. Some of those people might have an idea where to start looking for her. Since you're familiar with the players, you can help me sort out which of those tips might be helpful and which of them are just gossip."

Jessica nods as she kisses me lightly and then backs away. "You're right. I'm just so scared. What if you don't find her? What are we going to do then? I have no idea where she could be… What was I thinking, being gone for so long? This is all my fault. If I'd been around to watch her, maybe she wouldn't be so sick—"

"Jess, please stop beating yourself up! Think about it this way. Because you found us, Hope is here. Does your police force have its own search and rescue dog?" I ask bluntly, hoping to snap her out of the panic that's overtaking her.

She stops for a moment as she thinks. "No. In fact, Billy Foster is the Sheriff. He used to throw spitballs at me when the PE teacher wasn't looking and he put a snake in my desk in the fourth grade and I got in trouble for it. I can't believe he's the Sheriff. I hope he has changed a bit. If not, things could get interesting."

"Well, thank goodness I'm not the same person I was in the fourth grade. So, I think there is hope for recalcitrant little boys everywhere."

I kiss her one more time before I say, "I need to get moving because I only have limited daylight left. I'm going to try to save my cell phone battery. So, I'll only call if I have some really important news. The rest of the time I'll update you in texts. I don't know what the coverage is like out here. I'll try to update you every half an hour by text. If I miss a check in, it probably means I have no service. Hope has a GPS device on her service vest. I've turned it on since we're on an official rescue now. You can follow the progress if you'd like. It should show up on your tablet or cell phone. It works like those EPS locators you rent at the ski places."

I'm not exactly sure when Walter became my cheerleader and ally but, he pats me on the shoulder and says, "Son, I have faith that God puts people in our lives for a reason. There is a reason my granddaughter found this poor bedraggled pup and brought her to you and God gave you the talent to train her the way you did. I have to believe that he didn't bring all of you this far without a reason. Godspeed, Son."

Even though his thoughts echo what I had just mentioned to Jessica, hearing them come from him give them added weight. I've been downplaying my concerns about Wilma's blood sugar because there isn't anything any of us can do about that until we find her. Upsetting them wouldn't serve any purpose — still, it adds a certain urgency to this situation. Hope is watching me with alert eyes as I pull out a Ziplock bag from my backpack. I present the garment to her and give her the command to seek. I don't know if she can read the tension in my body language or if she just knows that this isn't just a drill, but she takes a long time sniffing the sample before she circles around behind me and takes off across the backyard. Hope pauses for a while near a garden area. I notice that there is a pair of gardening gloves lying on the ground. I pick up one glove and see that there is a spot of blood near the fingertip — consistent with where Wilma might have poked herself to take the glucose test.

I send Jessica a text message and ask her to meet me in the garden. It doesn't take her and Walter more than a few minutes to catch up to me. Walter is nearly breathless when he demands, "Did you find her? Is she here?"

"Unfortunately, no — not yet — but I think I'm on the right track. Are these her gloves?" I ask as I hold up the bright yellow gloves with purple ladybugs all over them.

Walter has to sit on a little gardening wagon when he sees what I've found. He wipes away tears with the back of his hand and nods as he explains, "Yes, those are her new gloves. I had to get her them new gloves because I ran hers over with the ride-on lawnmower. She was so unhappy with me. She had just

147

broken in her old ones just the way she liked them and then I went and ruined them so she had to start over again."

Jessica is studying the garden intently. "Mitch! Look, it looks like she was cutting chives for the mashed potatoes, but I don't see them anywhere," she exclaims.

I examine the neatly tended herb garden and realized that she has a point. "You're right, Red. They don't seem to be here, but the cuts are fresh and the potatoes were only scorched when we came in. She couldn't have been gone long. Call the Sheriff and let them know that I think this should be the starting point of the search. I'm going to see where Hope wants to go next. Hang in there, Walter — I think we're pretty close to bringing Wilma home."

Before Walter and Jessica can even answer me, Hope is on another scent trail. Just like the other day in the busy public square, she is picking up speed rapidly. I have to run to keep up with her. At one point, she is able to zigzag through a cattle fence while I have to stop to unfasten a gate. She is standing in the middle of the yard, looking back over her shoulder as if to say, 'What in the world is taking you so long? I thought we were in a time crunch here.' After I refasten the gate, she takes off like a shot. Much to my surprise, over the rise I see another house which looks remarkably similar in style to Walter and Wilma's except that it looks like the before version in some home makeover show. It is in need of a paint job and the shutters are about to fall off and the doors and windows are largely missing. It's as if whoever was living here just up and left in the middle of the night.

Hope is frantically trying to push aside what's left of the front door. Gingerly, I pull it open as the last hinges give way. I have to balance the weight of the door against my body weight as I push the door back against the side of the house and I carefully follow Hope inside trying to avoid dry rot as she bolts through the dark and dusty interior.

Hope barks sharply. This alarms me because it's not her usual signal when she finds her bounty. Usually, she just sits calmly and waits for me to find her. It's almost as if she's telling me to hurry up. As quickly as I can, I make my way to the back of the house. I really wish I had my rescue gear on right now with my ultra light headlamp and my walkie-talkie radios. Even heat sensing lights would be good in this pitch black atmosphere. I can't even see my hand in front of my face effectively. The silty atmosphere renders the air in the house nearly intolerable to breathe and makes navigation nearly impossible. Finally, as I almost reach the kitchen it appears that a portion of that roof has been peeled back like a lid on a sardine can. The kitchen is well lit but completely destroyed. Eerily, I can see that there are cereal bowls and boxes of Shredded Wheat and Raisin Bran sitting out on the table as if a family is expected to arrive at breakfast any moment.

Hope's bark grows more urgent by the second. Stepping over some two by fours and roof tiles, I finally make it to where Hope is sitting. Oddly enough, there's water running into a pan with raw potatoes in it. Reflexively, I turn the water off before I reach down to take Wilma Walker's pulse. I know that to do a full set of vitals, I need to take my backpack off. For my own peace of mind, I need to do this cursory search to calm myself down. Intellectually, I know she's got a pulse because I can see her chest moving — just barely — but it's moving. Yet, I still grab her wrist and place my fingers just below her palm. *Man! That's weak.*

I throw off my backpack and dig out my glucose tablets. As low as her blood sugar is, she's gonna feel like she's sucking on a mouth full of marbles, but she's got to bring her blood sugar back up quickly. I kneel beside her and directly toward her face, "Mrs. Walker, Wilma? Can you hear me?"

"Tom?" she whispers weakly.

"No Ma'am, my name is Mitch. I'm a friend of Walter and Jessica's, they sent me to find you. I have some medicine here and it will help you feel better. I need you to chew on these while I give Walter a call. If I don't call him and tell him that I found you, he's going to be pretty upset with me."

I tuck the little orange glucose wafers into her mouth. Unfortunately in order to bring her blood sugar up where it needs to be, she has eat about five of them. After she's chewed on a couple of them, she asks me, "Are you a doctor? These are the same kind my doctor's office gives me."

I shake my head as I answer, "No, I'm not a doctor. I've had some paramedic and EMT training though. It's part of my work in search and rescue."

She just blinks and mumbles "Oh... okay."

I am busy trying to get a message to someone about Wilma. My phone isn't working. There doesn't seem to be any service even though the battery is charged. I send both Jess and the Sheriff's Office text messages letting them know that although Wilma is conscious she could probably benefit from an evaluation at the hospital and to please send an ambulance as soon as they can. I have no idea whether my text messages are even getting through or whether they are getting gobbled up into cyberspace because I am receiving nothing back from anyone and my phone isn't giving me the usual message confirmations or error messages.

I'm just about to give up on modern communication and just go outside to let off some emergency flares when Wilma rouses a little and asks, "Was there a tornado? Was that why I had to be rescued? Is Walt okay?"

I glanced up at the missing ceiling as I respond, "Well, I can't speak to what happened to this house before, but there wasn't a tornado today. I think that maybe you got a little confused because of your diabetes and you ended up at the wrong house after you went outside to pick some herbs from your garden. Your blood sugar was critically low and that can cause you to do some strange things."

"You mean all this fuss and muss was caused because I ate too many goodies?"

I smile at her as I respond, "I suppose in a roundabout way. You need to keep closer tabs on that blood sugar, Wilma. You've got to keep it in the normal range, anything else is very dangerous and can get you in a world of hurt."

Wilma frowns at me as she asserts, "What do you mean? Walter is always after me to eat healthier. I thought it was like my weight on a scale. Lower is better isn't it?"

Before I have a chance to give Wilma the correct information, Jessica bursts in with Walter and the Sheriff is hot on her heels ready to take Wilma to the hospital.

Jessica

15

WITH EVERY FIBER OF MY BODY I'm trying to quell my internal drive to pace, but I've just about reached the end of my rope — both literally and figuratively. I'm having a weird sense of déjà vu. Nothing has changed and yet everything has changed in the blink of an eye. As I sit here, tying knots in the macramé rope and listening to my grandma counsel characters as if they have real life problems, I remember doing the same thing when I was ten years old, sitting in the middle of her cheery farmhouse with its pale yellow carpet and marigold drapes. If it weren't for the beeping of the various machines, it would be easy to forget how much time has passed and the fact that we're sitting in a hospital room waiting for the doctors to decide how they're going to treat her worsening diabetes. For some reason, they can't seem to stabilize her blood sugar. Sometimes it's dangerously low and other times it's frighteningly high. No one can seem to agree on what to do about it, although there's been some talk about an insulin pump. My grandma and grandpa have met with an army of doctors, dietitians, nurses, specialists and occupational therapists to try to come up with plans to better manage her disease.

At first, Grandpa was on board with this proactive approach but, after they suggested that perhaps he meet with a marriage counselor to help reduce the stress in their relationship, Pastor Walker decided he had enough. My poor grandma looks like she's been attacked by a porcupine. She's got bruises everywhere from where they've taken blood samples. On top of that, she sprained her wrists pretty severely when she passed out. She's pretty lucky that she didn't have even more severe injuries.

The only thing that everyone universally agrees on is that Mitch's quick action probably saved her life. My grandpa thinks he deserves some sort of commendation or medal of honor. Mitch, of course, doesn't even want to take credit for the rescue; he just considers it part of what any decent human being would do.

After meeting with Sheriff Foster (who turned out to be a pretty decent guy), Mitch and Billy decided to make the rescue part of the public record because Sheriff Foster is trying to petition the county for a canine officer position and an official record of a dog being used in a rescue bolsters the need for the K-9 officer, especially if the dog is cross trained.

Finally, I can't deal with it anymore. I tie the last bead on my plant holder and stuff it into the canvas bag. For the most part, I've learned to deal with most of my hyperactive tendencies as an adult, but confined spaces like this, where I can't get up and move around, are my Achilles heel. Just as I feel like about ready to pull my hair right out of my scalp, my grandpa pops his head into the room. "All right, Buttercup, time for you to skedaddle. I love you and all, but you're crampin' my style. How am I supposed to flirt with my beautiful wife if you are always underfoot?"

His statement takes me so off guard that I can't help but giggle, but I'm not the only one. My grandma looks at him with open-mouth astonishment as she just blushes prettily and chastises him, "Walt, you know as a minister you're not supposed to lie and I know I'm not looking very pretty these days."

My grandpa gently kisses her on the cheek as he says, "Willie, you'll always be the prettiest thing I see in the morning and the most beautiful thing I see before I close my eyes at night, no matter how long I live."

I can't help it, I have to look away to hide my tears. My grandpa is not a grand gesture kind of guy. He and my grandma have the same gold bands they had when they first got married. They don't go on fancy trips much — well, except for the time that Isaac and Rosa got married — and he doesn't shower her with elaborate gifts, but those small nuggets of love that they share almost casually are so valuable. When I find love, that's the kind of love I want. Love in small, steady heartbeats.

I retrieve my purse from the little closet and announce over my shoulder, "Okay, see you guys later. I'm going to go take a walk."

"Don't forget to enjoy yourself for a change," my grandma calls out the door.

I'm so caught up in the emotion of the moment, I don't even notice when I walk smack into the middle of Mitch's chest.

To make matters worse, I lose my balance and inadvertently step on Hope's tail. She shrieks in pain. Immediately I drop to my knees and hug her. I bury my face into her neck and whisper over and over, "I'm so sorry, Baby, I'm so sorry. I didn't mean to hurt you. I never mean to hurt anyone." Hope tries to lick away my tears. People are starting to stare at the pile that we make in the middle of the hospital hallway.

Gently, Mitch coaxes me to my feet and escorts me out the door. "Come on, Red. I doubt Hope is really hurt. I think she's just going for sympathy. She and Lexicon play a lot rougher than that. Hope is in the mood to play. I bought a few Frisbees for her to destroy. Does that sound like fun? Do you have any wide-open spaces around here?"

I snort back a laugh as I gesture in a big circle. "Mitch, I hate to tell you this but you're not in Florida anymore — look around this is Kansas — you'd be hard pressed to find a space around here that's not open."

"Okay, point taken, this is a tad different from Tampa. I'll let you be my tour guide," he concedes. Mitch fishes something out of his pocket and tosses it at me as he warns, "Walter said to remind you the clutch sticks a bit."

I open my hands; a wave of nostalgia hits me as I see the key ring. I remember how proud Grandpa was when I won that silly little glittery musical note at the fair by shooting water at a clown's mouth. Of course, what I didn't know was that it was all an elaborate set up. Grandpa had purchased this old beater Jeep to help teach me how to do things like change my own tires and check my oil. I had a whole year to learn to do those things; I was supposed to learn to drive on my learner's permit before the car became mine. Of course, I was less than impressed because my friends at school were getting new cars and this thing was an eyesore. Let's face it, it was little more than just an eyesore, I didn't understand how it was ever going to be anything more than destined for the junk pile. Grandpa tried his best to show me that you couldn't judge a book by its cover or a vehicle by its dented, scratched part. He would show me how to take a part off and sand it down and re-finish it. At first, I was interested enough. It was fun to have his undivided attention as we worked together. We would sing old B.J. Thomas songs to the radio while we worked miracles and fought rust. B.J. Thomas was okay in my grandpa's book because sometimes he sang gospel and sometimes he sang country. Soon enough, Dex came along and I was convinced that no one could ever love me like he did and my grandparents couldn't love me like my real parents did. Following Dex blindly, I abandoned everything I ever knew and found myself stranded in New York. I know now that that was probably one of the dumbest things I could've ever done, but in a weird way it led me to Mitch so it's hard to know how to feel about that.

I feel Mitch tap me on the shoulder. Startled, I look up at him. Grinning, he asks me, "Are you going to look at those keys all day or are we going to go somewhere?"

I must have looked confused because he guides me to a shiny red vehicle about fifteen feet away. "No! You're kidding me!" I look up at him and back at the car. "This is Candy Apple Junk Five?" I ask.

"Well, I'm not privy to all the details, but on the way over, Walter did tell me that this was the Jeep that you helped him restore when you were a teenager."

My eyes mist over a little as I clarify "I think he's being too generous. I helped him sand a few parts before I abandoned him in the middle of our big project. He finished the rest of this himself. It's absolutely amazing. This was what my dream car was supposed to be like before I gave up on the dream. I can't believe he saw it all the way through. This belongs in some sort of antique car magazine. I can't believe he's letting me drive it!"

"I know I didn't know you back then, but I know you now and I can't imagine that you're all that much different —"

Exasperated, I twist out of his hold as I argue, "How can you say that? I was shallow and stupid. You would've hated me as a teenager; I'm not even sure I didn't hate me as a teenager."

"Jessica, how old were you when you learned to belly dance for your roommate?"

I blush as I intentionally answer vaguely, "I don't know if I was even eighteen yet. I think I must've lied about my age so that they would let me do it."

"Hmm, I don't know if I remember this correctly — but, the last time I checked, when you're eighteen you're still a teenager. Funny how that works," he teases. "Doesn't sound too terribly shallow and vapid to me. In fact, it sounds pretty heroic to do something you're absolutely terrified of and completely bury your own fear to do something in a different social group than you typically hang out with to support someone who is terminally ill just to put a smile on their face. I'd go so far as to say that you are the anti-shallow role model."

"Okay, you might be right about that, but my grandpa doesn't know anything about all that and I haven't done anything to make amends for all the pain I've caused him and my grandma. Yet, they're still the most supportive people I have in my life. I just feel really awful about that," I add with a wistful sigh.

"Jessica, have you stopped to consider that your grandpa might have a few regrets over the way he handled it, too? Like you said, phones go both ways and he didn't call you either. I think that him refinishing this car is his own apology card to you for all of the misunderstandings you guys had when you were younger. I think he recognizes that maybe he was a little hard on you and may have had some unrealistic expectations given the circumstances of your life. Just viewing the situation from the outside, I think that one of the reasons the two of you clash a lot is that maybe in a lot of ways you are very much alike. You both have gigantic hearts that feel everything one hundred percent and you don't know how to give half of your heart to someone. When the two of you are together and on opposite sides of an issue, neither of you are going to give it up easily. No matter who 'wins' there is always going to be someone who has their feelings hurt one way or another."

I melt back into his arms and rest my head against his solid chest. For a moment, I just absorb his warmth and support. "Where were you when I was an angsty, angry teenager? Maybe if you had been in my life, I could've avoided this whole crazy blowup with my grandparents."

Mitch's chest rumbles like an earthquake as he chuckles, "I'm not so sure about that, Red. Even if we didn't live half a nation apart, I wasn't really in touch with the real world back in those days. I had a fantasy relationship with a girlfriend who belonged to someone else, remember? Does that sound real balanced and healthy to you? I lived on wishes, could-be's and should-be's. I didn't even have the guts to go after what I really wanted."

"When you put it that way, it doesn't sound real great — but I don't know if you were all that different from most high school guys. Most of the guys I knew in school weren't dating the girl they really wanted to be dating. They were dating a stand-in until the one they really wanted became available. I always thought that was a pretty sad way to live your life."

"Don't women do that, too?" Mitch asks. "I can't tell you how many people asked me out just so that they could get a shot at Stuart. It was like I was some weird 'gateway' date for the Prom King."

I pull his arms around me and squeeze them as I admit, "I suppose I should be more sympathetic, but all I can think about is how glad I am that some smart, pretty cheerleader didn't snap you up along the way. Even so, I'm really glad that I don't have to go back and relive my high school days. Although, I'm grateful I went through those experiences because I learned a lot about myself and I'm a stronger person because of what Dex put me through."

Mitch rests his chin on the top of my head and nods as he responds, "Life has taught me some pretty hard lessons too. Mostly, not to take anyone for granted. I just sort of figured that Nora would be in my life forever and then she wasn't. Looking back, as much as I loved Nora, I think my dream of love was mostly built on childhood loneliness and innocent crushes. I don't know that a real relationship would have survived if we'd have ever had a chance to be together, because truthfully, Nora lived her life far too close to the flame for me. Even as kids, she was a thrill seeker like none I'd ever seen. I can't tell you how much of my childhood was spent trying to keep her and Stuart out of trouble. Still, like you, her presence in my life taught me a great deal about myself and I wouldn't trade it for anything."

As much as I try to impassively listen to him talk about his love of another woman, my body involuntarily stiffens and I flinch when he says the word love. Mitch is quick to pick up on the subtle shift. He spins me around in his arms and pulls my baseball cap off. My hair cascades over my shoulders and he plunges his fingers through it. He leans down until his mouth is just a fraction of an inch away from mine. "Loving and losing Nora taught me all the important things," he murmurs before he tenderly kisses me. He is in no hurry to stop, even though we're standing in the middle of the sidewalk.

As he pulls away, I fan myself and quip, "Please tell me she didn't play spin the bottle with you, because if she was responsible for teaching you that, I might just cry."

Mitch blushes as he admits, "I did play spin the bottle with Nora. In the fourth grade she refused to kiss me — she insisted I had cooties. The next time we played, we were under the bleachers at the Sadie Hawkins dance. She pretty much gave me an air kiss, but it didn't matter, I was smitten anyway. You know the rest from there. She didn't teach me to kiss, though," he informs me as he opens the door for me and helps me untangle the seatbelt.

I wait for him to walk around the jeep and fold himself into the passenger side before I ask, "Really?"

He grins and winks, as he retorts, "Nope, I learned that particular skill during a bet in college."

"You lie!" I accuse, sticking my tongue out at him, barely stifling my giggles.

"True story," he asserts, nodding his head. "You'd be surprised by how valuable my ability to scale the side of a building without ropes is to a sorority sister whose keys and I.D. had been thrown on the roof. I was able to negotiate a sweet payout."

I raise a skeptical eyebrow. "Were you the one who threw the keys?"

"Of course not!" he exclaims. "What kid of cad do you think I am?"

"The kind who would barter for kissing lessons," I reply pointedly.

"I guess you're right, but that's not the point here."

"There's a point?" I ask, still snickering.

The laugh lines that had been radiating from the corners of Mitch's eyes a few moments ago are now gone as he studies me intently. "Yeah, there *is* a point. I want you to hear the lessons Nora taught me."

As much as I try to hide it, Mitch catches my wary grimace. I don't want to be that kind of woman who is jealous of her guy's every ex, but apparently my body hasn't gotten the memo.

Mitch runs his fingers along my jawline and shakes his head 'no' as he replies, "Red, don't do that to yourself. Nora was my past, you are my present and I hope my future. That's what I'm trying to tell you. Nora taught me to laugh in the face of my fear and to never take a second of time for granted with someone I care about without letting them know what they mean to me."

"Oh," I breathe quietly as the potential implication of his words sink in.

I mindlessly put the Jeep in drive and the gears grind as I shift. I look over at Mitch and comment apologetically, "Yikes, I forgot about the clutch."

I'm lost in thought as we silently drive through town listing to the old a.m. radio. It's hard to make out but I think it's an old Bob Seger song playing. Near the outskirts of town, I bring my Jeep to a stop. It's funny, I wasn't intending to come here; it's almost as if the Candy Apple Junk Five knew to come here all on her own.

Mitch surveys the area and glances back at me with befuddlement as he remarks, "It's nice here but, it doesn't look like a very good place to play Frisbee. There are too many trees and windows around."

Hope sticks her head between the seats and I give the scruff of her neck a rub as I respond, "I hope she doesn't mind too much but I think I need something different right now. I don't know that I'm up to a rousing game of Frisbee right now."

Hope sticks her head through the seats and places her head on my shoulder. Mitch observes the interaction and he comments with a crooked smile, "Somehow, I don't think she's all that upset with you. Whatever you have planned seems to be okay with her."

I get out of the car and do some back stretches like I do before I do any complicated yoga moves or belly dancing. Sitting around the hospital room has made me really antsy, and I feel like I need to decompress. I guess that's how we ended up in this place. Perhaps my subconscious mind needed something that I wasn't fully aware of. As I finish up a neck and shoulder roll, I look up at Mitch only to discover him watching me with complete fascination.

"I just love how you move your body. It's like watching artwork come to life. I feel like you could be the inspiration for a work of Degas or something."

His complement is so beautiful and unexpected that I actually have to catch my breath. I am hot, sweaty and upset. I certainly don't feel very beautiful or graceful. I feel like I might shatter like a snow globe. I feel like the weight of the world is on my shoulders. When I finally meet his gaze, there are tears in my eyes as I say, "Wow, you do have a lot in common with Walter. You don't say much but what you do you say packs a real wallop."

"I didn't say a word that wasn't true, Red," he insists as he looks up at the building in front of us. "Are you going to tell me about your little hideaway?"

I shake my head at him as I answer, "No, I have a better idea. If you know the art world well enough to compare me to a famous artwork from Degas, I think you'll be able to fully appreciate what I'm about to show you."

Mitch

16

I'LL FREELY ADMIT THAT I'M usually one of those guys who likes my life neat and orderly with a certain degree of precision. It's one of the reasons that I like mathematics and accounting. Generally speaking, there's a predictable answer at the end of every problem. I cringe when I think how many of those tendencies have bled into my real life. Even my free time is governed by my hyper-organized self. I'm not generally a person who strays from my plans. So, an impromptu trip through town to an unknown destination is pretty unusual for me. Had I planned this trip, I would've researched every stop along the way and known every bit of background about it.

When Jessica first pulled up in front of this property, I thought she was having problems with the Jeep. There doesn't appear to be anything around here within miles. This looks like an abandoned farm. The walls are old, tattered and aged by the sun. The grass is overgrown by several feet and what was presumably intended to be a wildflower walkway has overgrown to resemble a jungle of flowers.

I'm a bit concerned about our safety, but Jessica confidently walks up to the big heavy wooden door and opens it as if she's been here hundreds of times. For a moment, I'm spellbound by the intricacy of the ironwork on the latches of the wooden door. It's such an incongruous sight to see such delicate iron work together with such a dilapidated door. I've seen this exact move many times in horror movies and I half expect someone to come lurching out of the darkness.

What I don't expect is a quaint room with wood polished floors and intricately carved pews on each side. However, what makes this room even more breathtaking are the huge stained-glass windows and the elaborate engraved crown moldings. Sunlight is streaming in from outside, creating beautiful patterns on the floor and the walls. It's almost as if the window at the front of the church is acting as a huge sundial. I spend several minutes just looking around at all the beautiful woodwork and stained glass, the crown molding, books original and hand hewn. I'm completely fascinated by how someone could let such fine woodwork and art glass just set unused. I turn to Jessica and say, "Wow! This is beyond incredible. Why is it just sitting here?" I ask, incredulous at the wasted old space. "Is there a parsonage like this too?"

Jessica flinches and nods her head as she answers in a low broken whisper, so quiet I have to move closer just to hear. "We used to live there when I was a little girl." She wipes away tears. "I never knew the whole story and the parts I remember are probably sketchy," Jessica explains as she sits on a pew and folds her knees up to her chest and crosses her arms around them tightly. "All I remember from when I was a little girl was that my grandpa needed a bigger church and a historical preservation company offered to come in and buy the church out with the promise that they were going to renovate the church. They just flat out lied and when a group of church volunteers tried to fix it themselves, the company tried to have them arrested for trespassing."

"So why are we here now?" I ask. "Aren't we technically trespassing?"

"I guess karma finally caught up with the cheaters; that company went bankrupt and our local bank took over the note and they really don't care what happens to this place. In fact I'm probably the only person who remembers this place is even here. It only means something to me because it was the first parsonage I ever lived in. I remember Grandma and Grandpa were so proud when he graduated from seminary school and got this place. This was their home and they were so proud of it."

As Jess walks over to the piano, she points to an instrument built into the wall.

"I don't think they knew this, but when I was a little girl, I hid in the organ pipes and I watched my grandparents cry at the pulpit where my grandpa remembered every baby who had ever been born while he was a minister here. It was the saddest thing I've ever seen. I felt like my grandpa was having a funeral for this little church. It made me so mad when they didn't keep their word," she explains, as she wipes some dust off the piano. "Actually, I'm surprised it's still standing. I'm shocked someone hasn't come and stripped out the stained-glass windows. It would seem that they would be pretty valuable to a museum or something."

"I'm surprised by that, too. I would've thought that a salvage company would've come through and taken the antique wood work," I comment, as I run my hand along one of the wooden pews.

Jessica slowly gets up and starts to wander around the old church. "The church looks like someone has come to clean it every once in a while. I wonder if it's Grandma and Grandpa? If it is, I bet it breaks their heart."

Jessica sits down and plays a few notes of *Amazing Grace* on the piano. Much to my surprise, it doesn't even sound out of tune.

"When I was a little girl and my grandpa was practicing his sermons, I liked to pretend that I was getting married. I would take my grandma's rain bonnets — you know, those cheap plastic ones that you buy at the discount store — I would fold them together to make a veil. I'm sure it used to drive my grandpa nuts when I would interrupt his sermon practice and ask him to perform a wedding ceremony between me and my Care Bear."

"You married your Care Bear? I thought all little girls wanted to grow up and marry their Ken dolls."

"Are you kidding? Those things are hard and plastic and no fun to cuddle with," she responds with a laugh. "I was all about Sunshine Bear. I wonder if my grandma still has him?"

"I bet you were an adorable little bride," I comment. "I suspect your grandpa might be grateful for all that practice since you've grown up to be so beautiful."

She stumbles over the notes she's been playing. "Thank you, I guess I just don't see myself that way."

"Maybe it's time you did," I respond. I find it fascinating when she gets uncomfortable over a simple compliment. In some ways, she's so bold and confident, but in other ways, profoundly shy. It's intriguing. She's had a tough day, so I decide to let her off the hook. "How long have you played piano?" I slide in beside her as I start to play a very rudimentary form of *Chopsticks*.

She glances up at me in shock. "You didn't tell me you play. I thought you said you weren't musical."

I choke back a laugh as I respond, "Look, I can play *Chopsticks, Twinkle, Twinkle Little Star* and *Jingle Bells*. I don't think that's going to get me on a concert stage anywhere. I think I learned it about the time I learned to play the recorder in the first grade. It's weird, the stuff that sticks in our heads."

"Do you have any other hidden talents?" Jessica teases.

"When we were sophomores in high school, Stuart tried to teach me how to play the guitar, so I could pick up girls. I think I probably remember about four cords. I also can shuffle two decks of cards at the same time. I can crack eggs with one hand, so I make a mean omelet. As you already know, dogs and kids kinda like me."

"That's a pretty impressive list. See, that tells me an awful lot about you, because I have never met someone who plays the guitar who doesn't actually sing. I actually thought you did a more than admirable job at karaoke. You more than held your own that night. Are you sure that you're not just holding out on me? Do you wish to declare any other secret habits?"

Jessica hops up from the piano bench and disappears for a few moments. When she comes back, she is carrying an old dusty guitar case. The minute I see it, I am instantly reminded of the time that I went home on spring break with great pride after learning to play. I was so excited to show my family my new skills, but my grandfather told me that we were not from the Glen Campbell side of the Campbell family and there were not going to be any slacker musicians in his family. He actually went as far as breaking the fret of my new guitar. I had never been so humiliated. I took the money that I had been saving for a new car and bought a replacement guitar. To this day, I've never told Stuart what happened because I was so ashamed of what my family did. Jessica would be astonished if she knew how close her guess came to the truth. I actually enjoy singing a lot. I just can't because it's not worth the conflict.

After some difficulty with the latch, Jessica opens the case. It's fortunate that I'm fascinated with her beautiful eyes because had I not been watching so closely, I would've missed the spark of pain that zips through them as soon as she sees the guitar. "Red, what's wrong?" I ask, as I see her grow pale.

"I just haven't seen this since I was really little and I guess I just didn't expect it to be so painful."

"What hurts, Jess?" I ask as I gather her in an embrace.

"Daddy asked me to keep that for him until he came back and he never came back for it or for me, that's all. Some days, I'm over it and other days, not so much."

"Jess, I don't even know that I remember how to play. You don't need to torture yourself this way," I declare as I kiss her temple and hold her close, trying to absorb her pain.

"No, it's not fair. His guitar is a beautiful instrument. It deserves to be played and it didn't do anything to be sentenced to death in the closet." Jessica answers tearfully. She takes a cloth from the guitar case and wipes it down as she expertly re-strings it. When I give her a questioning glance, she shrugs and says, "I was the equipment manager for band camp during my freshman year at school before I decided that I should be all bad-ass. Yes, it was probably the geekiest thing that I've done my whole life. But, it was also one of the most fun. I got to learn to play so many instruments. I am truly a band nerd in the geekiest sense of the word. But what do you expect? Grandma taught piano lessons for more years than I can remember to help make ends meet when the crops were less than spectacular. Let me tell you, as a hyperactive kid, piano practice was not my favorite. I think that's why I got into theater — I need to be able to move while I make music and sing."

Jessica hands me the guitar. It feels really foreign to me because I haven't held one in years. It's beautiful and perfectly weighted. I play a few notes. The first few are discordant, but eventually they sound a bit better. "I have to warn you, my skills are going to be rudimentary compared to yours. I don't really know all that much. I can't make chord changes very quickly. I have to think about it pretty hard," I warn.

Jessica kisses me quickly before she pats me on the shoulder and says, "I happen to know you have a habit of underestimating yourself. I think you're going to do just fine." In a flash, she's gone and sitting back at the piano. Jess looks back over her shoulder at me as she offers, "Any requests?"

At this particular moment, I'm regretting my decision to step out of my comfort zone and live on the edge. This is so much farther over the edge than I ever wanted to go. What is it about Jessica that makes me go places that I've never gone before? I've never performed with anybody else. Sure, Stuart knows that I can play because he taught me. Singing in front of Jessica and accompanying her on the piano is a whole different ballgame. What am I thinking?

"Mitch! Stop thinking so hard. We're going to make some music. We're not balancing the federal budget here. You can do this! Come on! I love you, I'm not going to hurt you—," she says as she continues to play through some elaborate scales to test all the notes.

"That's not what I'm afraid of," I confess quietly.

"What?" she asks, seemingly confused by my response.

"I'm not afraid that you're going to hurt me, but did you mean what you just said?" I ask, almost afraid to hear the answer.

"Yes," she responds tentatively, "I hope that's what you wanted to hear."

"It is. It just seems like such a random time to say something. I feel like I'm not in a great position for you to love me yet. I haven't gotten everything all sorted out with my parents, my job or my life yet. I don't know that I can offer the life you deserve right now," I babble unable to stop the words free flowing out of my mouth like lava from a volcano.

"Mitch, that's *silly*. Love isn't like an ice cream treat you get at the end of a doctor's office visit after you've been good for your shots or something. It's what sustains a friendship, a relationship — it's the meaning of life. It's the heartbeat of togetherness. You don't save it up and give it when everything is perfect. Love is best served when things are chaotic and uncertain because it's the glue keeping everything together."

After I put the guitar back in the case, I walk over to stand behind Jess and I put my hands on her shoulders as I confess, "That kind of love sounds amazing. If I forget that this kind of love is out there, you'll have to remind me. I was raised with the idea that the only time you could get love was if a certain standard of perfection was met and if you failed to do that, love and affection was withheld. I don't think my parents were intentionally cruel, I just think that that's what they learned, and they just passed it down. I'm looking forward to changing the family legacy."

"I guess that's the bonus of being raised the way I was. Every week, I got a different lesson about what love is," Jessica explains as she leans her head against my stomach. She sighs deeply. "I only wish that I had understood the value of those lessons more when I was growing up. Did I just blow it between us by talking about this too soon?"

I gently turn her so she's facing me and I pull her down on the steps so she's cocooned between my legs. "Jessica, nothing could be further from the truth. You were the answer to a prayer I never even knew I had. I never planned to fall in love with you, but I'm so grateful and honored that you chose me. My life is so much better with you in it. I hope you can say the same because I'm in your life. I've been feeling this way for a while and I've been looking for a way to tell you; but like usual, you were just a little braver than me."

Jessica

17

TODAY STARTED OUT PRETTY CRAPPY, but now I'm grinning like a high school girl who just got asked out by the most popular kid in class. In a sense, I suppose I did. Adrenaline is pumping through me like I've just had four or five energy drinks. Of all the things I expected to happen today, this wasn't one of them. Today worked out better than I could've ever expected, it does not always work out as well. My mouth can get me in massive amounts of trouble. However, today I'm glad that I didn't stop to think about what I said out loud and just followed my heart. As I'm pondering the events of the day, Mitch is still playing the guitar, and I have a newfound appreciation for how my mom fell for my dad. Even though Mitch doesn't think of himself as much of a musician, there's something inherently sexy about a guy with a guitar when he's listening to his own internal beat and strumming along with the music. He misses a chord and the strings fire discordantly. Mitch looks up to see if I've noticed. When he observes the pensive expression on my face, he immediately stops playing. "Hey, I know I'm bad, but I thought I was getting better," he comments with an air of self-deprecation.

I'm startled out of my private thought bubble by his little joke. "Oh, no your playing is great. It has nothing to do with that. I'm just really worried about what Grandpa is going to say about what happened here today. He is big on tradition. My grandpa is going to be understandably curious about what happened today because I'm not going to be able to hide my happiness because I'm over the moon about what happened today. Even though I am an actress, my happiness is going show all over my face and I am a terrible liar especially to my grandpa. So, he's going to know exactly what happened today. As silly as it seems, I don't want him to be disappointed with how our love story progressed. I know, I'm being a dork. You can tell me that now. I've pretty much come to that conclusion. My brain does this sometimes, it just goes around and around and around like a hamster in one of those training balls. I guess I should've told you that about me. My timing probably could've been better, right? I should've told you about my weirdness before you fell in love with me."

Hope, who has been lying in a patch of sunlight filtered through a big stained-glass window, jumps up and walks over to my side. She places her paws on my shoulders and her head next to my neck. It's a little startling. She's not a very big German Shepherd, but she is still pretty imposing and she's almost as tall as I am with those long, lanky legs.

Mitch snickers at the sight. "Hope, how many times do I have to explain to you that you are not a psychotherapist or a lap dog?" Mitch just shakes his head when Hope looks over her shoulder and wags her tail. Mitch's voice turns stern as he issues the command, "Off!"

Hope gives me a look of indignation as if she's saying, "Thanks a lot, I was only trying to help." She walks back over to the patch of sunlight and curls into a small ball with her back toward me.

As she pouts, I look at Mitch helplessly. "I didn't mean to upset her."

Mitch sets aside the guitar and laughs as he responds, "Don't buy her act. She's a huge drama queen. She thinks she's going to get some more dog treats out of you. She has a total agenda. She probably did feel your stress. About that, the only thing we have to tell Walter is that we took Hope out to go play Frisbee and it was really fun. The rest of it, we can sort out between the two of us. You can share your news if you want, or we can wait until things have settled down a little."

Mitch stands up and rakes his hand through his hair as he starts to pace. He looks at me and shakes his head in bemusement. "You are really hard on a guy who likes to make step-by-step plans, do you know that? I used to be that guy before I met you. You've changed me in all sorts of little ways. Believe it or not, at some point, I intend to make things more official. This wasn't really the environment where I had planned to make lifelong promises. I figured it would be a little more formal than this — but, if today meets all your criteria for swoon-worthy romantic moments, so be it."

My brain is busy trying to put together all of what he said, sort of like sprockets and gears. The first thing that clicks is the phrase 'swoon-worthy'. It's absolutely the last thing I ever expected to hear coming out of Mitch's mouth. Before I can stop myself, with a little amused grin, I ask him, "Swoon-worthy?" As soon as I ask him that, I want to kick myself in the brain. Of all the things he said, on a scale of -5,491,975,386 to a million, that was the least important thing I could ever ask him.

Lucky for me, Mitch doesn't seem offended by my goofy question. He just shrugs and explains, "My grandfather might've been wound tighter than a Swiss pocket watch, but my grandmother was a real pistol. She used to keep a collection of amazingly dirty historical romances hidden from him. I know they were pretty steamy, because when Stuart and I were in the seventh grade, we both came down with strep throat and his mom had him stay at our house while she worked. Everyone thought we were sufficiently sick that they could safely leave us alone without us getting into much trouble. We took that opportunity to investigate the interesting fiction laying around the house. My grannie could never understand why Stuart and I couldn't manage look her in the eye after that when she would tell us that we needed to grow up to be 'swoon-worthy' young men. I'm sure she didn't mean it in the full context of those books. Still, we could never quite get those images out of our minds after that."

I clear my throat lightly as I respond, "Um… I'm not exactly sure how to take that. Was that a threat to be a gentleman or a promise to be a scoundrel?"

Mitch grins. "Don't you mean that the other way around?"

I wink at him. "I don't know. How do you want me to interpret it?"

Mitch looks around the sanctuary and remarks, "Probably in ways best not contemplated here. What do you say we blow this popsicle joint?"

I just roll my eyes and respond, "We haven't even been here two whole weeks yet and the quaint ways of Walter Walker are already starting to rub off on you. The man is a force of nature."

I have to stop and rub my shoulder; I had forgotten how much effort it takes to throw a Frisbee. Still, it's worth it to see Hope have so much fun. It's startling to see the difference in her behavior when she is wearing her work harness and when she's free just to be a goofy German Shepherd. If I didn't know they were the same dog, you would have a hard time convincing me that they were even related. Even more evident is the change in her demeanor from the time that I found her. She is a happy, confident dog. Her tail is wagging and her ears are perked up and alert. She clearly worships the ground that Mitch walks on. Although, I can't blame her. I watch his every move as well.

A group of teenagers have joined our game of Frisbee. A few of them want to run roughshod over a shy girl with glasses who isn't as skilled at playing. They start to exclude her from the game and not let her have a turn. However, Mitch isn't allowing that to happen. He is taking the time to show her how to play. I like how he is subtly showing her how to throw without making a huge deal out of it and embarrassing her.

Suddenly, my phone rings. My heart stops when I hear my grandpa's ring tone. I notice that Mitch has a similar reaction as he throws the Frisbee to the kids and tells them to continue the game without him. He runs over to my side to make sure I'm okay.

Holding my breath, I hold the phone up to my ear. Mitch puts his arm around my shoulder and rests his head against mine so that he can also hear the conversation. I have to swallow hard before I can properly greet my grandfather.

I must sound odd because he responds with "Buttercup? Is that you? You don't sound like yourself."

I clear my throat and try again, "Yeah, Grandpa, it's me. Is everything okay?"

"I suppose it's okay — but you should've warned me you were expecting company. Normally we welcome everyone at our table, but with your Grandma in the hospital, it is a little bit of an issue."

"Company? What company? Grandpa, I live thousands of miles away and I haven't seen anybody from church in years," I insist. "I'm not expecting any company. Are you sure they even know me?"

"Pshaw, now you're just being silly!" he replies with a laugh. "Of course I know these kids. It is kinda hard to forget that one blond kid, he likes to hang fishing lures from his ears and color all over his body and the other girls look just alike. I was even the minister at their mama and daddy's wedding, even though they were already married, so it kinda sticks in a man's head, you know?"

"Ivy and Marcus are here? In Kansas?" I clarify.

"It's what I said, isn't it? Did you fall and hit your head this morning? Ivy and her sister are here with their intendeds. I guess Mr. and Mrs. Roguen were supposed to be here too, but they got bumped off the flight," my grandpa explains in a tone he usually reserves for the children's service in church. "I guess they'll be here shortly."

"What about Tristan's private plane?" I ask inanely.

"Something about FAA maintenance logs. That Marcus kid just about busted a gut when I responded 'hashtag richguyproblems'. Come on, where's the respect for your elders? I run a farm worth some decent change and they think I live in a hay igloo with no Internet access?"

"I'm sorry, Grandpa, they just don't know. Why did they come all the way here?"

"Well, Buttercup, I don't rightly know. That Tristan kid, now he strikes me as pretty bright, he said it was something he could only tell you in person. I don't know exactly what he does for a job but he acts like he's some agent on one of those television shows Willie likes so much, you know like Agent Mulder? Anyway, he just said it was personal and he wasn't able to discuss it with me."

"I'll be right there, Grandpa. We'll hurry as fast as we can," I reply as I start to throw things in the back of the Jeep.

The last piece of advice I hear from my grandpa before the phone goes dead is, "I expect that might be the smart thing to do. This feels like it might be important stuff."

Once again, it's completely apparent why Mitch is so gifted at his job. Unlike me, who has completely fallen apart the second my phone rang, Mitch has become more focused. I'm not even going to try to drive home. I just hand the keys to the CJ over to Mitch. Forget butterflies in my stomach, I think I have a flock of emus in there.

On the drive home, Mitch reaches over to hold my hand as he says, "Jess, I know you're scared, but you don't know. It could be happy news, for all we know. They've all been engaged for a while. They might have baby news or something. Didn't I read in the news that something was going on with a baby theft ring that involved Ivy and Rogue when they were infants? It's possible they reached a settlement," he offers, squeezing my hand as a gesture of support.

I roll my shoulder in a half shrug as I respond, "I suppose so — but it feels like I'm just waiting for the other shoe to drop, this doesn't feel like it's going to be good news at all. My stomach feels like it did right before my grandparents called me into the living room to tell me my parents packed up everything they owned and left the house. That's the way I feel right now; I don't know why, and I don't know how — but I just know that this can't be good news."

Mitch lifts up my hand and kisses my knuckles before responding, "Jessica, I'm not asking you to disregard what you're feeling. You're right, it could very well be awful news. I just want you to know that whatever the outcome, we are partners in this. I'm here for you. You don't ever have to wonder about that."

"Basically what you're saying is, you're not going to get bored with me like my parents did and ditch me?" I ask trying to sound disaffected and humorous, but failing miserably.

Since we're stopped at a stop sign, Mitch takes a moment to kiss me before he declares, "That's exactly what I'm saying. Got a problem with that?"

A horn blares behind us. I glance up at the kitschy makeup mirror I attached to the visor when I was a teenager and I notice that it's Betty Sue, the hairdresser I've gone to since I was a little kid. She starts to yell random statements out of her big pink pickup at a frightening clip just like she used to at her station at the beauty salon, "Who-ee, Girl! Walter's description didn't do you any justice. You are downright gorgeous, you should go on one of those shows, you know with Tyra. You could win the whole shebang. Is that your firefighter guy you're kissing on? You know, Walter says he saved Wilma's life? Is that true?

That's just an answer to prayer right there. Can I scooch right on by? I gotta get to the store. I'll let you get right back to kissing, and I won't even tell Walter. If my man looked like that, I'd be kissing him in broad daylight too," she admits with a laugh.

Much to Mitch's credit, he doesn't act embarrassed at all. He just gives her a friendly wave and yells back "Thank you for the compliment. I do believe I chose one of the finest women Kansas had to offer. We need to be getting home ourselves. Thanks for chatting."

As we drive off, I pat Mitch on the knee and proclaim, "You are the master, I bow to your skills. You have absolutely no idea how good you are. Not only did you effectively shut down the town's biggest gossip, but you did it with extreme deftness and exemplary politeness. That will help Sheriff Foster out because her husband is the chair of the City Council and her brother is the mayor."

"I guess that's helpful to know, but I was just being polite—" Mitch asserts with a small shrug.

I grin widely as I respond, "I know, that's what makes it so deviously clever. It's too bad all of your hidden political skills are wasted on big city life."

By the time all the polite greetings have been dealt with and Tristan and Mitch had gone to go get Isaac and Rosa from the airport, I've practically worn a hole in the carpet. Grandpa has opened up the church rec room for us to use today, so the twins went and got chicken and ribs from the local barbecue place and we've set up a pretty decent impromptu picnic for everyone. We even had time to go see my grandma at the hospital. I don't know how my grandpa is going to feel about this, but after she saw Ivy's new tattoo, she's decided that she wants one to commemorate all of her years of teaching music. I can only imagine what my grandpa's response to that is going to be. At least, there seems to be some good news from her camp. The doctors seem to have found a combination of medications that is effectively controlling my grandma's blood sugar so she should be able to come home tomorrow. They want to do twelve more hours of testing to make sure that her blood sugar is indeed controlled.

Apparently, Ivy has had enough of my endless laps around the big empty room. She steps in front of me. I have to stop to avoid running over her. She leads me to a couch in the corner of the room. After we sit down and she pins me with a narrowed gaze and asks, "I've been your friend for years and I've never seen you this wound up. What's wrong?"

"The last time I had to wait for a big talk like this, you know that my life was practically ruined," I explain dramatically. Even as the words come out of my mouth, I know they're a tad over the top.

"Yeah, we figured out a long time ago that your parents are not the brightest bulbs on the Christmas tree, but that's not what this is about," Ivy replies as she hugs me.

"Do you know what this is about?" I demand.

"No," she answers tentatively, "not entirely. Although, what I do know is that when our guys tell you they've got your back, they entirely have your back. Every single one of them, Mitch included. They are professionals at other jobs and they've got you covered. If they didn't have you covered, they'd just let some random stranger deal with this."

"Deal with what?" I practically screech.

Ivy pulls a Kleenex out of her pocket and offers it to me, "Jess, it's not my place to tell you. I know better than anybody how hard that is to deal with. Remember all those times you were beside me when I knew part of the story but not all of it? I was about ready to pull my hair out. I know how hard it is to wait. Everyone should be back in just a few minutes. They'll explain everything to you then. Until then, do you want to tell me what's going on with Mitch? I just think it's pretty amazing that the two of you are together — but I guess in another way it's almost not so much of a shock. You were fascinated with him from the first moment you saw his profile on BrainsRSexy. It's almost as if you were drawn to him way back then — before you even actually spoke to him. Isn't that weird? I wonder if online dating works that way for everyone else?"

For a moment, her question takes me back in time to when I first saw Mitch's profile on the BrainsRSexy site. I remember pointing him out to Ivy and then fervently wishing that she would not at all be interested in him. I don't know if it was my prayers or just dumb luck, but she didn't even seem to think that he was all that interesting or handsome. I, of course, thought she was absolutely crazy when she ignored such an engaging and clearly gorgeous man. After I watched her heart melt at the mere sight of Marcus, everything became clear. Marcus and Mitch are just about as different as daylight and dark.

I take the Kleenex from Ivy as I respond, "I don't know. All I can tell you is Mitch is the real deal. He's as heroic as he advertises — if not more so. After a lifetime of wondering where my heart belongs, it's nice to know it finally has a home."

Ivy blinks away tears as she tries to fix my makeup. "There you go then. Just remember to trust that even when it's hard."

The doors burst open and there is immediate chaos as the room suddenly erupts in a cacophony of conversation. My grandpa is holding full-court and is fully in entertainer mode. He is currently showing off all of the recent renovations that the local youth program helped him complete on the building. I suspect that Rosa may not care quite as much about the weight of the felt under the roof tiles as my grandpa, but he doesn't seem to notice her inattention. Mitch has taken up his usual station behind me and slightly to my left. He has learned the hard way that I'm right-handed and I often gesture wildly when I speak. Consequently, he has learned to stay out of the line of fire.

Isaac comes over and kisses me on the cheek as he quietly observes, *"Mi Pequeña,* those must have been some powerful wishes. I see that Mitch is much more than your friend now. You used your wish wisely, I know him to be a good man."

"Thank you, Isaac. I know him to be a good man too. I have to ask though, how did you know he's what I wished for at my birthday party? Mitch and I had only been going out for a couple of months; and you and I barely knew each other," I respond.

Isaac gives me a knowing look as he smiles slyly. "I have two daughters who are very much in love and I have loved my wife ever since I found her upside down in an ice storm — it wasn't a very hard puzzle to solve."

"Speaking of puzzles to solve, why is everyone here, Isaac?" I ask firmly.

Isaacs scrubs his hand down his face before he nods to Tristan and points to a nearby table. "Ahh, *Mi Pequeña,* that is a much more difficult thing to share. There are days that I do not

184

care for the responsibilities of my job. Today is one of those days. Shall we go sit and discuss what's going on?" he offers.

My knees buckle at Isaac's serious tone, as I process what he's actually saying. It's a good thing that Mitch is standing behind me because I collapse against his frame like an origami crane. For a few moments, it feels as if his bones are holding me up. My knees are so weak that I cannot get them under me. Mitch seems to understand what's happening because he threads his fingers through my belt loops and securely holds on to my waist until I can collect my strength. After I catch my breath, my brain rewinds a bit and focuses on what was just said. I know it's a rhetorical question, but part of me wants to scream, "Oh *hell* yes! Why do you think I've been waiting hours and hours?"

Mitch knows I'm on the edge because as Isaac collects his briefcase and grabs a cup of coffee, Mitch murmurs in my ear, "Red, take a deep breath. He's got protocol to follow. You'll have answers soon enough. Roguen has a job to do and we have to let him do it by the book even though you guys know each other. Otherwise, we could pay the price later."

Of course, I know he's right. I can't let my impulsivity ruin everything — whatever this is. But, I'm about to blow a gasket here. Mitch walks us over to the table and pulls out my chair so that I can sit down. As he does so, he fishes something out of his pocket. I am amused when I see that it's a bright yellow stress ball made to look like the classic happy face. It's a very small one; perfectly proportioned for my small hands. "Some boyfriends would get their girlfriends fancy earrings or a dozen roses — I love the fact that you know me well enough to know that the most romantic gift you could get me would be a yellow smiley face stress ball. It just says something special about our relationship," I tease.

Tristan smiles at me as he responds, "Hey, don't knock it. The other day, Rogue got me these kick-ass earplugs to use at the gun range. They work better than anything I've ever tried before. She got the fact that I need them because I was always complaining that I had a headache after going to the gun range. I hadn't put it together with a need for better ear protection, but Rogue did, because she knows me so well and loves me. Here's to partners who know us better than Hallmark and Teleflora."

"Not that I don't appreciate the marriage advice and all, but can we really get to the point of why we're here. I've been completely stressed out all day. I think I'm going to get an ulcer or throw up or both. Why did you guys come halfway across the United States to talk to me? You know that we have the Internet even all the way in Kansas. You could have called me, sent me a text message, Skyped me or video called via FaceTime or something. Why did you all come here en masse?" I inquire, my voice getting louder with every suggestion.

Tristan shuffles some paperwork before he looks at me and responds, "Jessica, you're right. I would be frustrated too. We all wanted to come tell you that there have been three arrests in the animal cruelty case involving Hope."

When I hear those words, all the angst and worry that I've been carrying around all day just seems to drain out of me and I almost slide out of my chair. It's almost as if my backbone just dissolves. It's like I have fallen apart and I need to be put back together. As the initial shock wears off, I start to look around and I realize there isn't a look of celebration on everyone's face. "Let me get this straight —you arrested the bad guys, so why isn't everyone happy?" I ask, feeling like I'm on some strange reality show like *Punk'd* or *Jackass*.

Isaac reaches out to squeeze my hand as he continues the explanation, "*Mi Pequeña,* I wish that was all there was to it, but the way they were arrested gives us grave concern."

"Sir, with all due respect, we need it all on the table—" Mitch warns with a sharp edge in his voice.

Tristan picks up the story, "Jessica, the teenagers were picked up because they were trying to vandalize your car while it was parked in your driveway and they were tampering with the bird feeders."

"Why would anybody want my Jeep? I ask incredulously. "It's orange and obnoxious; it even has daisies on it. Even Ivy laughed when she saw the decals I found for it. Were they trying to hurt the birds in the bird feeder? They're just poor little hummingbirds! That's just sick!"

"Apparently they are part of the local gang and they had at least one accomplice on the inside of the police department. They found out that you were attached to the case and helped rescue Hope. They were intent on destroying your vehicle because their vehicle was impounded by the police department as part of the investigation. It seems, their vehicle is viewed as high profile within the gang units and revered so, having it taken away by the police department was considered a huge dishonor and a badge of betrayal."

"That's insane!" Jessica insists. "Do they know that I don't even have a license plate number or anything else on their car! All I did was identify a patch of color that may or may not be on a license plate. I know nothing else. It could be any license plate from any state."

Isaac chuckles as he responds, "You and I know that, dear little one, but those we pursue don't know that". He turns to Mitch and comments, "Campbell, you were spot on about the leather harness. We found a receipt when we got a search warrant. We're chasing down the financials on that."

"What about the hummingbird feeders?" Mitch asks, still trying to piece together the story.

Isaac breaks out into a large grin as he responds, "They either watch a lot of television documentaries about crime or they have a very inflated view of their criminal stature because they believed that there were hidden cameras in them and that they were being taped as part of a sting operation."

"How did they get caught? I wasn't even there. Midnight is being kenneled at a friend's house."

Tristan snickers as he responds, "It seems our junior criminals, who are so camera shy are not so shy about bragging and posting Snapchat videos."

A chill goes down my spine. "What does this mean for me?"

"Unfortunately, these kids are part of a well-known street gang. Marcus helped us identify their tattoos. Even though they're young, they're not playing around. They've issued some serious threats against you. The Hillsborough County Sheriff's Office and the FBI contacts Isaac has spoken with would feel much more comfortable if you would stay here in Kansas until we can figure out where the threats are coming from and determine how deeply within the organization they're coming from."

From all the way across the room, I hear my grandfather declare, "What do you expect from a place called 'The Armpit of Satan'!"

I roll my eyes as I respond, "Grandpa! You never did give Florida a fair chance. It's really nice there!"

"If it's so nice there, why are all of your friends here warning you about a bunch of teenage punks terrorizing you in your own driveway?" he counters.

I fall silent because as usual, the man makes a good point

Mitch

18

I FEEL LIKE I'VE BEEN stranded in the middle of some strange movie scene where everyone has the script except me. After Tristan and Isaac dropped their little bombshell, everyone seems to be treating this little get together like it's an impromptu family reunion instead of a potentially life-changing, catastrophic event. Although Jessica is a little teary-eyed and pensive, she seems to be in much better spirits than she was earlier in the day. I can't help but wonder if I'm blowing things out of proportion or if everyone else can't see the ramifications of what's just happened.

Hope places her paw over my foot to gain my attention. Glancing at my watch, I realize that it's been several hours since I've taken her out to relieve herself. Catching Isaac's eye, I show him Hope's lead and tilt my head toward the door to show him that I'm leaving. He nods and goes back to speaking with Marcus and Walter.

After Hope takes care of her needs, I realize that I'm just not up to socializing so I let myself into the church sanctuary. Although this is a really nice sanctuary with padded pews and a beautifully appointed altar with lush ferns and inlaid wood, I prefer the atmosphere of the quaint little church that we visited yesterday. There is just something about old historic buildings and the stories contained within their walls that speak to me. I sit in the back pew and rest my head on my arms as I tried to marshal my thoughts. Quite literally they are all over the map.

Suddenly, I have new respect for my father. Several years ago, there was a threat issued against all firefighters in our county after a cadet failed to pass all of his training through the Academy. My father is an instructor and was one of several who failed to advance the applicant through the program. He took it personally and issued death threats against the instructors and their families. I remember my father being absolutely terrified to let my mom go to the grocery store or to church alone or with me; he even asked to have a police escort accompany me to school and to after school activities. Of course, he couldn't tell us what was going on at the time. As a result, we were both alarmed and half convinced he was overblowing the situation. However, now that I'm living through this scenario from the other perspective, I can understand my dad's hyper vigilance. Right now, I would like to borrow Tristan's fancy aero-plane and fly Jessica to some artsy European villa somewhere and let her draw, paint and belly dance to her heart's content and forget the evil in the world.

I don't even know how I'm going to deal with my real world. Even before this newest development, I had pretty much decided that I wasn't going to go back to my job with the school district. My unscheduled rescue of Wilma underscored a few things for me. I like taking dogs who were considered worthless and giving them lifesaving occupations. I like the feeling that what I do matters to somebody. Now the only question that remains is how do I accomplish that? This whole gang issue with Jessica has put her life in danger so, now more than ever, the where becomes as important as the why. I'm not even sure I know how to process that information. Is there any place that's safe or is this gang nationwide? I simply don't know the answer to this. What about my commitments back in Florida? Can I simply drop those? More importantly, with Jessica's life being threatened, can I afford not to?

These questions are spinning around in my head like some deranged one-armed bandit and they just won't stop. Every time I contemplate an answer, I come up with a slightly different configuration. One thought occurs to me — I don't even want to consider it although Jessica might think it's within the realm of possibilities. With Jessica's past, I wonder if she even trusts me enough to keep her safe after the parents who were supposed to love her and keep her safe decided to leave her behind. I hope she understands that I'm not them and I wouldn't make those kinds of selfish decisions, no matter what the danger.

I'm still trying to organize the chaos that's in my head when I hear the door to the sanctuary open.

"I see I've found a kindred spirit," Isaac comments, as he sees me sitting alone on the pew. "Rosa loves these social events, but they are not my favorite thing to do. I would much rather be at home in my wood shop. Though, I sense that something more is going on with you today," he observes as he comes and sits down beside me.

I can barely remember to hold my tongue because that's such a bizarre question given all that he and Tristan dumped on me. Of course I have a crap load of things bothering me today! How could he think anything different? Although I don't say anything, I think Isaac could read it in my face.

He chuckles wryly as he says, "Okay, my small talk skills are a little rusty. I should ask you how you're doing with that mess we handed you."

"Isaac, how do you think I'm doing? How would you handle it?" I ask, unable to keep the edge of sarcasm out of my voice.

"Son, the very last thing you want to do is take advice from me on this subject. I did the worst thing you could possibly do. I tried to protect my family by going away from them. As a result, I almost lost my wife and my two daughters in the process. It was the most heartbreaking thing that I could have ever done. I'm just lucky that Rosa came back into my life. So, my advice is to never leave the side of the woman that you love — regardless of what threatens to come between you. This is a lesson I learned the very hard way."

I nod as I agree, "No, Sir, I don't ever plan to leave Jessica. The complication comes in deciding how to stay. I have commitments back in Florida, but I need to stay here to keep her safe."

"Are your commitments in Florida worth losing Jessica over?" Isaac asks, giving me a shrewd look.

"Absolutely not. It's not even a close call."

"Then, I think you have your first answer. What would you like to do instead? I suspect that Walter could use some help on this farm."

I grimace slightly as I acknowledge, "That's probably true enough, but I spent enough time in Florida doing a job that I didn't really like to know if I'm going to relocate, it needs to be in a field that I want to pursue."

"I understand that. So, I'm guessing that working with the dogs is what you want to do," Isaac states.

"It is. There is a need nationwide for well-trained search and rescue dogs and shelter dogs like Hope and Lexicon are being put down all the time because landlords are excluding breed types that they think pose a danger to the public when it's simply not true. The dogs just don't have the proper training. By using rescue dogs, I'm saving dogs and educating the public. It's a win for everybody."

"It sounds like you have a pretty good plan. Why are you concerned?"

"A couple things. First, I have to quit several jobs in Florida. The school district counts on me, the shelter needs me, and I don't know that the second-in-command at the training program is quite ready to step up to the helm yet. The guy that I've been working most closely with at the training program, Stuart, is actually still in veterinary school. He graduates this year, but he was planning to start his own practice separate from our work with search and rescue. Stuart and I have been friends since the second grade and he's going to be pissed that I haven't run this decision by him first."

"Even all of that doesn't even begin to unravel the mess that is my family. If they thought they were disappointed when I dropped out of college, this is going to push them entirely over the edge."

Isaac studies me carefully before answering, "The one thing that my family and I have learned through this ordeal was that most of what we thought we knew about each other was based on layers and layers of misunderstandings. That may very well be the case in your family. However, if they're already disappointed in you, it can't get much worse. You just need to go and talk to them and make sure they hear what you have to say. They will either accept or they'll reject it, you are not in charge of their reaction to your news. You must do what is right for you and Jessica. As a father myself, I can't imagine that your family would be disappointed with all that you have accomplished, and Jessica is a delightful young woman. Your heart has chosen well."

"I can't believe how much better this airline is treating Hope than the last one. I think that the flight attendant would've put her in first class and left us in coach if we would've let him," Jessica jokes as she sips her Pepsi.

"I don't know. James Joseph was pretty nice to you too. I'm not sure you actually needed three pillows. I think he was flirting with you. Not that I blame him. You look beautiful. I like the haircut that Betty Sue gave you," I remark, as I watch her read a book on her Kindle.

"Thank you, I wanted to look good for your mom. Can you believe that this is my first time with the whole meet the parents thing, I never did that with Dex. I am surprisingly nervous. What if they don't like me? What does that mean for us? I wouldn't want to make you choose between me and your mother if she hates me. Oh geez, listen to me ramble again. It's like I can't control it…" she trails off.

"First of all, my parents are going to love you because everybody loves you. Even if they don't, that's their problem, not yours. If they choose not to love you, I will choose you. Always."

"Really?" Jessica asks, shock evident in her voice. "I mean, I hate to sound dumb about this. In case you haven't noticed, my life is pretty short on people that have chosen me. I'm a little afraid to trust that."

"I understand that, Jess, but the people who have chosen to stay in your life are people of amazing caliber. I only know a few great people in my life, so I have a theory that a few great people outweigh a crowd of average folks every day of the week."

"What if your parents think I'm only average? I don't want you to have to be embarrassed about me," she frets. "You always seem to know the right thing to say, whereas random things just fly out of my mouth without any control. You are always so composed, it's amazing."

I laugh out loud before I admit, "You wouldn't think I was so composed if you knew the thoughts that swirl around my brain all day. I'm so nervous, I haven't been able to eat right in two days. The reason I'm not too worried about choosing you over a relationship with my parents is because I haven't really had a relationship with my parents in a few years. I can't seem to find common ground with them over anything. We don't see eye to eye. Everything I do with them seems to not meet their expectations. That's the reason that Stuart and I are such good friends. I had to turn to someone to communicate with because every conversation I had with my parents when I was growing up seemed to result in the silent treatment. Nora and Stuart became a sounding board for life. It was the three of us as the Three Musketeers. We became our own little family.

If I'm nervous about this meeting, it has nothing to do with you. I'm just so lucky you are here by my side. I need a champion and a number one fan. 'Composed is not at all what I'm feeling. 'Completely and totally freaked out' would be more in line with my emotions," I admit in a rush of words that I didn't know was going to erupt so violently. I have been trying to be so strong for Jessica that I hadn't shared any of this. I guess it's all been building up for a while; I'm not typically one to talk about feelings but I guess maybe I should do it more often.

Jessica looks a little stunned by my admission, but she has taken her headphones out and she is fully engaged in our conversation. She leans forward and whispers, "Mitch, it's okay."

Now that I've opened up, I can't seem to stop talking so I just keep going, "Just so you know, this meeting where I'm going to announce that I'm going to completely abandon everything that I've built in Florida and once again completely change the direction of my life is going to be a complete crapshoot. I have no idea how they're going to react. When I had to make a similar decision after Nora's death, I thought that they might never talk to me again."

"But they did, right?" she probes.

"They did what?" I reply, too upset to properly track the conversation.

"Your parents eventually started talking to you again, right? That means that there is always hope that whatever differences you have, you'll be able to set aside and have a reasonably normal relationship. I have a hard time believing that they wouldn't when someone as phenomenal as you are in their lives. Come on! You help save people for a living. That is beyond awesome. If they can't get that through their noggins, as my grandpa says, then they don't deserve you in their lives, and I'll make the same offer to you as you made to me. I'll stand by your side, always."

I wish we weren't in these cramped airline seats, there is nothing I would like more than to pull her onto my lap and show her how much I appreciate her complete and undivided support. She makes me feel like I can conquer the whole world with one hand tied behind my back. It's the most exhilarating feeling in the whole world.

The email app on my iPad suddenly beeps repeatedly, indicating that I must have multiple emails. I guess the airline Wi-Fi must've finally kicked in. I've spent the better part of the last hour trying to make it work. I'm waiting to hear from my former supervisor at the school district. I offered to help train my replacement if she needed me to. However, much to my surprise, the email contains a letter of recommendation for a grant that I applied for the new place in Kansas, we've named Hope's Haven. I'm grateful, but surprised since I expected my former supervisor to be more upset with me for leaving her in a lurch.

The next email is from my father, informing me that they are going to be late picking us up at the airport. For some reason, that doesn't surprise me at all. In this case, it actually works in my favor. It will give me a chance to decompress a little from the flight and grab a bite to eat, among other things I'd like to accomplish today. Although the flight attendant offered to bring Hope some food from first class, he did not make the same offer for Jessica and me.

Normally, shopping is not an activity that I truly enjoy, but there's something unique about shopping in airport stores. It's almost like a grown-up treasure hunt. Jessica's eyes are sparkling with joy as she explores each store with eager anticipation. She is beside herself with joy when she finds handmade postcards painted with water colored fireflies and butterflies. When we pass a jewelry store, a hummingbird necklace catches her eye. "Wow, isn't that pretty?" she comments.

"They have some really nice stuff here," I agree. "It looks like they might be having a sale, do you want to go in and check it out?"

Jessica's eyes grow wide as she exclaims, "Really? You wouldn't mind?"

"No, I don't mind. As you may recall, I owe you a proper birthday present?"

"This is probably wrong and materialistic of me, but don't mind if I do," she replies with a grin as she skips into the store.

As she goes in search of a salesperson, something draws my attention and I turn to an older gentleman sitting quietly at the counter. "May I see these two in our sizes?"

He looks up at me over his spectacles and asks, "Are you sure? Most folks your age are looking for something a little more flashy."

"No, these are perfect. I've actually gone to three or four other stores looking for something just like this and I haven't had any luck."

"Funny thing is, these were a custom order and they never came back to pick them up. I have had a Dickens of the time selling them because the woman's fingers were so tiny, much like your gal over there and there's just not much call for these plain gold bands anymore. Everyone wants glitter these days."

"Jessica and I are not really into much glitter. She's got enough sparkle all by herself."

The gentleman behind the counter glances over at Jessica and remarks, "That she does. Have a seat and I will polish these up for you and be right out."

I walk over to where Jessica is looking at the hummingbird necklace. "What to do you think?" I ask.

"It's pretty, but I don't know if I need it," she replies wistfully.

"Come here, I want to show you something else I was looking at," I say, as I guide Jessica to the counter where the salesperson is waiting. When Jessica sees what I've found, she looks at me with total astonishment.

"Does this mean what I think it means?" she asks in a voice barely above a whisper.

"Red, if this comes as a complete and total shock to you, I haven't been doing a very good job of making my intent clear."

"I know you love me, you've made that plain enough, but there's promises between us and then there's telling the whole world. That's an entirely different thing!" Jessica stammers. She focuses on the ring display. "Mitch, I can't believe how much these look like Grandma and Grandpa's set. It's almost as if they were cast at the same time."

The salesperson that was helping Jessica comes over and whispers something in the gentlemen's ear. He pauses for a moment and then looks at Jessica, "I'm sorry, Ma'am but I need a private moment with your young man, please. Tracy here can show you some more things around the store."

A look of complete befuddlement crosses Jessica's face and I'm sure a similar one is on mine. I have no idea what this salesperson is up to. Shrugging, Jessica gets up and follows Tracy to the other end of the store.

"Don't worry, Tracy is my daughter and I won't let anything bad happen to your fiancé — you do intend to make her your fiancé, correct?" The salesperson laughs as he sticks out his hand, "I'm sorry, I did not introduce myself, I'm Gene, the owner of the store. I noticed the search and rescue badge on your dog and I just want to say thank you. My son was lost while hiking and was saved by a search and rescue dog. We owe you everything."

"You're welcome, Sir. I'm honored to be part of the group of people that do this for a living. Is there a problem with the rings?" I'm curious as to why he sent Jessica away.

"No, there's no problem. I just thought perhaps you might want to think about an engagement ring as well as a wedding set. Tracy pointed out to me that your girlfriend is very much enthralled by the hummingbird necklace. I have a very graceful gemstone ring that compliments the hummingbird pendant that would serve as the perfect engagement ring. I have been waiting to find a home for that wedding set for many years. I had just about given up hope. I am willing to negotiate a very good price if you want to purchase an engagement ring with the pendant and the set." He writes down a number on a business card and slides it in my direction. I pick it up with some trepidation, but I'm more than a little gob-smacked when I see the number. I've been doing enough ring shopping to know that he must be giving me the jewelry at nearly wholesale prices.

"All I can say is, thank you. If Red likes those pieces as much as I do, consider it a deal."

"No, the pleasure is mine. All I'm doing is paying it forward. One day a few years ago, a young man not unlike yourself, put his life on the line to help my family. It's just time for me to return the favor."

"Your generosity isn't going unnoticed, that's for sure," I comment.

Gene looks a little uncomfortable with the praise as he looks through his inventory for the engagement ring. When he opens the box, I can immediately tell that Jessica is going to love it. The stones are delicate teardrops overlapping to form a band in the bright jewel tones that she was wearing the first day I saw her in her belly dancing costume. As he sets it back on the counter, Jessica sits down beside me as she remarks, "Did you guys finally get done talking about all your 'guy' stuff? If you would've let me wander around the store much longer, it could have been dangerous to my budget. There is just too much pretty stuff in this store."

Tracy laughs at Jessica's remark, drawing her attention away from me. This allows me to get the ring out of the box and quietly leave my chair. Gene motions for me to give him my cell phone, so I gently scoot it across the counter to him. I'm not even listening to what Jessica is saying to Tracy, she could be plotting to buy all of the inventory in the store for all I know. My heart is in my throat. Suddenly, I'm shaking, even though I've been planning to do this for weeks. I could use some of my famous nerves of steel right about now.

Despite my online dating thing, I'm still pretty much an old-fashioned kind of guy. So, I drop to one knee and wait. Tracy's sudden gasp clues Jessica in that something is happening. Jessica spins around and looks at me kneeling on the ground. "Oh my *gosh!* You are so doing this! I'm kinda sad that Ivy and Rogue aren't here. My grandma and grandpa should be here too. I should probably shut up and let you do your thing, shouldn't I?" she asks with an ear to ear grin.

I smile up at her as I joke, "I'm not an expert in this by any means, but I think that it might actually go smoother if you let me talk."

She sticks her right hand out and waves it in my face as she replies, "By all means, please proceed."

"Jessica Lynn Walker, as we long ago established, nothing about our relationship has gone according to any sort of traditional plan from the way we met to the way we've courted. For a by-the-book, plan ahead, organized guy like me, it should've been the scariest thing in the world, but that didn't seem to matter to my heart. As you said, I fell in love with you one heartbeat at a time when you provided my heart with unexpected shelter. Because of your warmth and love, I've discovered how to be who I need to be and I need you beside me every day. Would you please do me the honor of agreeing to be my wife?"

Jessica swallows back tears as she nods and whispers, "In a heartbeat." I place the ring on her finger and stand up to fold her into tight embrace.

I'm a little startled when our celebratory kiss is interrupted by an enthusiastic round of cheers and applause. After I catch my breath, I am surprised to look up and see my parents watching the whole proceeding through the glass windows in the concourse of the airport. I excuse myself and run after them to invite them into the store.

Just when I think my day can't get anymore unpredictable, my dad spends several awkward moments studying Jessica and Hope before he gives me a hearty slap on the back and announces, "I see you've finally settled on a good woman and a career in search and rescue instead of pussyfooting around in a classroom with dusty old books. It's about time you made up your mind and followed your heart."

"You mean, you're not disappointed in me?" I practically stutter. Something about interacting with my dad always makes me feel like I'm nine years old and just got caught with a roll of toilet paper and a flashlight on the way to the neighbor's house.

"Are you kidding me? We've been waiting forever for you to grow a backbone and make a decision based on what was best for you instead of everyone else. Do you think your grandfather wanted me to teach firefighters for a living? Every son needs to make his own way for his own reasons. How could I ever be disappointed in you for that?"

"I think that my lovely fiancée, Jessica here was right and we need to talk. We probably should've done it a long time ago, but now is a good time to start," I admit.

Jessica

19

I'VE BEEN BACK FOR A little over a week and every day as the excitement wears away, a feeling of discontent and restlessness settles over me. It occurs to me that I'm actually feeling homesick for Florida. I find this a bit shocking since most of the time I spent in Florida, I felt like the only place I wanted to be was back home. I never expected that I would miss Florida — yet, somehow I do. I suppose I feel less autonomous here. Every place I go, from the grocery store to the library and the bank, everyone is reminding me of the person I used to be when I was young. Sometimes, those memories are not always flattering or pleasant. I've tried really hard to become a bigger, better person and to make up for the mistakes that I've made. It seems like I might not ever outgrow them around here. I'm starting to feel really self-conscious, yet when I tried to speak to my grandma and grandpa about how horrible I was to them back in the day, they just laughed it off and told me that there really isn't anything for them to forgive.

I'm feeling a little bit at loose ends because I feel like I never got to say goodbye to my old life and I don't really have anything other than Mitch to embrace in my new life. I could help Grandpa out with church business, but he has volunteers at the church that help him with those tasks and I would feel like I was taking away someone's job. They count on that work to be able to develop work skills, so I don't want to be taking away someone's career aspirations just to create busywork for myself.

Mitch doesn't seem to be having the same problem assimilating to life in Kansas. He has found opportunities for himself literally left and right. First, Tristan wants him to join the company that he and Isaac have formed to work with law enforcement agencies. They want to capitalize on his ability to work with search and rescue dogs and expand that into providing companion animals and personal protection dogs for women who have been traumatized and soldiers returning with Post Traumatic Stress Disorder; it sounds like a huge undertaking. Mitch hopes he'll be able to start a whole training facility and bring on a couple trainers for Hope's Haven within a few months. He's really excited about the opportunity. I can tell he's nervous too, he keeps trying to steer Isaac and Tristan to more established programs that have a more favorable record of long-term placements. However, they pretty much told Mitch they were willing to take the risk on him and his work ethic.

As if that weren't enough responsibility, when Rogue saw the little church and parsonage that I grew up in, she showed it to Tristan and suggested that they start a new satellite center of Elliott's Center. At first, the connection went over my head. I had to ask her what Elliott's Center was. She reminded me that it was formed to honor Tristan's half-sister who had unexpectedly passed away leaving her son behind who didn't know how to grieve. They have set up a charitable foundation to help kids and their parents learn how to process the loss of a parent or other close family member. As soon as Isaac saw the parsonage and the chapel, he fell in love as well. Grandpa and the guys have been meeting with all of the city officials to try to come up with a plan.

Even my grandma is well enough to go off to her ladies club. Feeling out of sorts, I decide to go to the local public library. Jotting a note to Mitch and my grandpa, I grab my keys and head out the door. All of this down time with nothing to do is driving me crazy. I miss having art and dance classes everywhere I turn or the ability to see a movie twenty-four hours a day or even the ability to go have ethnic food in a dozen different varieties at the drop of a hat. Assimilating back into small-town life is harder than I would have imagined. When I pull up to our small town library, I realize that they've remodeled quite a bit since I used to hang out here as a kid. This place used to be my refuge from life. My grandparents are amazing people, but they were not always aware of how profoundly lonely I was as a kid. I used to come to the library and read books about faraway places and famous people. I loved reading biographies of Hollywood stars and imagining that one day I would be one of them. I think that's what sparked my interest in theater; I thought that playing characters would be a way to live in someone else's shoes. When I was really young, I thought perhaps if I were someone else, my parents would love me more. I would spend hours in the mirror practicing all sorts of faces, expressions and voices trying to perfect the art of acting.

I cautiously open the door. The sensory memories are almost overwhelming, as the smell of old paper and carpet glue come rushing at me. It looks like they've recently remodeled. Instinctively, I look up at the reference desk. I remember spending so much time there, asking my favorite librarian to look for specific books for me. Much to my shock, Mrs. Turner is still here. She looks equally stunned to see me. "Jessie? Jessie Lynn? Well, look at you all grown up with a ring on your finger. I guess the rumors around town are true."

"I don't know what you've heard, but yes, I'm going to marry a very wonderful man, Mitch Campbell."

"The rumor mill didn't exactly spit out his name, but it told me that he did a mighty fine job of rescuing your grandmother."

"He did at that," I acquiesce. "Mrs. Turner, do you have anything interesting for me to read? I'm going a little stir crazy."

"I just got a few new books in on Lady Gaga. You might find those interesting since she just won a bunch of awards in Hollywood."

"Thank you, I'll take a look at them," I answer with a smile.

As I'm about to take the stack of books from her, a rambunctious youngster comes barreling through the library and practically knocks me over as he is shrieking at the top of his lungs. In fast pursuit behind him is a slightly older girl screaming, "You are in so much trouble. My homework was on that disk and you went and ruined it. Now what am I going to do?"

The little boy sticks his bottom lip out as he replies, "I just wanted the metal part for my airplane."

"Oh my goodness! These two are supposed to be keeping themselves occupied and quiet while their mom gets ready for a job interview."

"Is everything roughly where it used to be?"

Mrs. Turner looks at me a little skeptically as she nods and answers, "Yes, I suppose it is. Mostly we've added to the reference section and put in space for computers. Everything else is pretty much the same, it's just spiffed up."

I set the book down and turn to the kids. "Hi," I greet, "I'm Jessica. Do you mind showing me where your mom is?"

The older girl looks dubious as she responds, "Don't think I should. Mom said not to bug her. She's studyin' for a job."

I nod solemnly as I respond, "Oh, I know all about studying, I just graduated from college. I'll be really quick, I promise."

I look over the top of the little girl's head and wink at Mrs. Turner as the little girl cautiously holds out her hand to me and leads me deeper into the library.

When we approach the table, I instantly recognize its occupant as soon as I see her beautiful waist length hair the color of corn silks. She was a couple years ahead of me in school and then suddenly disappeared. Rumor had it that she was going out with some college guy from a couple of towns over and that she had gotten pregnant. From the looks of her family, it appears that there might've been some truth to the small town chatter. I have to mentally bite back the phrase, "Janice Franks, as I live and breathe!" It's true, I have turned into my grandmother. I can't even pretend that I haven't.

I'm saved from having to form a socially acceptable, age appropriate greeting when the little girl announces, "Mama, somebody came to the library to see you. Is it somebody from your new job?"

Janice looks up at her daughter with a confused expression as she explains, "No, Sweetie, I don't have a new job yet. I'm still trying to get a job. That's why I'm trying to study these interview questions. I need you and your brother to stop bothering me so I can concentrate."

"But, Mama—" the little girl starts to protest.

I step forward to rescue her as I say, "Hi, Janice. I am sorry for any confusion. I'm afraid I'm the one who asked her to break the rules. I just wanted to ask you if it was all right if I borrowed these two. I don't know if you remember me, but I was a couple years behind you in school. I'm Pastor Walker's granddaughter."

She smiles at me as she responds, "Of course I remember you. You and I were hair spirits because the only person that got made fun of quite as much as I did for my hair was you. I figured that made us sisters of the heart. What did you have in mind?"

"I just thought maybe I would take them down to the reading corner. They have a bunch of puppets and kids' books over there. Truth be told, I am going a little stir crazy being all normal and straight-laced at my grandpa's house. I need to let a little bit of my acting skills surface and take them out for a spin or I'm going to go a little nuts. I just can't be this normal for this long, it's driving me absolutely crazy. I'd like to read your kids a story or two if you don't mind? I'll just be right over here in this room."

"You would do that for me? I mean, we were friends, sort of, but you didn't really know me like a best friend or anything."

I chuckle as I respond, "Well, quite frankly I'm a little bored, but you also look like you're a little frazzled and look like you could use some help. I am a sucker for kids, I totally love them. Ask Mrs. Turner, I love books, especially kids' books and I was really bummed out when I got too old to read them. I'll use any excuse to go back to the kids' section."

Janice giggles at my antics and replies, "Okay, okay you don't have to work so hard to sell me. If you want to entertain my kids for a while, knock yourself out." She looks at the kids and warns, "Craig and Lissa, try not to kill each other. That's Mrs. Wilma's granddaughter. You guys better be nice to her," she warns sternly as the kids run off to the reading room.

I wink at Janice as I remark, "If you remember, I used to be the original wiggly kid, so I've got this covered. Nothing much upsets me. Just do whatever you need to do. We'll just be in the kids' room having fun.

Her shoulders slump slightly as she says, "Okay, thank you, I don't know that you understand what you're getting into but if you're willing, I can't even tell you how grateful I am. All I can say is 'Good luck'."

I shrug and say, "I think I'll be okay." As I enter the room, I realize that the puppet collection has expanded a great deal since I was a little girl. I glance around a little in awe as I see the vast variety of puppets. I find one that resembles Lissa and hand it to her. "Lissa, it's been a really long time since I've been here. Do they have puppets that look like your brother and me?"

Lissa grins and runs off to a different puppet rack. Craig is waiting for me to address him. He looks like he's afraid that I'm going to leave him out of the fun. "Craig, I need you to pick out some puppets that look like you and your sister's favorite animals. Let me see if you can guess some of my favorite animals too," I challenge. "I'll meet you back at the reading mats."

Lissa returns with the puppets and asks, "Will these work?"

She actually did a really great job. One puppet looks like an exaggerated version of me. The puppet of the little boy looks even more like her brother. The only thing missing is his freckles.

"Those are perfect," I proclaim. "Can you do me a favor and find some books for us to read? I don't really know what you and your brother like."

"That's going to be a really big problem. My brother and I like really different stuff. He likes dinosaurs and trucks and stuff like that. And I don't like that stuff so much. I like books about animals like dogs and cats and horses," she explains with all the exasperation common to big sisters everywhere.

"How about this? You get some of the books you like and some of the books he likes and we can switch back and forth," I suggest.

"You sound just like my mom," she laments.

"I happen to think your mom is a pretty nice lady so, I'll take that as a compliment. We have lots of time so make sure you choose lots of books," I say, as I carry the puppets over to the mat and lay them down. Craig comes in with an armload of animal puppets. I take them from him and set them down beside the puppets that resemble us. When I pick up the parrot puppet, I ask him, "Whose favorite is this?"

"Yours, Ma'am," he mumbles around his thumb.

"Really? How did you know that birds are one of my favorite animals?" I reply.

He gives me a look like I am one of the most dimwitted creatures he's ever run across as he mumbles, "Umm… I sawed one on your necklace."

I reach up and place my hand over my hummingbird necklace. "So you did. I forgot I was wearing my necklace today. That was very clever of you to notice."

Lissa brings me a large stack of books. Many of them are among my favorites and I smile as I pat the mat next to me and start to hand out puppets. "Have you guys ever watched the Muppet Show?" The kids nod with a look of puzzlement on their faces. "You know those old guys who criticize everything that happens in the show and tell funny jokes? You guys can use your puppets to pretend to be like that when I read the stories if you want. That way if you don't like the way I'm reading a story, you can just let me know and I'll do something else."

"What are the amminals for?" Craig asks stumbling over the word.

"You know in some movie scenes there are lots and lots of extra characters? Sometimes, they have extra lines. I may need your help with some of that, so I had you pick some extra puppets for you to use."

"Miss Jessica! He don't know to read yet! He's too little," Lissa informs me.

"That's okay, we'll help him along. This is all supposed to be about fun and imagination anyway, right?"

Lissa looks at me as if I've lost a few marbles in my old age and responds, "If you say so, Ma'am."

I've got to hand it to Janice; her kids have good manners. Then again, they haven't seen the full force of me yet — I wonder how they're going to react.

After about two and half hours, I have discovered a few things. First, kids' books can be really funny. My sides hurt from laughing so much. Lissa lost much of her reserve around me after the first few minutes and it turns out this little girl has a wicked sense of humor and is smart as a whip. She had me in total stitches. Craig might not have been able to read much, but he was a whiz at funny voices and sounds and enthusiastically picked up on the spirit of our activity. He didn't even seem to mind much when we were reading stories about horses, dogs and cats. Finally, I had to cry uncle when we read the Monster at the End of the Book for the fourth time.

Janice finally came and collected the kids with a grateful smile and a promise to exchange emails and text messages to let me know if she got the job. I was really touched when both kids took the time to hug me goodbye and thank me for their adventure in books. That was one of the most rewarding things I have done in quite a long time. I forgot how much fun it was to act out stories and use different voices. I haven't had a chance to be really creative in forever, so it felt like finally letting my hair down after I've worn it in a bun for many months on end.

When Mrs. Turner beckons me into a back office, my heart sinks. It feels like it did when I was a little kid, often sent to the principal's office for squirming too much in class. I wonder what I did to upset her. I'm surprised when I see a large grin on her face. *Okay, I'm totally befuddled.*

"Did you have fun today, Jessica?" she asks, as she sits in her old-fashioned wooden swivel chair.

Even though part of me is sending out warning signals that I should probably be circumspect and listen to what she has to say before I open my big mouth, I can't seem to help but gush, "Oh yes, Mrs. Turner, I had the best time. Those kids were awesome and their imaginations were great. It was so much fun to introduce them to the joy of reading — I had forgotten what a new reader is like. It's amazing to be able to encourage someone to think about things in a different way, through words. It was phenomenal to see her learn to pronounce new words right in front of me," I reply, letting my speech trail off as I realize I'm just rambling as usual.

My stomach clinches as I realize that Mrs. Turner has begun to write on a yellow legal pad. Usually, when people start to write things down in meetings that involve me, it's not a good sign. She looks over the top of her reading glasses at me as she inquires, "I understand that you recently earned your college degree?"

"Yes, Ma'am, I have finished the coursework. I still need to go back to Florida to march in commencement, but the school has awarded my degree."

Mrs. Turner smiles at me as she remarks, "Walter is so proud of that degree, you would think he earned it himself. Theater Arts and History, correct?"

"Yes, Ma'am," I confirm. I can't help but ponder the question, if my grandfather is so proud of me, why did I never hear that from him for all those years?

"I understand from your grandfather that you may actually stay in Kansas for a while," Mrs. Turner says.

"Yes, my fiancé is opening a training facility here to train search and rescue dogs. I will definitely be moving back home." At this point, I'm not even trying to disguise the fact that I am searching Mrs. Turner's face for clues about why she's asking me such a series of strange questions. Finally, I can't contain my curiosity any longer and I blurt, "I'm sorry, Mrs. Turner, but am I in trouble for something?"

"Goodness gracious, Child, why would you think you're in trouble? I brought you in here to see if you wanted a job," she exclaims.

Now, it's my turn to be stunned as I reply, "Wait... I'm not a librarian. Don't you have to be a librarian to work in a library?"

"In most cases, it's very helpful. For now, this is just for the summer reading program. We may evaluate it later, but for now, this is our immediate need. You remember Caitlin Jones? Well, now she's Caitlin Nelson. Anyway, she got pregnant and no one was expecting her to have twins. She and her husband have decided that it's cheaper for her to stay home with the babies than to pay for daycare, so I lost my program manager for the summer reading program. I think you would be the perfect match. I don't have time to do a long exhaustive search and you have the perfect qualifications to run it. You know this library frontwards, backwards, and inside out. You love books and children. Most importantly, you value reading and you can instill it in kids and help make them enthusiastic readers just like you are. I was watching you in the reading room, and you're absolutely perfect. What made it even more remarkable was no one had to push you into doing what you did this afternoon, you volunteered to do it because you love books and reading — that spoke volumes to me."

"What you're telling me is that my little impromptu trip to the library this afternoon with my ratty old clothes with no makeup on was actually a job interview?" I ask incredulously.

Mrs. Turner gives me a sly grin as she responds, "Yes, that's exactly what I'm saying. Wasn't that crafty of me? You didn't even have to worry about dressing up. Think of all the stress and anxiety I saved you. I think after you start your new job, that should earn me a piece of Chocolate Silk Pie at Sally's Bakery. You are taking the job, aren't you? Someone else didn't snatch you up first, did they?" she asks insistently.

My thoughts are racing a million miles an hour. Mitch and I haven't even talked about this. I know that Isaac and Tristan don't want me to go back to Florida. I can't imagine that working in my small town library with kids would be dangerous. I think I'm probably safe to work here; they didn't say I couldn't work. Besides, if I stay at home all day, every day doing nothing, I'm going to go absolutely bonkers. I can't stay home with Grandma and watch soap operas every day. There is a hard limit to how many things I can macramé. There just is. For my own sanity, there is only one decision I can make. I take a deep breath and try to keep my voice steady as I answer, "Mrs. Turner, you know since I was a little girl, this has always been my home away from home. I would be honored to lead your summer reading program."

Mitch

20

TO SAY THAT THIS HAS BEEN A roller coaster of a week is the understatement of the century. Small town life is both amazingly simple and complicated. Jessica was so excited when she was offered the position at the library. It's fascinating how small town gossip works. She hadn't even been home more than a half an hour before word started to circulate that she was actually going to kick Mrs. Turner out and take over the entire library. I swear word gets around this town faster than a Facebook message. Walter had to call a few well placed sources with the correct information to quell the rumor mill to restore Jessica's good name in the town. After Walter's intercession, Jessica became something of a local celebrity and news of her hiring became the top news story in town and we were like, the hottest couple around.

I'm starting to feel a little more sympathy for Stuart and Nora. This must've been what it was like for them in high school. It's odd to be in demand because you're a couple and to have people want to be in your presence because they heard that other people want to be near you. Jessica says I need to play along because sooner or later I'm going to be asking these people for funding for Hope's Haven so I need to be in their good graces. For a shy, awkward guy like me, it's my definition of torture.

For now, things seem to be progressing pretty well on every front, although we are insanely busy. Tristan brought his dad and his brother who own a construction business to refurbish the old parsonage and church. Tristan is a fascinating guy. You would never guess that he has developed a half a dozen really successful software programs and a gaming platform. The guy is totally normal, unless you count the fact that he owns a plane.

The permitting process is progressing really well with the search and rescue business too. I've developed a really good working relationship with the shelter in the next county so they are beginning to get a feel for the types of dogs that I will be looking for when I have the facility to house them. In fact, they began to pull a few out and keep them in foster homes until I'm ready for them. In a development that I did not expect, Walter said that if I can find a way to develop the land or fix up the house that I found Wilma in, Jessica and I can live on the property next door and put Hope's Haven there. I'm still trying to find a way to make that happen.

I'm on my way back to Tampa to essentially close out my life in Florida. The most difficult part of this trip will be saying goodbye to Stuart. I can't really remember a time in my life when Stuart wasn't in it. I don't even know what I'm going to say to the friend who has been with me through the best times of my life and without question, the worst. How do you say goodbye to a friendship that basically was responsible for keeping you together when everything else in your life was completely falling apart?

As I disembark the plane, Hope's tail is wagging against my leg so hard that I will probably have bruises in the morning. I look up to see Stuart holding up a sign that says, "You were supposed to fly over, not stay. Welcome back home!" I smirk at his reference to Jessica's ring tone. Stuart has disdain for all country songs so this is a direct jab at Jason Aldean too.

"Very funny!" I retort as I give my best friend a hug. "I missed you too."

"You missed all the drama. They arrested some of those kids from the gang. When I say 'kids', I mean it. The youngest was like, thirteen or something. You'll never guess why one of them is saying they took the puppies. I guess one of them saw a news story on YouTube that there were service dogs that could sniff out cancer and his mom hadn't been feeling well and so he thought maybe she was sick with cancer so he was going to teach the dog to sniff out illness. Unfortunately, he didn't know how to train dogs or even how to treat them humanely. When Hope didn't know how to behave properly, his older brother and father decided to 'discipline' the puppy."

"We heard that they had been caught, but this is the first time I've heard any explanation about why they took the puppies. That's quite a leap for a kid to make, but I've heard stranger things, I guess," I remark. "What's going to happen with this whole mess now?"

"Since you decided not to come back as trainer for the Search and Rescue program and the original executive director was planning to semi-retire, they brought in a new director and hired a new Board of Directors. The new executive director has experience at one of those wilderness camps for kids so he has an agreement with the youth correctional facility to take the kid under his wing and let him volunteer his community service time to help train the dogs correctly."

I bristle at the thought of that because I remember the condition Hope was in when Jess found her. She still tears up about it when she encounters Hope's scars as she's brushing her. "Do they even remember what the dog was like when she came to us? Wasn't he responsible for her condition?" I ask harshly. "I thought the police said a whole bunch of kids were in on the scam at the shelter the day Hope was stolen."

"I know where you're coming from, that was my attitude at first too. I was told the investigation determined that it wasn't this particular kid. I guess that he was the one that pushed the dog out of the car because they were on their way to shoot Hope somewhere in the Everglades. In some obscure way, he actually saved her life by getting her out of the car. It also turns out that some of the tape was an attempt to bandage up the burns that his big brother had inflicted. Unfortunately, the rest of the tape was placed there so that they could throw her out of the boat once they shot her in the Everglades. It was just a sick and twisted plan altogether. In the overall scheme of things, J.J. was actually trying to help. According to everyone that I've spoken with in the program, he actually adores the dogs. Although he's still new, he shows some aptitude and he's exceptionally patient with the slower learning animals. The only open question right now is his own personal safety. I guess the older members of the gang are pretty upset that he is openly working with our side and I suppose the S & R could be construed as law enforcement. His probation officer has some real concerns about his well-being."

"There have been some really specific, personal, deadly threats against Jessica by some pretty senior members of the gang as well. It's enough that some senior members of the FBI have alerted Isaac to be on the lookout," I explain, running my hand down my face in frustration.

"That sucks. I just have to tell you, it sucks to be the one left behind. I really figured that we would all be friends — you know, like when you were friends with Nora and me. I didn't leave you just because I got a girlfriend," Stuart declares with a definite edge in his voice.

"I know you didn't. I didn't ask you to either and maybe that wasn't the best situation for any of us in retrospect. I didn't plan for it happen this way, but I have to move for the safety of the woman that I love. You get that, right?" I ask as I struggle to explain all the upheaval in my life.

"I just thought it'd be cool to be the kind of friends our parents are when we're eighty and trying to run the dogs on the beach. I hope Jessica is worth all the sacrifice," Stuart answers as he reaches down to pet Hope even though he knows she's in harness.

"Breaking up our team is the hardest part of this move for me. I hope you'll stay in touch. You know we can still do video calls and Facetime and texting and stuff. As you have pointed out to me, I don't really have to fall off the edge of the planet just because I'm out of town. We'll be back to visit. Jess has friends here too."

"What am I supposed to do? Who's going to keep me from eating myself into a sugar-induced food coma?" Stuart complains.

"It's funny that you should ask, you know I'm starting up this fancy training facility for search and rescue dogs. Dogs that will need lots of top-notch care and someone I know like a brother will be a vet soon—"

Stuart groans as he answers, "I don't even know what it takes to pass the boards in Kansas. I've spent more than a year studying so that I can get my license here."

"It's just a suggestion — that's all I'm saying," I answer.

I'd wondered how long the peace in Kansas was going to last. I soon found out that answer is eleven days. I'm just sitting down to dinner with Wilma, Walter and Jessica when the call from Sheriff Foster comes in. Apparently, there was a freak lightning strike that started a house fire and a young toddler was missing from the home. Recently, I lost Dizzy, my most experienced search and rescue dog. I knew that day was coming, I just didn't expect it to occur right after we moved. I'm not confident Lexicon is quite ready to handle a chaotic scene yet, so I harness up Hope and hop into the CJ and head to the scene.

As we arrive, the fire department is still mopping up hotspots and various factions of the family are outside shouting at each other. Hope is more disconcerted than I have ever seen her. I thought that I had put her in just about every conceivable situation she might encounter, but I have never seen her quite this distracted. Hopefully, she will settle down and act like her usual self. The sheriff greets me with the child's blanket that they retrieved from the car. He explains that in the rush to get everyone out of the house, the child simply wandered away and no one has been able to locate Sebian in the chaos.

After putting on a reflective vest and hardhat with floodlight, Hope and I set off to find the missing toddler. Usually, after getting a scent off of an exemplar, Hope is pretty confident about what direction to go in, but tonight she seems to be going around in aimless circles. I'm trying not to project my frustration through my commands or through her tension in her lead, but as time wears on, it becomes increasingly difficult to keep my body language neutral. As we take one last pass along a low-lying creek bed a sick feeling overtakes me when I see a flash of red. I don't even have to consult the victim description to know Sebian was last seen wearing Spiderman pajamas.

Dammit all to Hell! Why didn't I bring both dogs? I should've brought Lexicon with me just in case. If I had, as soon as Hope started acting squirrelly, I could've switched dogs and maybe we could have found Sebian faster.

I mark my location on GPS and send it to the rest of the rescue team. I radio for backup and then run to Sebian. When I see that he is completely submerged facedown in the water, I have to repeat the mantra in my head 'cold and not breathing is not dead'. They drum that into us in EMT training. It's not necessarily too late and we might still be able to help him if we can get him to a trauma center. I have to keep myself calm and thinking even though it looks dire.

As gently as I can, I scoop him out of the water in put him on his back on the shore and begin the procedures that I've been taught. I have barely begun when the fully trained rescue team comes and takes over for me. After the toddler has been rushed away with full lights and sound, Sheriff Foster comes over to my rig to debrief. He is visibly pale when he updates me on Sebian's unresponsive state. "It's a really good thing that Susan was on call. If that little guy stands any chance at all tonight, it will be due to her."

"Susan?" I ask, totally confused.

"She worked in Portland at one of those big teaching hospitals and flew on the crew of a Life Flight helicopter before she got married and her husband got transferred here; she's some fancy trauma nurse, you know the kind they write movies about."

"That's good because this little guy is going to need a classic Hollywood ending with a miracle or two thrown in for good measure."

Unfortunately, little Sebian didn't get his happy ending either at the local hospital or when they, in a last-ditch effort, tried to life flight him to an advanced trauma center.

Somehow, I've found myself over at the Totter place again. I don't know, there's just something about this place that draws me like a magnet even as dilapidated as it is. I didn't intentionally come over here today but my mind is so full that I need a safe place to empty it. I'm sitting on the dilapidated porch watching a mama barn cat play with a litter of kittens. I can't help but think how much a little boy like Sebian would enjoy playing with a bunch of little kittens like this.

I can't stop running last night's call in my head over and over. If I had thought about it more carefully, I probably shouldn't have relied on Hope to be rock solid in that kind of environment. I knew that she had been burned. Sure, I had put her in fire rich environments before but nothing that big and smoky. It likely triggered some bad memories for her when paired with a loud arguing family. I have had her in loud environments as well but never the two together. I should have had the foresight to combine both environments. I worked Hope in training environments that contained fire trucks and fire, but never with both darkness and distraught family members. I think it just overwhelmed her. Had I been thinking ahead, I should have thought to bring all of those elements together and maybe taken her on a few actual fires.

What if all this is my fault because I didn't thoroughly test her enough? I'll never know whether a child lost his life because I didn't run every single scenario by my dog in advance. I can't go back and test whether Lexicon would have performed better under pressure. He might not have collapsed emotionally, but his talking skills aren't quite as good as Hope's. Either way, in retrospect, I should've had both dogs there. There's just no way to escape that conclusion.

I'm so lost in my thoughts that I don't hear Walter approach. "You can't let the bad days eat you," Walter advises, as he lays a hand on my shoulder. "I've been through enough farming accidents and counseled enough grieving families to know that you'll find enough would've, should've, could'ves to last a lifetime, but they won't change the outcome."

"But what if I should have done things differently?" I argue.

"You'll do them differently next time, but you gotta forgive yourself," Walter declares softly. "The Lord knows you tried your best. As long as you don't ignore what you've learned, that's all anyone can ask of you, including yourself."

"What if I'm not ready for all of this?"

"If you truly believe that, you do what it takes to get ready. After my granddaughter brought you home with stars in her eyes, I did some research about what it is you do and from what I understand, you were facing about the worst conditions you could face that night with wind, fire and rain. It's possible that no decision you made or didn't make would've changed the outcome. That little boy could've already been resting in God's arms before you ever got the call from Sheriff Foster."

"You know what, Walter? I'm beginning to understand why my fiancé thinks you're one of the smartest men she knows. Thank you for the words of support. I'll work on the whole self forgiveness thing, unfortunately it doesn't come very easily for me."

"Well, you're worth it. Anybody who loves my granddaughter as much as you do deserves to be given the benefit of the doubt. By the way, I've noticed how much you like this place. You know, the banks in this town kind of like me. They make a lot of money off of me. They probably wouldn't bat an eyelash if I were to say, sign a home improvement loan for you to fix this place up and Tristan's family have done a right fine job with the old parsonage and sanctuary.

You know, I was all kinds of skeptical. I already had one place lie to me so much they practically set their britches on fire, so I wasn't holding out any great hope that I was going to be treated any better by this out of state company, especially when they claimed to be friends of Buttercup's. Not to be mean or anything but that girl's got a heart as soft as butter so I worry about people taking advantage of her. I was tickled pink to find that Tristan and his family are good people. If you want to use them to fix up the Totter place, I would fully support that and I'd be happy to help you kids get that done."

I give the mama cat a scratch as I try to formulate a polite response that won't offend Walter, "I really appreciate your offer, I don't want you to feel like I can't carry my own weight and with the uncertainty of Hope's Haven, a house might be to much for me to tackle right now," I admit.

"Since I already own the place and a lot of it's going to be reimbursed by insurance for the tornado that swung through a couple-o-years back, I'm not terribly concerned about your ability to pay me back right now. I consider the fact that you brought my Jessica home to me to be the most priceless thing you could've ever done, so if anything, I owe you a big favor. The bottom line is I trust it all to work out in the end. The fact that you guys are here at all is the answer to hundreds of prayers. The rest of it is all just a matter of paperwork between us and the bank."

Jessica

21

PLACING FRESH CANDLES IN THE votives along the edge of the altar, I can't help but marvel at how much has changed in just a few months. My little humble church doesn't look so humble anymore. Even though Tristan's dad and his brother worked really hard to keep the original character of the old church house, if you look hard enough, there are modern touches everywhere from the eco-friendly recessed lighting to the additional outlets to accommodate modern electronics. I guess the biggest surprise has been the high degree of historical accuracy. Isaac went as far as bringing in members of his wood crafting guild to carve some replacement pieces to fix some of the damaged crown molding. After the nightmarish experience with the other company, the town was relieved and amazed when Tristan hired Janice to help his dad with all the historical research to make sure that everything was restored correctly. The result is the stunning environment that I'm currently decorating for Ivy and Rogue as a trial run for the real thing in a few months since it's only May now.

When they told me that they were both getting married on Thanksgiving, I was really surprised. As far as I know, from the moment Ivy found out that she had a twin, she was dead set against having a stereotypical twin wedding. Last I heard, Rogue and Tristan were going to get married in Paris like Isaac and Rosa did. I haven't really had a chance to clear up my confusion because we've been trying to figure out all of the wedding stuff over Skype. Skype might be fine for business meetings, but have you ever tried to pick out a bridesmaids dress over Skype? It's a little insane. Still, flying all the way to Kansas just to check out the decor and eat some cupcakes seems a little extreme to me, but I guess that's the lifestyle they lead now. Mitch opens the back door of the sanctuary and about scares me to death. "What are you doing here? I thought you had a meeting with your new board of directors."

"I thought so, too. Apparently, the Chairperson contracted a wicked case of the Norwalk virus and wisely decided not to expose everyone. It's been rescheduled for next month."

"That sounds terrible," I empathize, remembering the reports I've seen on the news.

"What are you doing?" he asks, looking around.

"I'm just trying to do last minute stuff. I still can't believe they want me to set all this up as a trial run, but they do. They want to see what it looks like in the church. I guess I don't blame them because it's hard to see custom ordered samples over Skype. There's not really much more I can do. I've tied up all the tasks I can think of. It's not as if I can taste the cake and order desserts for them."

"Wait a second, don't orders have to be ordered like, months in advance. When my mama ordered one for her class reunion, she had to order three months in advance. How can they taste cake they haven't ordered yet?"

I shrug as I respond, "I'm guessing that this is probably Rogue's influence on the situation because she's pretty laid-back and casual."

"What's her influence, Red?" Mitch asked, still baffled by my strange ramblings.

"Oh, I thought you knew that they're having different kinds of cupcakes instead of one big cake. That reminds me, I need to stop by the bakery and make sure that she has samples of everything available for when everyone comes in tonight."

Mitch removes the candles from my hands and escorts me out into the sunshine as he says, "Come on, you need to get out a little more. Even though it's been snowing, it's still nice out here. See, the sun is shining. I don't know about you but I miss the thought of warm sun. Although, snow is cool, too."

"Where are we going?" I ask with trepidation in my voice. Yet, there is a bigger part of me that pokes fun at myself. It's so funny how our lives have kind of switched places. I used to be the one who would go anywhere, anytime with questions asked. Now, I'm the one with the calm, sedate office job and Mitch is the one working outside with the dogs, traveling around the country, giving demonstrations. There's something inherently funny about that. I felt compelled to laugh at myself.

Apparently, Mitch's thoughts are running along the same vein as he comments, "Wow, look at me doing something impulsive and off-the-cuff. I hardly know what to do myself — maybe I've earned the right to throw myself a little happy parade. Anyway, I just wanted to show you something that Tristan's brother, Elliot built. Do you want to stop by the bakery before or after?"

I stick my hands in my pockets to warm them as I decide, "I don't think I need to come back here, I've done about everything that I can do. Let's stop by Sally's on the way and then I'm done for the day. For once, I think I'm totally free to play hooky with you."

I dressed in layers today, but I didn't dress in enough layers to be traipsing around outside. Even though I was raised here, being in Florida has made me spoiled to the cold weather. I had forgotten how cold it still is in May. However, watching Hope, Lexicon and the newest member of the group, Remington, frolic around with Mitch makes me forget about how cold I am. After Sabien died, I was beginning to wonder if Mitch would ever wear a carefree smile again. It's almost as if the little boy's tragic death was a ripple in the pond that caused Mitch to question everything he ever believed about himself or anyone else. It was a profoundly scary time for me. I didn't know if I was going to be able to reach him and find the man I fell in love with again; nothing I said or did seems to make any difference. During his lowest time, he barely even seemed to notice that I was there beside him.

Eventually, my inability to help him started to stress me out. Surprisingly, it was my grandma that came to my rescue. She pulled me aside one day as we were trimming flowers in her rose garden. Apparently, she runs into the same problem with my grandpa when he has to help a parishioner through a difficult illness or a suicide. Even as a pastor with all the faith in the world, it's sometimes difficult for him to absorb all the pain of his congregation and it can affect him. My grandma looked me in the eye and said, "Make sure your heart is coming from the right place so that you can be strong when they are not, so that you can provide shelter for their heart when it feels like weeping."

My grandpa is really well known for being a person who knows what to say, but those words from my grandma have had a profound impact on me. As hard as it's been, I've taken a step back and just stood by Mitch's side and waited for him to find his stride again. Little by little, he's been able to do that with the help of his friends and family; he seems to be rebuilding his life and his confidence.

I was incredibly proud of Mitch when he finally went to the doctor and admitted he was struggling with the pain of losing Sabien on his watch. Once Mitch started reaching out to me and others while working through his pain, we started talking about deeper, more important things. We talked about fear and pain and loss. We both have a lot of issues around guilt and fear of failure in being left behind. It's incredible how much more we learned about each other after we fell in love.

One really big part of Mitch's new success has been the hiring of Devon as a new trainer at Hope's Haven. Devon's specialty is training dogs to work with veterans returning from overseas with Post Traumatic Stress Disorder. Swapping stories about successes and failures within the dog training world has helped to give Mitch some much-needed perspective about where his responsibility begins and ends and helped him realize that every dog training team feels some sense of guilt over a failed rescue whether it's misplaced or not. Devon and Mitch play the same kind of video games as well, so they've done some socializing outside of work. Although Mitch reports that it's not quite the same as having Stuart around because Devon is really a health food nut and won't let sugar pass over his lips so Mitch doesn't have to play the role of food police. In fact, the roles are often reversed and Devon is often trying to get him to drink kale smoothies.

I'm trying to hold my phone still as I'm videoing the antics of the dogs with Mitch and suddenly all three dogs gang up on Mitch and knock him over onto his backside. I start to laugh so hard that I can't hold my phone still. Mitch looks up at the sound, "You think that's funny? Do you want to join the fun?" he threatens.

"No, that's fine, thank you very much. I'm not dressed for baptism by snow," I reply primly

"Lucky for you, I have other plans for you. Otherwise, you would be making snow angels with the puppies," he threatens.

"If you're trying to scare me, Mitchell Carver Campbell, you're going to have to try harder than that because I really like to make snow angels," I tease as I stick my tongue out and run around to the other side of the wraparound porch. I can do that now because Tristan and his dad replaced it.

The house is starting to look like something out of one of those southern architecture magazines now from the outside, it just seems like it's merely waiting for a coat of paint but, it doesn't take very much imagination for me to envision what it's going to look like finished. Actually, it does take a little bit of an imagination because I love colors so much that I can't settle on a paint color. It's driving Mitch crazy. I keep looking at historical references to trying to determine what is appropriate. It's the downside of being a History minor. I want to be accurate for once in my life, but every time I come up with a new source, I change my mind. Mitch has been living in a little apartment above the veterinarian's office, so he just wants me to make some decisions and get on with life so that we can start our lives together.

I start to run away from Mitch and the dogs as a fun game of chase, but as I round the corner, I stop dead in my tracks. I gasp before I blurt, "Is it too late for me to be in love with Tristan's brother?"

Behind me, I hear Mitch choke back a startled laugh as he responds, "Yes, Jessica Lynn, it is very much too late for you to fall in love with Elliot. If I remember correctly, I think he might even still be in high school. Besides that, there's the teeny tiny technicality of the engagement ring on your finger!"

I swing around to look at Mitch as I point to the object of my awe. "Yeah but he can build that —" I counter with a starry-eyed gaze toward the gleaming white gazebo with upholstered cushions with a brightly colored batik pattern that mimics my necklace. There are hummingbird feeders hung all the way around the gazebo just like the ones I left behind in Florida.

I watch with amusement as Mitch puffs out his chest and replies, "True, Elliott built it — but, you happen to already be in love with the guy who told him to; I say you're well ahead of the game. Do you want to go check it out?"

"Is there casserole at a church potluck? Of course I do!" I answer with a breathless giggle.

Mitch grabs my hand and I practically drag him across the lawn to see the new gazebo. It looks like something out of a fairytale. I've never seen anything quite like it. The one in my yard in Florida was nice enough, but it pales in comparison.

Mitch helps me up the little step to the gazebo and suddenly backs me up against one of the pillars. He pulls my knit hat off and threads his fingers through my hair. I wince a little as his gloves catch. He notices and pulls his gloves off and tosses them aside before placing his hands at the nape of my neck. I don't even try to suppress my contented moan as he kisses me deeply. He pulls away a fraction of an inch and whispers, "You have no idea how much I miss you. It's been crazy at Hope's Haven. I feel like I saw you more when we lived forty-five minutes apart than I do when we live two miles apart. It's crazy, but I feel like I never see you and I haven't even gotten a chance to say thank you for being such a rock. I love you, Jess." Mitch kisses me again, this time much more tenderly, as if he's trying to convey more words than he can say.

I rock up onto the balls of my feet as I try to increase the intensity of the kiss because Mitch is not the only one with a message to convey. "I love you, too. You're not the only person in our relationship with the crazy job. I have been pulling some insane hours too, there's plenty of blame to go around. I keep thinking that eventually things have got to settle down. We won't be remodeling things forever, starting a new business and learning new jobs, right?"

Mitch nods and backs away as he motions for me to have a seat. I'm puzzled when he doesn't sit down beside me but walks over to the other side of the gazebo. It looks like there are cup holders over there similar to the ones next to me. I watch as he opens a funny little cupboard and a speaker emerges with a cord designed to attach to his phone. I smile when I hear Eli Mattson's version of *Favorite Things* being piped throughout the gazebo. Mitch leans down and pulls out a bowl of fruit and a bottle of something from a small refrigerator. He hands the bowl to me and sets the bottle down on a little end table. "I guess I forgot the cups, I suppose we'll have to improvise," he comments, as he looks around the gazebo.

"Look at this place! It's amazing. Do I look like I'm even going to care about a couple of little cups? I can't believe you planned this. I totally love it."

"I love it, too. I had a vision in my head of what I thought it might look like, but this is even better. I knew that you would want someplace for hummingbird feeders and I wanted to make you a private spot where you could come out and read your books so I thought that this would be a great way to combine the two ideas. Elliott worked really hard to get this done before they have to go home for their busy season, just in case you wanted to have it available for your friends to use for their wedding. To be honest, I'd really rather be selfish and keep this as our special spot. I'm afraid that makes me sound awful." Mitch opens a bottle of sparkling cider and offers it to me as he unwraps a bowl of chocolate covered strawberries and holds one up for me to take a bite.

"I have really great memories of the first time I saw you lost in the world of music by yourself in the gazebo and I don't want to share those memories with anyone. I know that you have your idea of what your perfect wedding looks like. Mine looks like a beautiful summer day with just you and I and a few of our closest friends out here in our backyard with your hair down flying in the wind with you wearing white lace and me wearing comfortable jeans when we say our promises to each other in front of the people we love."

My eyes tear up as I think about his vision of our love story. I swallow hard before I answer, "Well, then I guess I better choose a great color to paint our house that looks really good in wedding pictures because next summer seems like the perfect time to tie the knot."

Mitch

22

I ROLL MY SHOULDERS AND watch Jessica as she tries to figure out which graduate is Stuart. It's going to be a long weekend. The flight wasn't as smooth this time. I'm working with a very smart dog named Tucker, but I discovered today in a really awkward encounter that he's not fond of people with crutches or white canes used by people with visual impairments. This could be the factor that excludes him from being a service dog of any type. Unfortunately, you take rescue dogs however you get them and sometimes they have pre-existing hang-ups; it's something that I'm going to have to discuss with Devon. Devon was planning to use him as a PTSD dog. However, if he reacts negatively in public, that could be a real problem. This weekend was his test to see how he handled flying; although he did fine on the airline test, he flunked other parts of his exam.

Abruptly, Jessica lets out a gasp followed by a big sigh as she turns to me and states, "You know, I was beginning to think that all of this stuff was over. When were you going to tell me that they were still doing all this crap?"

I pull my head back into the conversation and look around quickly as I try to figure out what she's talking about. I apologize, "I'm sorry, I wasn't really paying attention, what were we talking about?"

She points to a woman with uncovered dark hair even from our high vantage place, I can vaguely make out suspenders. I have to admit, Jessica has a point, even from the nosebleed section, that looks suspiciously like Darya next to a grad who looks very much like Stuart. Now that her suspicions have been raised, Jessica is carefully studying every single guest. When she sees both Tristan and Isaac, her eyes swing back to me as and she narrows them suspiciously. "When were you planning to inform me?" she demands.

"I'm not exactly sure what I'm supposed to be telling you, Red," I protest.

"For one thing, I didn't realize that Stuart and I were traveling with our own security detail. It would have been nice to know that. If nothing else, I might've worn more practical shoes."

"I thought the answer to that question was pretty obvious since we moved all the way to Kansas," I reply dryly.

Admittedly, I am very tired, but I probably should've thought about that one before it came flying out of my mouth, it sounded a whole lot meaner than I intended and Jessica looks like I just verbally backhanded her.

"Wow! I get extra asshat points for that one, don't I? Look, I'm sorry. That was way out line. As far as I know, they still haven't figured out who issued the threat against you in Hope's case. There haven't been any new threats so, I think they're just being really careful."

"Why is Officer Virk guarding Stuart?" she asks.

"I bet they're watching Stuart since this is such a high-profile thing for him and because he gave testimony in the juvenile proceeding about Hope's condition. That's all."

Jessica groans softly as she replies, "It's just so easy to forget all of this when we're back home. I mean, if you think about it, I literally live in a fantasy world all day. I read lovely stories to largely happy kids all day. We are going to live in an idyllic house next to a guy who pretty much believes the best about everyone."

"True, Walter is a glass half-full kind of guy," I interject.

"Right now, the most conflict we have in Kansas is among my grandma's soap opera characters. Even though raising funds for Hope's Haven is a little stressful, even that's not too bad because Janice is doing a pretty phenomenal job. It's easy for me to believe that my life is just about as perfect as it gets — knock on wood — so, I don't even want to think about how ugly it could be. I don't want to think about it ever. I especially don't want to think about it this weekend. Stuart and I have worked too hard to not graduate. Well, Stuart has worked a whole lot harder than me, but — still, you know what I mean."

I hug her closer to my side as I respond, "I understand what you mean. Sometimes, I feel the same way. I feel like I have won the lottery because you are in my life. My life is perfect in ways that I couldn't have imagined a couple years ago. I don't feel torn apart in a million directions anymore. Thanks to you, I have direction, focus and mission — and when Sabien died and I almost lost it, you stayed the course and never lost the vision or your belief in me. Your faith in me and in Hope's Haven allowed me to go get the help I needed to cope with what happened and move on so that I could help other people. Without your support, I don't know that I could've reached out and gotten help. Depression is a scary thing. Things are better now and Hope's Haven is growing and Devon and Zoe are training other dogs."

Jessica kisses my temple and whispers, "I'm sorry it hurts so much."

I gently kiss her and then continue explaining, "No matter how perfect Kansas is and how much I love it, it's not all great because you're not safe. Not until Isaac or the law enforcement officers in Florida find every person who has threatened you. This stuff keeps me awake at night. I never expected to find you but now that I have, I never want to think about living my life without you. I want the kind of love story that Wilma and Walter have. It's exactly like you always say, one small gesture at a time, one small smile at a time, one heartbeat at a time."

"That's how I see our love story, too. I can't tell you how much I wish that I had never seen that stupid car. This is so *crazy*. I never even saw anything that the police could really use."

"Jess, think about it though. If you had never seen that car, you probably wouldn't have gone chasing after Hope. If you hadn't gone chasing after her, you and I may have never met. Whether it's God's intervention, answered prayers or random fate, you were meant to see a mud covered license plate that day that caught your eye so that Hope would have a new lease on life and I would too."

Jessica smiles at me as she concedes, "That's true, you did rescue more than just Hope that day although, you were kind of a jerk about it."

A huge section of the graduating class sits down and we can finally see the veterinary school standing there. I now understand how my diminutive fiancé was cast in so many plays during her academic career. Her voice projects like you would not believe. The crowd around us has their jaws open in collective amazement as she shouts her congratulations down toward Stuart. I see both Tristan and Isaac shoot me twin looks of alarm; they are clearly asking me to keep her as quiet as possible as to not draw attention to herself. Well, that mission was blown all to pieces the minute she decided to become a super colossal fan of my best friend. I glance at her with desperation as my eyes plead for her to stop. She's having so much fun, there is not a whole lot I can do other than just give her a celebratory kiss.

The sense of déjà vu is strong. Same hard bleachers, same crowded environment, same crowd noise, different day. This time, it's Stuart sitting next to me asking me questions. Although, I have to admit his are a little more amusing.

"Why am I using this cane again? I mean, it's cool and all but it's little weird," he states looking down at the black walking stick sitting in the chair beside him.

"I'm testing Tucker, remember? He has a thing against canes, sticks, and crutches. I'm trying to acclimate him to them so he doesn't think they're scary. Face it, you're just a prop today."

Stuart grins as he responds, "I can live with that." When he moves, Stuart moans. He stops to takes a couple aspirin and a swig of 7-Up. He glances over at Darya and back at me as he says, "Buddy, what are you doing to me? I'm aware that I may have indulged a tad too much in liquids of a celebratory nature last night while you were cuddling with your gal pal, but did you really have to sic the thin blue line me?"

"Relax, she's just here to help keep you safe, not be a buzz kill," I explain.

"Dude, there were two of them. It was completely killing my game," he laments.

I snicker as I reply, "I hate to break it to you, but you don't have any 'game'. You eat Coco Pebbles with strawberry milk and still have a nightlight in your bedroom."

Stuart suddenly seems angry as he replies, "I don't do that stuff anymore. Maybe I want to attract a higher class of woman like Jessica so I'm adjusting my sites a little. Who's to say I don't deserve what you have?"

His mercurial mood shift is a little out of character and takes me by surprise. It makes me wonder what else is going on. We used to poke fun at each other all the time and he never used to respond this way. "Hey, I didn't mean any harm. I was just flicking you crap. You know me, I'm happy and in love, singing nostalgic Coca-Cola commercials. I want everybody in the same boat as me. Nothing would make me happier than for you to find somebody who makes you as happy as Jessica makes me."

"Yeah, I get that — but did you really fall in love with someone whose last name is Walker?" he asks with exasperation.

"Well… I don't know… yes… no… I don't know! That's her name. Why?" I stammer.

"Buddy, you just killed our chances of ducking out of this graduation early, I hope you know that," Stuart quips.

"You better get used to this whole graduation thing, did I tell you that once Hope's Haven is up and running, I plan to go back to college and finish my degree. I'm still trying to decide whether I'm going to change my major to Criminal Justice or Forensics," I announce.

Stuart high-fives me as he advises, "I vote for forensics because you can cut up dead things. That was my favorite part of vet school. Besides, it's fun to chase the girls around the classroom with slimy eyeballs."

Darya raises an eyebrow at me as she asks, "Is your friend always this charming?" She turns to Stuart and declares, "You know, not all *women* are afraid of that kind of stuff."

I wink at Darya as I defend Stuart, "Generally speaking, my best friend can be a pretty charming guy, if you can overlook his addiction to sugar. He also dresses quite sharply." I look over at Stuart and advise quietly, "Stuart, you know that game you were trying so hard to have? You might want to 'up it'. Women don't get much classier than Darya. Especially if you like them smart, capable and lethal."

Stuart straightens in his chair as he holds his hand out for Darya to shake, "Nice to meet you, Ma'am, I'm Stuart Eastwood. *Dr.* Eastwood. I'm especially kind to animals and small children."

Darya tries unsuccessfully to hide her grin as she responds, "I am aware, Dr. Eastwood. You made that abundantly clear at two o'clock this morning when you were arguing with me about whether the live-action version of *101 Dalmatians* was better than the animated one."

Stuart turns a little green as he replies, "Really? I can't even imagine which side of the argument I would be on."

"I guess technically, you could say you won the argument because throughout the whole night you were on every side of the argument and by the end, you finally threw in the towel and decided that you were solidly in the *Lady and the Tramp* camp as best movie of all time involving animals," Darya responds with a laugh.

"You heard my very persuasive arguments, what do you think?" Stuart asks facetiously.

"Oh, no, not me — you're not drawing me into this. I'm Switzerland. My only job is to protect your backside, as handsome as it is," Darya responds.

For the first time since we were about thirteen, I notice my best friend is blushing

Jessica

Epilogue

ISAAC CATCHES ME IN THE little kitchen of the parsonage when I duck out of all of the bridal preparations to grab everyone some bottled water.

"How are my daughters? I didn't think it was possible, but I think I am more nervous today than I was the day I married my Rosa."

"Aside from a little drama over a dropped earring, everyone is holding up beautifully. Your daughters look stunning as usual. They are very happy that you are in their lives so that they can have this father-daughter moment," I reply, trying to disguise my own pain over the fact that I probably won't be able to have a similar moment at my wedding.

Isaac notices my pain and says, "Don't be sad. If your father can't get his head screwed on straight by the time your wedding comes, your *abuelo* and I will work something out, I promise."

He suddenly starts to pat his pockets as he says, "Speaking of the earrings, your friend Sam said to tell you that he hopes that this is the last time you ever have to be a bridesmaid and that he wanted me to give you these as congratulations for graduating from 'perpetual bridesmaid' to bride to be. He's sorry that he won't be able to see you the next time you come to Florida because he has been selected to take over a store in Portland. He said it's not fair that you get romance and he gets rain." Isaac laughs at Sam's joke as he hands me the little box.

"Oh, wow! That's even further from Florida than Kansas. Good for him for getting a promotion. He's been with that jewelry company for a while," I remark. "I'm a little sad that I didn't get a chance to say goodbye to Sam. He's been a really good friend."

"He did seem like a remarkable young man. I've never seen someone quite so knowledgeable about gemstones and I've worked with some pretty qualified experts throughout my career."

I unwrap the tiny little box and I'm stunned to see sapphire and diamond earrings. They even match my engagement ring and hummingbird necklace — right down to the teardrop shape of the stones. I look at Isaac accusingly and ask, "Did you have a hand in this?"

Isaac shakes his head 'no' as he responds, "No. I did not. On this mission, I'm only the message carrier. The package came to me already wrapped. Although, the young man said to me that he chose these particular earrings because they would look beautiful with your hair. Now that I've seen them, I have to agree with his assessment."

There's just something about men in suits that can render a girl speechless, and these four men are striking. Make it five; Grandpa looks pretty good too. Elliott is standing up for his brother as best man and honestly, I've never seen Tristan have a bad day. Mitch looks stunningly handsome as usual. But, the most amazing transformation is in Marcus. He looks like he could have walked right off the pages of GQ. Even his usually wild, spiky hair looks artfully arranged and his nice, sedate black gauges complement his conservative suit. The only embellishment of color is the dragonfly, which has been skillfully embroidered on his charcoal colored tie.

Originally, my grandma was going to play piano today, but she was feeling a bit shaky this morning so she asked me to fill in for her. It's interesting to be both bridesmaid and accompanist at a wedding. I've been in lots of weddings before, but I've never had to play dual roles. Fortunately, Rogue chose not to wear a dress with a long train, so Jade only has to tend to one train.

As I play the wedding march and watch Isaac proudly march up the aisle with a beautiful woman on each arm, it's all I can do not to cry on the piano keys. After my friends have reached the front of the church, I grab my flowers from a front pew and go stand beside Jade.

My grandpa steps up to the pulpit and comments as he surveys the wedding party, "You know, you guys are really good at confounding me. I've encountered more things with you that I've never run into before in all my years as a minister. First, it was Isaac and Rosa already being married and now you all are throwing two at once at me. I'm not even sure I want to know what comes next."

"I believe that's going to be Jessica," Marcus answers with a wink in my direction.

"Son, I already know her wedding is going to be a wild one. She was practicing for that long before she ever met the likes of you," he quips with a smile. "I apologize for missing the wedding rehearsal last night. Mr. Baumgartner had a heart attack at a rather inconvenient time, but he is feeling stronger this afternoon. I'm not sure of the order you've all worked out, so I'll let you take the lead; just let me know when you want me to say my parts."

"I get to go first since I was the one that started this ball rolling," Ivy responds looking at Rogue. "When I first set out to find you, I expected the worst. Yet, what I found was the absolute best. I found the best sister in the world. Neither of us expected to find our other half, literally. I also never expected to find a beautiful bonus set of parents whose love story inspires me every single day. However, the biggest surprise of all was that I found a man who takes my breath away and helps me find it again. I never expected to fall in love in the middle of an asthma attack, but if I'm truly honest with myself, I really did." Ivy turns to Marcus and traces the edge of a tattoo that is visible under his shirt cuff with her fingertips as she says. "You were everything I didn't expect but everything that is absolutely perfect for me. You encourage me to be bold and outrageous. Rogue once told me that your specialty would be teaching me to color outside the lines. It turns out that pushing boundaries and living life in full color is my favorite place to be. I'm so glad you encouraged me to be my true self. Marcus Brolen, I love you so much," Ivy whispers softly.

A tear slides down Rogue's face as she hands Ivy a Kleenex and wipes her own face before picking up the complicated love story, "Before you found me, I was busy pretending to keep it together, pretending that I had it all. That I needed no one. But, I was carrying around a lot of hurt and anger that I hadn't shared with anyone. I had physical pain I couldn't describe and I was angry at a nameless, faceless man I never knew." Rogue turns to Tristan. "When you came into my life, I wanted to hate you and everything you stood for, yet somehow I couldn't. You were so different from what I expected that I couldn't seem to muster the proper level of hate for a man who clearly had money but had the morals to match. As time went on, I fell head over heels in love with you but was still afraid to trust what was right in front of me. Watching my sister fall in love with my best friend helped me realize that no relationship is perfect or has the perfect timetable, love just is. You were everything I needed you to be, strong and steady and there when they needed you to help me reunite my family in ways I never dreamed possible and helped me fulfill dreams that without your help, would be unreachable. Without even realizing was happening, I went from skeptic to your biggest cheerleader to your partner. Thank you for loving me through it, Tristan Macklin."

Watching my friends become emotional is hard for me to watch. This is especially true when it comes to Rogue because it's such an atypical reaction from her. She's usually so calm, cool and collected — it's like she's got ice water running through her veins. As I look around, I realize that I'm not the only person affected by the emotional words from the twins. Of course, Isaac and Rosa are crying; but Devon, the new dog trainer at Hope's Haven is surreptitiously wiping away tears as well and he doesn't even know any of these people.

Tristan loosens his tie a little before he begins to speak, "At first, Rogue was just another puzzle for me to solve, but, it took almost no time at all for me to figure out that she is actually the missing piece of the puzzle in my life that makes the whole thing makes sense." He leans forward and places a kiss on Rogue's cheek as he murmurs, "I love you, Rogue Medea Sisneros Betancourt."

Rogue smiles with a teary grin as she responds, "I love you too, Mr. Super-Secret Spy Guy."

Marcus elbows Tristan in the ribs as he quips, "I knew I should've gone first, you all are like Shakespeare compared to me. First, you have the super romantic proposal and then you take my best friend to Paris to get engaged; it's a lot for a guy to keep up with, you know? I'll give it my best shot though." He turns to Ivy and says, "You know, for many years, I began to wonder if I was even capable of falling in love. I didn't know if it was because of my 'troubled past', the odd way that I perceive the world or just because I was weird, but love just never seemed to happen for me the way it did for everyone else. When Rogue became my best friend and everyone started to wonder why we weren't together, I just gave up the thought of finding that perfect match, the person who sees the real me. Then Tristan found you. I know the real story is that he found Rogue for you, but in my mind, he found you for me. From the moment I looked into your eyes while we counted breaths when I was helping you through your asthma attack, you owned my heart and everything else I have. I'm so lucky to be here on this day with you, I could've never dreamed it. I love you, Ivy Montclair."

Ivy rushes forward and gives him a brief hug as she whispers, "It's funny, I was just thinking the same thing about you."

Grandpa clears his throat as he turns to Marcus and remarks, "Mr. Brolen, I know you were nervous today, but I'm not sure what you were worried about; it seems to be you did just fine. That sounded pretty poetic to me. I've been through lots of ceremonies and that one seemed very heartfelt to me. Now, since Ivy and Marcus went up first last go around, I'll let Mr. Macklin and Miss Betancourt have the honors this time." My grandpa looks at Jade and Elliott and asks, "I presume you fine people are the keepers of the rings?"

Jade winks at my grandpa before she answers, "I am, but for the life of me I can't understand why because I lose everythin— "

Suddenly, from the back of the room there is a commotion. We crane our necks to see what's going on. All of the members of the wedding party blanch a little when my grandpa asks, "What in tarnation? Are you here to object to one of these marriages? I've never in all my years of performing marriages had one of those. What is going on here?"

The woman takes her parka off and I realize that it's Janice as she gasps and declares, "Oh no, Pastor Walker. I'm sorry to interrupt — but it's an emergency."

"Well, why didn't you say something? Go on, don't stand on formalities," Grandpa demands impatiently.

"It's Craig. I can't find him anywhere. I'm afraid he overheard his father make some threats over the phone and who knows what he thought about them. I didn't even know he was home. I thought he was with my mom at the movies."

Sharlene runs in behind Janice as she confirms, "I'm so sorry. I planned to take the grand babies to the movies, but they were sold out of the kids' movie so I brought them back home. I didn't know Calvin was going to be on the speakerphone."

"Mom, that's okay. I just do it that way so I can record it in case I ever need it for court. None of us knew he was going call. Still, I think Craig heard Calvin say he was going to get rid of his little child-support problem."

I hear Grandma exclaim from the back of the sanctuary, "To think that Calvin was one of my best students in bible study."

Grandpa looks at the wedding party and asks, "Any objection to postponing these proceedings for the moment? It seems that all you really need to do is sign paperwork anyway. You guys have done the mushy feel-good part."

Almost in total synchronization, Ivy and Rogue turn to Isaac and Tristan and issue orders, "Go!"

Mitch

Epilogue

IT TAKES ME HALF A second to go from wedding mode to rescuer mode and when I do, my heart drops to my knees. I know I have every bit of training that I need to do this correctly, but after what happened the last time I tried this, my head and my heart don't necessarily agree. I know I need to nix that attitude in a hurry. I concentrate on my breathing for a moment while I mentally catalog what I need to do in the next five minutes to make this happen.

When I look back up, Devon is standing right in front of me, "Boss? What do you need me to do first?"

I look down at my dark suit and survey the rest of the wedding party. Nearly everyone who would be a key player in the search is dressed just like me. It's perfectly appropriate for the wedding, not so appropriate for a search at the end of November. Devon on the other hand is dressed in khakis and a turtleneck and sweater.

"Devon, please tell me that you didn't have time to unload all the training gear from the rig last week," I mutter as I shed off my tie and fancy cufflinks.

"It's all still there. I got interrupted by a reporter the other day and didn't get around to unloading it. All I need to do is go back and get the dogs. Tucker is solid with the seek command and we can also use Hope and Lexicon."

"Do you need the Polaris?" Walter offers as he walks up behind me.

"Actually, I do. I'm really concerned about the water level in the creek at this time year and the weather is not working in our favor. If you can cover the water line, I'll take the dogs and cover this area since it's the start of the search. With three dogs, we should be able to cover quite a bit of distance."

"How will you manage three dogs with two handlers? I've watched you enough with them that I could probably direct Hope well enough," Jessica offers as she takes off her high heels and her jewelry. "I'm going to run over to the parsonage and change. I've got a pair of ski pants stashed in the Jeep. You know what a packrat I am. I've got everything from bikinis to a pup tent in there."

"I know, I can't believe at some point I thought your disorganization was going to drive me nuts, but it's saved my backside more than once. I think Hope will do just fine with you. Some days she listens to your commands better than mine anyway," I admit.

Loud enough for the rest of the room to hear, I announce, "We'll meet back here in ten minutes in more appropriate clothing to start the search. Has anyone called Sheriff Foster and his team?"

"Nobody needs to call me when I'm sitting right here," Billy says. "I've already called in backup."

After we've reassembled, relief courses through my body when it becomes apparent that it doesn't take the dogs long at all to hit on the same scent. Wherever Craig is, he likely went there on foot.

I'm certain to the non-trained observer, we look like some sort of performance art as all of us are parading down the street. Cars are stopping in the middle of the street to watch our progress. However, the dogs are not deterred as they are charging down the street on a singularly important mission. Things get a little more muddled when we reach the city park; it seems as if Craig may have lingered here for a bit. However, Hope quickly picks up the trail again and we're having difficulty keeping up with her on the icy sidewalk. Suddenly, Hope veers off at an angle and runs up the stairs toward the library. Inexplicably, she sits down in front of the metal book return box.

It doesn't really make any sense that we would be here at all. The library is closed down for the holiday season and there isn't a soul around. It's closed up tight and there aren't even prints in the snow, although with the wind blowing like it is, the snow patterns are not a terribly reliable way to determine who has been coming or going.

I study Hope's body language closely to make sure that she isn't just stopping for a rest in the brutal weather. However, it is very clear that she is alerting us that she has found Craig.

"Jess, you know this little boy, right?" I ask over my shoulder. "Is he a large kid?"

Jessica shakes her head, as she answers, "No, he's built more like a soccer player than a football player. He's pretty tall, but very thin."

"How old is he again?" I ask as an idea starts to form.

"He's five, but he acts older because he has a big sister. He is always trying to keep up with her."

I call Devon over and point out the oversized opening to the book return box. "What do you think?"

He shrugs as he responds, "I guess anything's possible. I would trust Hope's instincts."

"We got bolt cutters?"

Sheriff Foster steps forward with a set as he says, "Way ahead of you." He snaps the padlock on the hitch and opens the metal book return cupboard. Much to our relief, Craig is curled up in a slightly awkward position, almost completely upside down and he's sound asleep.

Jessica squats down beside him and gently lifts him out and holds him in her arms as she murmurs, "Hey, Sweetie, the library is closed today. What are you doing here? It's not story day until next week."

Craig blinks in surprise at his change in circumstances and then buries his face in her neck as he answers, "I know, Miss Jessica — but I had to come here. 'Member when you said that the liberry is the place you can pretend to be anything you want to be and everybody loves all the books at the liberry?"

Jessica nods with a puzzled look on her face.

"I heard my daddy tell my mommy that he don't love me anymore and he don't want to be my daddy."

"I see. That must've been scary to hear," Jessica acknowledges.

"I comed here to pretend to be a book so everyone would love me again."

"Craig, can I tell you a little secret?" Jessica murmurs, as she sticks her forehead against his. "Sometimes, when grown-ups are really mad, we say stuff that's really silly and stupid. I bet your daddy never stopped loving you for a single second, even if you didn't pretend to be a book. You know what else? Your mom and grandma love you bunches and bunches because they sent all of us to come look for you."

Craig smiles shyly as he asks, "Really, Miss Jessica, or is you just making up one of your silly stories?"

Jessica grins broadly as she responds, "Do I do that? I happen to believe all my stories are true, especially the mushy ones about love, but this one is absolutely one hundred percent true. You were rescued by a dog nobody wanted. Hope was given a second chance and trained in the new job and she saved your life. Now, you can grow up to be anything you want to be. That sounds like a pretty awesome story to me. I think you should write it down so that the library can someday publish your book. Does that sound like a good plan to you?"

"Miss Jessica, can I put parrots in this story, too?" Craig asks.

Jessica comes over to me and puts a free arm around my waist as she says, "Why not, kiddo? We all have a chance to write our own happy endings."

THE END (for now)

(You can follow up the rest of the friends in Hearts of Jade, which is available now.)

Acknowledgments

Although I spend countless hours dictating books alone, writing is by no means a solitary endeavor. I have many people who help me along the way. Chief among them on this project are my editor, Lacie Redding, my beta reader, Kathern Watts, and my extraordinary cover designer, Ada Frost. Put quite simply, without the help of these wonderful women, this book would not exist. Also deserving mention are Heather Truett, Susan Pruitt and Tiffany Fox who do their best to inform the world that I write books. It seems simple enough to publicize books, but in a crowded field it's hard to help an author stick out. These ladies do their best.

As you may have noticed from this book, I am a huge supporter of service dogs. I got my first service dog in the mid-80s. Her name was Molly and I received her from the Assistance Dogs of America, back when service dogs for people in wheelchairs was an unusual concept. I'm also an avid fan of rescuing dogs. I have adopted several dogs from the Humane Society.

Your purchase of this book will help support Search and Rescue dogs of the United States of America. I will donate 15% of my profits to that organization. You can help maximize this impact by sharing the word about this book with your friends and family. If you like this book, please leave a review on Amazon, Goodreads and Twitter (If you don't like it, I need to hear that too).

I have had many positive influences in my life, but one of the most enduring is the pastor that I had growing up, Ken Knoll. I credit the marriage advice that he gave my husband and I in premarital counseling for the fact that I am still happily married after twenty-seven years. Pastor Knoll retired last year and I just want acknowledge the wonderful impact he has had on my life. Thanks, Ken.

Because love matters, differences don't.

~ Mary

About
the
Author

I have been lucky enough to live my own version of a romance novel. I married the guy who kissed me at summer camp. He told me on the night we met that he was going to marry me and be the father of my children. Eventually I stopped giggling when he said it, and we just celebrated our 27th wedding anniversary. We have two children. The oldest is in medical school, where he recently found and married the love of his life, and the youngest is tackling middle school.

I write full time now. I have published more than a dozen books and have several more underway. I volunteer my time to a variety of causes. I have worked as a Civil Rights Attorney and diversity advocate. I spent several years working for various social service agencies before becoming an attorney. In my spare time, I love to cook, decorate cakes and of course, I obsessively, compulsively read.

If you have questions or comments, please E-mail me at Mary@MaryCrawfordAuthor.com or find me on the following social networks:

Facebook: www.facebook.com/authormarycrawford

Website: MaryCrawfordAuthor.com

Twitter:www.twitter.com/MaryCrawfordAut

A
Final
Note

Being an author is a very isolating endeavor, since by nature we live in a world of fantasy. I take fan input seriously and I would love to hear yours. Sites like Amazon and Goodreads give you the opportunity to rate this book and share your thoughts on Facebook and Twitter. If you like this book, please take a moment to share your review and encourage your friends and family to share in the love of reading.

Thank you so much.

~Mary

Previews of
Current &
Upcoming
Books

If you enjoyed Mitch and Jessica's love story, similar adventures continue in the upcoming releases in **The Hidden Beauty Series** titles:

Until the Stars Fall from the Sky (A Hidden Beauty Novel #1) — Jeff and Kiera — June 3, 2014

So the Heart Can Dance (A Hidden Beauty Novel #2) — Aidan and Tara — April 24, 2015

Joy and Tiers (A Hidden Beauty Novel #3) — Heather and Ty — August 15, 2015

Love Naturally (A Hidden Beauty Novel #4) — Madison and Trevor— December 24, 2015

Love Seasoned (A Hidden Beauty Novel #5) — Denny and Gwendolyn—January 19, 2016

Love Claimed (A Hidden Beauty Novel #6) — Donda and Jaxson — June 17, 2016

Jude's Song (A Hidden Beauty Novel #7) —Tasha and Jude — Coming Late Fall 2016

If You Knew Me (and other silent musings) — Elijah and Sadie (A Hidden Beauty Novella)— Coming Fall 2016

Love Against Code (A Hidden Beauty Novel #8) —Matt and Devon — Coming Winter 2016

Paths Not Taken (A Hidden Beauty Novel #9) —Jordan and Cristiano — Coming Early Spring 2017

The Hidden Hearts Series:

Identity of the Heart (A Hidden Hearts Novel #1) — Ivy and Marcus and Rogue and Tristan — September 21, 2015

Sheltered Heart (A Hidden Hearts Novel #2) — Jessica and Mitch — March 28, 2016.

Hearts of Jade (A Hidden Hearts Novel #3) — Jade and Declan —July 31, 2016

Port in the Storm (A Hidden Hearts Novella) — Sam and Taylor — Debuting at Passion in Portland 2016

Love Is More Than Skin Deep (A Hidden Hearts Novel #4) — Shelby and Mark — September 7, 2016

Resources

Search and Rescue Dogs of the United States:
http://www.sardogsus.org

International Association of Assistance Dog Partners:
http://www.iaadp.org/access.html

Assistance Dogs International:
http://www.assistancedogsinternational.org/

Guide Dogs for the Blind: http://welcome.guidedogs.com/

Petfinder: https://www.petfinder.com/

American Society for the Prevention of Cruelty to Animals:
http://www.aspca.org/animal-placement

ADD & ADHD Health Center—WebMD:
http://www.webmd.com/add-adhd/guide/10-symptoms-adult-adhd